DEATH COMES
TO BATH

Center Point
Large Print

Also by Catherine Lloyd and available from
Center Point Large Print:

Death Comes to Kurland Hall
Death Comes to the Fair
Death Comes to the School

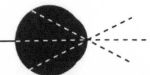

**This Large Print Book carries the
Seal of Approval of N.A.V.H.**

Death Comes to Bath

A Kurland St. Mary Mystery

CATHERINE LLOYD

CENTER POINT LARGE PRINT
THORNDIKE, MAINE

This Center Point Large Print edition
is published in the year 2019 by arrangement with
Kensington Publishing Corp.

The text of this Large Print edition is unabridged.
In other aspects, this book may vary
from the original edition.
Printed in the United States of America
on permanent paper.
Set in 16-point Times New Roman type.

ISBN: 978-1-64358-267-2

Library of Congress Cataloging-in-Publication Data

Names: Lloyd, Catherine, 1963- author.
Title: Death comes to Bath / Catherine Lloyd.
Description: Center Point Large Print edition. | Thorndike, Maine :
    Center Point Large Print, 2019.
Identifiers: LCCN 2019017953 | ISBN 9781643582672 (hardcover :
    alk. paper)
Subjects: LCSH: Murder—Investigation—Fiction. | Bath (England)—
    Fiction. | Large type books. | CYAC: Bath (England)—Fiction.
Classification: LCC PS3616.E246 D423 2019b | DDC 813.6—dc23
LC record available at https://lccn.loc.gov/2019017953

Many thanks to Sandra Marine and Ruth Long, who read this book for me and helped knock it into shape. I spent two very happy weeks in the city of Bath last summer making sure I walked the routes and visited the places Lucy and Robert would've enjoyed. If you ever have the opportunity, I highly recommend a visit to Bath.

Prologue

Kurland St. Mary
January 1822

R obert! *Robert,* can you hear me?"
Aware that something was vaguely amiss, Sir Robert Kurland attempted to focus on his wife's face, which appeared to be underwater. Something slobbered noisily on his cheek. He was fairly certain that *wasn't* his wife, and was one of his dogs. He blinked hard and pain shot through his limbs with such appalling agony that his back arched in instinctive protest.

"Robert."

In truth, he'd much prefer to sink back into oblivion and leave all the unsettling brightness concentrated around his wife alone, but she obviously needed him, and he could never deny her anything.

Where was he? The last thing he remembered was coming down the main staircase in Kurland Hall intent on taking his two young dogs, Picton and Blucher, for a short stroll down the drive before breakfast. The surface beneath him was hard and cold, which was a damned sight better

7

than being buried up to his neck in the mud at Waterloo, but still uncomfortable.

"Thank you, Foley." Lucy appeared to be speaking to his butler.

Robert groaned as something soft was placed beneath his head and a blanket was thrown over his torso.

"Dr. Fletcher is on his way, my lady."

"No." Robert managed to open his eyes. "*Damnation,* not him."

"Robert." Lucy leaned closer and a tear dripped from her cheek onto his. "Oh, my *darling* . . ."

He frowned at her. "My dear girl, there's no need for tears. I'm not dead yet."

She tried to smile and wiped hastily at her cheek. "I do apologize, but the sight of you on the ground has somewhat affected me." She turned her head. Robert followed the direction of her gaze and saw several pairs of muddy booted feet approaching.

"We can't leave you out here in the cold. If you can stand it, James and the other footmen are going to lift you and take you to bed," Lucy said.

Even though he was hardly in a position to argue, Robert still wanted to object. He tensed as the men gathered around him.

"On my mark." Foley took charge. "One, two, three . . ."

Even before Robert was lifted off the ground the pain swallowed him whole, and he knew no more.

The next time he opened his eyes he was lying in his own bed with the covers drawn back, and his blasted friend ex–army surgeon Patrick Fletcher was glaring down at him.

Someone had removed all of Robert's clothes except his shirt, and that was pulled up to expose his left hip and thigh.

"Why didn't you tell me about this?" Patrick demanded. His strong fingers gently probed the massive swelling on Robert's thigh.

"So much for your bedside manner, Dr. Fletcher. You will hardly make your fortune with the aristocracy if you shout at your patients," Robert murmured.

"I'm shouting at you because you are a special case." Patrick placed his hand on Robert's forehead. "You also have a fever."

"I *am* aware of that."

"You promised at Christmas that you would allow me to examine you properly."

"You're examining me now," Robert pointed out, and received another ferocious glare in return. "Where is my wife?"

"She is right here, sir."

Patrick stepped back, and Robert located Lucy sitting in a chair next to the fire, her hands twisted together in her lap around her handkerchief. The dogs were asleep at her feet. She looked remarkably pale but met his gaze resolutely.

"I know you said you didn't wish to see Dr.

Fletcher, but when one's husband is discovered unconscious on the drive, one is entitled to ignore his wishes."

"Indeed," Robert said. "Although one *might* have considered waiting awhile and consulting the patient first."

"Lady Kurland did the right thing," Patrick replied. "I know you don't want to hear this, Robert, but this swelling on your thigh is hot to the touch. I hesitate to literally reopen old wounds, but I've heard of cases like this before from fellow army surgeons, and I'd like the opportunity to drain the swelling and see what's going on."

Robert swallowed hard. The idea of a surgeon laying hands on him again made every cowardly impulse in him stir to attention. It was also why he hadn't mentioned the swelling to anyone, not even his wife.

"If I don't try something, you will probably lose the leg, and maybe your life if the inflammation spreads," Patrick continued.

Lucy came to stand beside the doctor and looked down at Robert. "As you might imagine, I would rather you continued your existence."

He reached for her hand. "Then I must agree to put myself in the good doctor's hands. When do you want to perform your butchery?"

Patrick shared a glance with Lucy. "Now if possible."

Robert nodded. "Then give me a moment with my wife, and I am all yours."

"I need to get some equipment and persuade Foley to give me the best brandy in the house." Patrick squeezed Robert's shoulder hard. "I'll do my absolute best to save your leg."

The silence left behind by the doctor was broken by the crackling of the fire and the whimper of one of the dogs chasing rabbits in his sleep. Lucy sat on the side of the bed and wrapped an arm around Robert's shoulders. He drew her close and kissed the top of her head.

"I do apologize for worrying you."

She cupped his chin. "You have always been a worry, but one that I willingly embraced." She searched his face. "Do you wish me to assist Dr. Fletcher or would you rather I took myself off?"

"I'd rather you were here." He hesitated. "Just in case."

"Then here I shall remain." She kissed him gently on the lips. "At your side." She glanced over at the fire. "The dogs, however, will return to the kitchen." She went as if to sit up, and he held her in place.

"If the worst happens, I've made provision for you and protected the estate as best as I can from Paul, but—"

She placed a finger on his lips. "Let's not worry about that now. I have every confidence in your ability to protect me, and I do not fear the future." She smiled and he stored the memory away like a precious jewel. Her strength and calmness had never been more vital to him than at this moment.

He kissed her fingers and then her mouth, deepening the kiss until she was molded against him and they breathed as one. Eventually, she eased away from him, her eyes grave, and patted her now disordered hair.

"I must look a fright."

"You look remarkably pretty to me," Robert said.

There was a knock on the door, and Silas, his valet, peered in. "Dr. Fletcher asked me to come and assist, sir. I hope that's all right."

"Please join us." Robert pointed at the dogs. "But take these two fine fellows down to the kitchen first and make sure one of the stable boys gives them some exercise."

"Yes, Sir Robert."

Foley came in with a bottle of his best brandy and placed the decanter beside Robert's bed.

"Good luck, sir. We'll all be praying for you."

Lucy pressed her lips tightly together and averted her gaze as Dr. Fletcher used his wickedly sharp blade to cut through the angry-looking flesh on Robert's thigh. Why hadn't her husband told her how bad his leg had gotten, and why hadn't she noticed? If Robert survived the good doctor's attentions, Lucy would be asking Robert those very questions herself.

"Hold him still," Dr. Fletcher instructed Robert's valet as his patient visibly stirred even in his drunken stupor. "Lady Kurland, I'll need that bleeding bowl positioned beneath the incision."

Despite being virtually insensible, Robert flinched as a stream of foul-smelling pus gushed from the small cut and eventually slowed to a trickle. Dr. Fletcher pushed gently on the swelling until it started to bleed.

"Ah, wait." He leaned in closely and used the tip of his knife to draw something out of the hole. "Look at that! Must have stayed in there all this time."

"What exactly is it?" Lucy inquired through her teeth.

"Looks like a piece of blue fabric from Sir Robert's hussars' uniform to me." Dr. Fletcher laughed, which struck Lucy as particularly insensitive at this particular moment, and typical of a man. "I must have left it behind last time I was in here. I'll feel around and see if there is anything else. You can take the bowl away, and I'll bind up the wound."

Fighting nausea, Lucy covered the bowl and placed it on a tray outside the door. She'd already sent a note to the local healer, Grace Turner, asking her to come and see Robert at her earliest convenience. Lucy had great faith in Dr. Fletcher, but it never hurt to consult an expert in *herbal* remedies. Grace's potions had done more to improve Lucy's well-being during the previous year than any of Dr. Fletcher's concoctions.

As she returned to the bedchamber, Lucy sent up a quick prayer to the heavens. If Robert could survive the almost inevitable fever from Dr. Fletcher's attentions, she had high hopes that the sheer stubbornness of his nature would ensure his continued survival.

Chapter 1

⟨❧⟩

Aond what if I don't want to go to Bath?"
Robert inquired, scowling at his wife as she
tidied his pillows. Rain spattered the diamond
windowpanes of their bedchamber, and a cold
draught whistled down the chimney, making the
wood fire send out sullen puffs of smoke. "What
if I prefer to stay here in my own bed, and in my
own house?"

"You've been skulking in that bed for weeks,"
Lucy said, pausing in her efforts to straighten the
sheets. "Dr. Fletcher believes the hot springs at
Bath will be beneficial to you, and I am in complete agreement with him. I've rented a house
close to the baths and Pump Room where you can
drink the waters and take additional treatments as
recommended by Dr. Fletcher."

"You've gone ahead and arranged all this without consulting me?"

Lucy met his indignant gaze. "If I *had* consulted
you, you would just have said no. It seemed far
more efficient to simply organize everything, and
present you with a fait accompli."

Robert sighed. "What about the dogs?"

"James will remain here, and he has promised me that he will look after them as if they were his own." Lucy offered Robert a cup of tea. "Foley and your valet will accompany us, as will Betty."

Robert sipped the tea and studied his wife's calm features. He had a sense that whatever objections he raised she would have answers for them. After Patrick had doctored his thigh he'd fallen into a fever that had weakened him considerably and he had no memory of the first few days after the operation. He still didn't have the strength to prevent Lucy from ordering one of his footmen to bundle him up in his blankets and deposit him in his traveling coach.

"Bath isn't exactly fashionable anymore," Robert pointed out. "All of society flocks to Brighton."

"Which is why I thought you would prefer Bath." She patted his hand. "I doubt you wish to meet the prince regent strolling along the promenade?"

"Good Lord, no." Robert shuddered. Even though it had been the prince regent himself who had awarded Robert his baronetcy he had no love for the royal buffoon. "That would not please me at all."

"Then that's settled." Lucy took his cup away from him. "We'll be on our way by the end of the week."

Robert lay back against his pillows and accepted defeat. If his wife had been a man and of a military bent, he reckoned she would've beaten Napoleon in a month. She stood to brush a kiss on his forehead and picked up the tea tray.

"I'm going down to the rectory to advise my father of our decision. Do you have any message for your aunt Rose?"

Robert still found it difficult to believe that his beloved aunt had married Lucy's pompous fool of a father, but they appeared to rub along very well together.

"Just give her my love."

Lucy nodded. "Do you wish to speak to Dermot Fletcher about the estate?"

"I'll do that later today. How long are you intending to keep me captive in Bath?"

She paused at the door. "At least three months."

"That long?"

"That's what Dr. Fletcher recommends." She smiled at him, and it occurred to him that it was the first time he'd seen her look happy in days. He was not an easy man at the best of times, and being an invalid made him ten times more cantankerous.

"Thank you," Robert said gruffly.

Lucy raised an eyebrow. "For what?"

"Arranging everything."

She had the gall to laugh. "Now I know that you are still unwell. Normally, you would be standing toe to toe with me arguing the matter out." She opened the door and left the room, leaving her warm amusement surrounding him.

It was good to see her laughing again—even at him. There was a time during the previous year when he'd thought she would never smile again. But she seemed much healthier now, and far more herself. Even if that self *was* somewhat exasperating . . .

After speaking to Foley, Lucy walked down the drive of Kurland Hall and took the shortcut beside the church that brought her out opposite the rectory. It was a brisk, cold morning that required a person to keep moving. The fact that Robert hadn't ordered her to cancel the trip to Bath had surprised her immensely. Perhaps despite his objections to leaving home he was as bored as she was staying put for three months since Christmas.

She was convinced that the change of scenery and the hot springs at Bath would help aid his recovery. Dr. Fletcher and Grace Taylor, the local healer, both spoke very highly of the notion, and that was enough for Lucy. She would never forget Dr. Fletcher's skill in preserving Robert's life and leg yet again, and would be forever in his debt.

At the rectory gate, she paused and decided to use the front door. The golden stone was now covered in reddish ivy, which softened the harsh lines of the ten-year-old exterior. The new building didn't impress Robert, but secretly, after living at the Elizabethan Kurland Hall for three years, Lucy rather appreciated the rectory's warmth and symmetry. But she no longer lived there, and her father had a new wife who should be offered every courtesy. She waited as the bell clanged in the depths of the house, and was surprised when her father opened the door himself.

"Goodness me, Lucy. How very pleasant." He pinched her cold cheek. "You look very well today, my dear. I was just about to go out for a ride. Did you wish to speak to me?"

Lucy followed him into the hallway as he shut the door. "Sir Robert and I will be leaving for Bath at the end of the week as planned."

"Excellent news, my dear." The rector rubbed his hands together. "I wish Sir Robert a full and vigorous recovery."

"Thank you. I assured him that you would offer Mr. Fletcher your assistance in estate matters if required." Lucy removed her bonnet and gloves and placed them on the hall table.

"Of course, of course." The rector surreptitiously checked his pocket watch, picked up his riding crop, and put on his hat. "May I take you through to the back parlor? Rose and Anna will be delighted to see you I'm sure."

Lucy allowed herself to be escorted down the

corridor as her father opened the parlor door wide enough for her to step past him.

"Ladies, here is our Lucy to see you." The rector smiled at his new wife. "She is leaving for Bath with Sir Robert at the end of the week. I have assured her that we will render Mr. Fletcher any assistance necessary."

He bowed and stepped back, but Lucy touched his sleeve.

"There is one more thing I wished to ask you, Father." She smiled up at him. "Would you permit me to bring Anna to Bath? I would value her companionship enormously."

The rector looked over at his new wife. "What do you think of this scheme, my dear? Can you manage without Anna for a few months?"

Rose smiled at Lucy and Anna. She was an attractive woman with Robert's dark blue eyes and a lovely smile. "It's about time I stopped relying on Anna to solve every domestic crisis large and small in this house, and took on the responsibilities of my new position." She patted Anna's hand. "If you wish to accompany your sister, I will gladly give you leave."

Anna glanced uncertainly from Lucy to Rose. "I'm not sure . . ."

The rector cleared his throat. "And I must be off. If you wish to accompany your sister to Bath, Anna, I give you my blessing and hope that *this* time you'll meet some young man you will be pleased enough with to marry." He bowed and departed whistling loudly to his dogs as he went out to the stables behind the house.

Rose patted the seat beside her. "Do come and sit down, Lucy. How is Robert faring? I am very glad that he decided to go to Bath to recuperate."

Anna chuckled. "I don't think Robert had much to do with it, Rose. Lucy organized everything and sprung it upon him at the last possible moment."

"Not *quite* the last minute," Lucy defended herself. "Although I did consider dosing him with a sleeping powder and loading him into the coach while he was unconscious if he disagreed."

Rose laughed. "My nephew is not an easy man to command, but you seem to have discovered the knack of it."

"Lucy is used to managing difficult men," Anna said. "Between my father, Anthony, and the twins she usually emerged victorious."

Rose rang the bell and ordered fresh tea before settling back in her seat. Despite her very recent and surprising decision to marry the rector, she looked quite at home in the rectory. Even more remarkably, perhaps, she seemed genuinely delighted to be married again. Her adult children from her first marriage had refused to attend the quiet wedding ceremony, but seeing as she was at odds with the lot of them that hadn't bothered her at all.

Anna poured the tea and offered Lucy a slice of cake. She'd arranged her blond hair in ringlets in a casual style Lucy could never have pulled off and wore a modest blue gown that still accentuated her exceptional figure. It *was* a shame Anna was not married yet. Despite Anna's objections, Lucy was determined to give her sister another chance to meet the man of her dreams. Bath was not London, but from what Lucy had discovered there was still a smattering of polite company, which might include any number of eligible gentlemen on the lookout for a wife. . . .

"I think you should accompany your sister, Anna." Rose accepted her cup of tea. "You have done nothing but look after me for the last three months." Her smile was full of genuine affection for her newly acquired stepdaughter. "I don't know *what* I would've done without your guidance. You deserve to enjoy your freedom for a few weeks."

Anna bit her lip. "I'm quite happy here . . ."

"*Please* come." Lucy leaned forward and took her sister's hand. "With Robert taking treatments every day I will be very much on my own. We can explore the shops, and libraries, and attend the theater together."

"That does sound appealing," Anna acknowledged. She turned to Rose. "Are you *quite* certain you can manage without me?"

"No, but I'll do my best," Rose said. "I'll have to learn how to be a good wife to the local rector at some point. It's not something I anticipated happening to me so late in life, but I've always enjoyed a challenge."

"Then I will accept your invitation, Lucy," Anna said with a smile. "And now I must go and consider the state of my wardrobe. I doubt I have a thing to wear!"

"We can purchase new gowns in Bath," Lucy encouraged her sister. "I certainly intend to."

When she'd finished her tea, Anna walked with Lucy through to the kitchen where Lucy spoke to the staff, and then out into the garden.

At the back gate Lucy stopped to consider her sister.

"Are you really reluctant to come to Bath? I have sometimes wondered recently whether life at the rectory has become . . . difficult for you."

"Please don't think that Rose has been unkind to me," Anna hastened to reassure her sister. "She is as lovely as she seems and works wonders with Father's somewhat difficult temperament." She sighed. "It's just that sometimes I feel a little de trop. They are so happy together, and after running the house all by myself I find myself resenting being expected to revert to the lowly status of unmarried daughter-at-home."

"I quite understand your sentiments." Lucy nodded. "I felt the same frustration." She kissed

Anna's cheek. "Perhaps spending some time away from Kurland St. Mary will offer you the opportunity to reflect on your future."

"Perhaps it will." Anna shivered and gathered her woolen shawl more closely around her. "Now I really must go and decide which garments I can bring that won't make me look like a hideous dowd."

"I doubt you could ever manage that," Lucy said as Anna retreated into the house.

Satisfied that she had accomplished everything she had set out to do that morning, Lucy walked back toward Kurland Hall with a smile on her lips, and a spring in her step. *Some* people might call her managing. She preferred to consider herself as a woman who accomplished the impossible. Robert would regain his strength, and Anna might finally meet her match. Perhaps at some point, both of them would be grateful to her.

As she turned onto the Kurland Hall drive a horse and rider came toward her and drew to a stop.

"Good morning, Lady Kurland." Dr. Fletcher doffed his hat. "I understand that you have persuaded my most difficult patient to take my advice and retire to Bath to recuperate?"

"I believe I have, Dr. Fletcher." Lucy looked up at the doctor, who was smiling down at her.

"Excellent news. I will join you there for the

first week and stay until I find a physician of worth in Bath to carry out the regime I wish Sir Robert to follow."

"You are welcome to stay with us, sir. I rented a whole house, and there is plenty of space."

"Thank you, my lady." Dr. Fletcher touched the brim of his hat. "That would certainly make life easier. My new apprentice here in Kurland St. Mary should be capable of dealing with any medical issues that arise while I am away."

"That is good to know," Lucy confessed. "I hate to deprive the whole village of your services."

Dr. Fletcher shrugged. "If it wasn't for Sir Robert, I wouldn't even have a community to serve. Not many land-owners would willingly provide room and board for a Catholic Irish-man—even one who served in the recent war."

"How is Penelope, Dr. Fletcher?" Lucy asked.

The doctor grinned. "You know my wife, Lady Kurland. She isn't one to suffer quietly, and the 'indignities of pregnancy' haven't sat well with her." He sighed. "In truth I'd better be off home before she comes looking for me."

"Indeed."

Lucy stood back to allow him to turn his horse and head off toward the village where he and his wife lived in a modest house between the school and duck pond. She considered sending her carriage down for Penelope to bring her back to the manor house for afternoon tea, but she had rather a lot of organizing to do, and Penelope wasn't one to take a hint when it came to helping out.

Lucy entered Kurland Hall through a side door and left her muddy half boots in the scullery before heading up the stairs to the main part of the house. The pleasant smell of beeswax polish and potpourri greeted her as she traversed the ancient medieval hall. She encountered Dermot Fletcher, the physician's younger brother and the agent of the Kurland estate, going up the stairs.

"Good morning, my lady," he said, bowing. "I hear you are going to Bath."

"Yes, on Friday," Lucy said.

Dermot nodded. "I'm just going up to see Sir Robert to discuss his plans for the months he will be away." He hesitated. "Unless you wish me to return later?"

"Please, go ahead," Lucy said. She had plenty to do before she saw Robert again. "And tell him I will join him for afternoon tea."

"As you wish, my lady." Dermot bowed and continued up the stairs, leaving Lucy to walk through to her study. She sat at her desk and considered the daunting list of tasks still required to move half a household to a new location for an entire three months. Refusing to be disheartened she reminded herself that the biggest obstacles had already been vanquished.

Robert had agreed to the trip, and Anna was

coming as her companion. On that thought, she took a new sheet of cut paper and readied her pen. There was one last letter she needed to write to a naval acquaintance in Bath. . . .

Chapter 2

⸙

W ell, it isn't quite up to my standards of cleanliness, but I think we can contrive to make it comfortable enough for Sir Robert, don't you agree, Foley?"

Lucy brushed down the skirt of her sadly crumpled traveling gown and looked at Foley, who had accompanied her on the tour of the rented property.

The town house, which was faced with mellow Bath stone, comprised of five floors, a basement, and attics, which meant that after climbing many staircases Lucy was breathing quite heavily, and Foley was positively wheezing. She'd left Robert on the couch in the drawing room on the first floor, which overlooked the street, and walked through the top floors of the house with the butler at her side.

Foley nodded. "I believe we will manage, my lady. I will set our staff to cleaning the place before they depart on the morrow."

"That's an excellent idea. At least we know they will do the job properly. I see nothing wrong in the *quality* of the furnishings." Lucy took off her bonnet. "Perhaps you might ask the kitchen to bring up some tea and sustenance to the drawing room?"

Foley bowed. "Of course, my lady. Cook seems an amiable person. Let's hope her cooking skills match her appearance."

Lucy made her way down the main staircase and went into the drawing room where Robert was standing. He turned when she came in, and she noted the dark circles under his eyes.

"There isn't much of a view, is there?" Robert said.

"Not much." Lucy joined him at the window and studied the grassy center of Queen's Square, and the identical houses opposite. "I decided it was better not to be directly facing any of the major attractions in the city because of the noise."

"Ah, good point." Robert shifted restlessly from one foot to the other and went to sit down. "I am delighted not to be in the carriage. I'd begun to fear the journey would never end."

Lucy sat beside him and smoothed his sleeve. "It did seem somewhat interminable. But we're here now, and I've set Betty and Silas to unpacking our boxes. Dr. Fletcher will be here tomorrow with Anna, and then we will all be settled."

She found a footstool and deftly slid it under Robert's left boot. "I've ordered some tea, and

I intend to interview Cook properly before we attempt to eat dinner."

"Poor woman," Robert murmured with a smile. "I do hope she doesn't leave in a huff."

"She came highly recommended by your aunt Rose so I doubt she will be an issue." Lucy frowned. "I wonder if we should ask Jeremiah and Benjamin to stay with us instead of returning to the hall. With all the stairs in the house, you might need some assurance getting around."

"I'll manage perfectly well, my dear. From what I understand the master bedchamber is on this floor, which means if I do wish to go out I only have to navigate one flight of stairs down to the hall."

Lucy glanced doubtfully at his leg but decided not to comment. She could only hope that he wouldn't rely on Foley to help him, and accidentally crush the old man if he fell.

A knock on the door announced Foley with the tea tray. Lucy thanked him and poured herself and Robert a cup. She also sampled the fruit-cake Cook had sent up and discovered it was both moist and flavorsome, which gave her great satisfaction.

"How far from the baths are we?" Robert asked as he ate a large slab of cake and finished off his tea.

"Within a few minutes' walk I believe." Lucy poured him another cup. "I was told that there is very little point in bringing a carriage and horses to Bath when walking or hiring a sedan chair is much quicker and far less expensive."

"I won't miss having my own horses around," Robert admitted. "Although the notion of entrusting my person to two hulking lads in this town of hills does somewhat worry me." He touched his knee. "Dr. Fletcher told me I should attempt to walk as much as possible and take the air."

"That reminds me," Lucy said, putting down the teapot. "I must prepare an additional room for Dr. Fletcher." She fidgeted with her cup. "I wish I'd brought one of our housemaids with us. I can hardly expect Betty to manage three rooms."

"As you have already observed, the staff here came highly recommended by my aunt Rose so I should imagine they are perfectly capable of dusting a room for Dr. Fletcher." Robert finished his tea, found his spectacles, and opened the newspaper Foley had somehow already acquired for him.

Knowing from experience that conversation would be limited from this point onward, Lucy rose to her feet. "I'll go and speak to Cook and the rest of the household, and then make sure our bedchamber is ready for occupation."

Robert nodded but didn't take his gaze away from the Arrivals column in the local newspaper. After one last glance at his serene expression,

Lucy congratulated herself on arriving in Bath with her husband not only in one piece, but also in good spirits. She had worried that the jolting of the carriage would set off his fever again, but he had survived the long, tedious journey with its many stops unscathed.

Lucy peered into the master bedroom where her maid, Betty, and Robert's valet, Silas, were busy making the bed with the Kurland linen, and then went down to the kitchen, which was below the ground level of the street. She was welcomed by Mrs. Meeks, the cook, and took a seat at the kitchen table where her fears as to the staff's competence were swiftly laid to rest.

Mrs. Meeks had dealt with many invalids and even had suggestions as to which of the many resident physicians in Bath were men of good character as opposed to charlatans. Lucy made a list she intended to give to Dr. Fletcher on his arrival.

After discussing the details of their dinner, Lucy climbed the stairs again, peeked into the drawing room where Robert had fallen asleep over his newspaper, and took herself off to bed for a nap before dinner.

Lucy jumped up to look out of the drawing room window as a carriage drew up outside their door. Dr. Fletcher got out and turned to assist Anna's descent.

"Robert! Anna and Dr. Fletcher are here!" Lucy spun around with a smile as Robert looked up from his newspaper. "I'll go down."

They had both slept well despite the slight noise generated by being in the middle of a town and enjoyed a hearty breakfast together. Lucy had already planned out her schedule for the next few days and was feeling remarkably optimistic.

"There's no need, my dear. Foley will dispose of their luggage and bring them up to us momentarily." Robert folded his newspaper and set it on the seat beside him. "In fact, I can hear them coming up the stairs right now."

He slowly got to his feet leaning heavily on his cane and faced the door as Foley opened it.

"Sir Robert?" Foley bowed. "Miss Harrington, Dr. Fletcher, and *Mrs.* Fletcher."

Lucy's mouth fell open as Penelope Fletcher elbowed her way past Anna and came over to shake Lucy's hand and press a kiss to her cheek.

"*Dear* Lucy, it is so kind of you to offer Dr. Fletcher and myself a place to stay in Bath. As you know, our situation is not as it should be, and with a baby on the way my dear husband insists that we be even more cautious with our finances."

Lucy looked past Penelope to Anna, who raised her eyebrows and shrugged.

"It is indeed good to see you, Penelope, and it was very kind of you to accompany Anna to

Bath." Lucy glanced over at Dr. Fletcher, who was talking to Robert. "Although, I have to admit, I was not *quite* expecting you."

Penelope seated herself on the couch with a flourish. Despite being pregnant she still looked her beautiful self-composed self.

"I could not allow Anna to travel by *herself.*" Penelope fanned herself with her gloved hand. "It would've been quite shocking."

It was on the tip of Lucy's tongue to ask Penelope whether she trusted her own husband, but for the sake of being polite, she restrained herself. If Penelope wished to spend a week in Bath at the Kurlands' expense, then Lucy would not deny her the treat. It wasn't easy being the wife of a local country doctor, especially when Penelope had once dreamed of marrying a duke.

When Penelope turned to greet her former fiancé, Robert, Anna sat beside Lucy and lowered her voice.

"I didn't *ask* her to come to protect my virtue. She was just *there* in the carriage when Dr. Fletcher came to collect me." Anna chuckled. "Although we were given the best treatment at all the inns because Penelope looked down her nose at everyone and they thought she was royalty."

"I can imagine," Lucy murmured.

"Dr. Fletcher did tell me that he was worried about her health and thought a change of air might suit her," Anna said.

35

Lucy sighed. "Then I suppose I will have to put up with her. It *is* only for a week, and we owe Dr. Fletcher so much."

"That's the spirit." Anna patted her hand. "I must say that I am looking forward to my visit with you. I'd forgotten how much I missed all the excitement of being in town."

"Tomorrow I intend to obtain a subscription to the Assembly Rooms and write our names in the visitors book so that any acquaintance of our family knows we are in town and can come to call," Lucy said. "And then there are shops to visit, dresses to purchase, and the theater!"

"I am glad to see you in better spirits as well, my dear sister," Anna said, smiling at Lucy. "Perhaps this trip will do us both good."

While Anna talked to Penelope, Robert came over to Lucy, touched her shoulder, and murmured, "What maggot in your brain made you invite Penelope Fletcher?"

"I didn't invite her," Lucy whispered back. "In her usual highhanded manner, she just decided to come along with her husband and take advantage of my offer of accommodation."

Robert sighed. "As that sounds just like her I forgive you."

"You won't see much of her while you are busy with Dr. Fletcher at the baths. That task will fall on Anna and myself," Lucy pointed out.

"Indeed." He winked at her. "I suppose I will

manage, and I have no doubt that you will emerge the victor in any skirmish."

Foley reappeared and offered to escort the Fletchers and Anna to their respective bed-chambers, leaving Lucy and Robert alone in the drawing room again. Penelope hadn't brought a maid so Lucy directed the girl she'd asked to look after Anna to share her efforts with the doctor's wife.

Within a few minutes, Foley reappeared with a calling card on a silver platter.

"There is a gentleman in the hall who wishes to pay his respects to you, Sir Robert."

Robert picked up the card and frowned. "Do we know anyone by the name of Benson, my dear?"

"I can't think of anyone." Lucy looked up from her embroidery. "Do you wish to see this gentle-man or would you prefer it if he returned at a more convenient time?"

"Send him up," Robert commanded Foley. "The day is already full of unexpected visitors so what's one more?"

Foley retreated to the door, a frown on his face. "He is an *elderly* gentleman, sir, so it might take him some time to ascend."

In truth, Lucy had begun to believe their visitor had run away before he eventually appeared at the doorway. He wore an old-fashioned wig and frock coat and was exceedingly large around the middle. A younger man in livery who was bearing most of his massive weight accompanied him.

"Let me be, Edgar," the older man bellowed as he pulled free of his servant's grip and managed a creaky bow, his round face glowing with exertion. "I'm not dead yet, lad!"

Lucy hid a smile as Robert inclined his head. "Good afternoon, Sir William. I'm Sir Robert Kurland and this is my wife, Lady Kurland."

"Pleasure to meet you both." Sir William nodded affably at Lucy. "I saw the carriage on my return from the baths and thought I'd step in and pay my respects."

"That was very kind of you, sir," Lucy said. "Would you care to sit down and take some tea with us?"

Sir William winked. "I'd much rather a glass of port than more tea to curdle my insides."

Lucy turned to Foley, who had remained by the door. "Perhaps you might bring a variety of refreshments for our guest, Foley?"

"As you wish, my lady."

Sir William slowly lowered himself into a chair, which creaked ominously, and set his walking stick against the fireplace. "I'm renting the house next door to yours."

"Ah, and how are you enjoying Bath, sir?" Robert asked.

"I'd much rather be at home. I'm only here because my wife and my damned physician insisted upon it."

"You have my sympathy, Sir William." Robert glanced over at Lucy, one dark eyebrow raised.

"I assume your wife and family brought you here because they were concerned for your health and well-being, Sir William," Lucy said. "I should *imagine* they only wanted the best for you."

"That's true seeing as they all depend on me to make them money," Sir William chuckled. He had a strong northern accent with a rich rumbling tone. "I'm not one of those namby-pamby gentlemen who likes to sit about doing naught—present company excepted, of course."

"Are you in the business of manufacturing, Sir William?" Robert asked. "My maternal grandfather made his money that way, which gave me the opportunity to live my life in relative comfort as a landowner and farmer. Whereabouts are you situated?"

"Yorkshire, lad. I made my first fortune in coal and then dabbled in building canals, and other local industries."

"My grandfather lived in Halifax in Yorkshire. I wonder if you knew him?" Robert asked. "His name was Samuel Milthorpe."

"Milthorpe?" Sir William patted his perspiring face with his handkerchief. "Aye, I knew a man called that. He owned a pottery or two, and mayhap a mine?"

"That would probably be him. He died when I

was quite young, but I remember being taken to meet him when he visited London. He was a large man and quite terrified me with his booming voice."

"Now that I look at you, I do see a likeness," Sir William acknowledged. "What happened to his business interests after his death?"

"My uncle Wilfred ran the business for some years, and now my cousin Oliver is in charge," Robert said. "I receive a percentage of the profits through his settlements on my mother, and I attend as many board meetings as I can."

"Good for you for taking an interest." Sir William favored Robert with a firm nod. "Some of my own sons are not so diligent. They enjoy the money, mind, but don't care to get their hands dirty."

Foley came in with the drinks tray followed by the parlor maid with tea. Lucy poured herself a cup, and Robert helped himself and Sir William to a glass of port. She didn't question Robert's unusual decision to join their guest in a drink this early in the day because it was such a delight to see him so interested and engaged.

She had no recollection of Robert's maternal grandparents visiting Kurland St. Mary when she was a child. She would surely have met them in church if they had. Had they stayed away not wishing to embarrass their daughter in her new aristocratic life, or had they simply not been interested enough to travel such a great distance? It was something to ask Robert when they were alone.

"And why are you here, Sir Robert?" Sir William asked. "Is your lady taking treatment?"

"No, it is for myself." Robert touched his thigh with his cane. "I injured my leg during my service in the war and have dealt with a few complications ever since which necessitated this trip."

"Which regiment were you in, Sir Robert?"

"The Prince of Wales Tenth Hussars." Robert shrugged. "A somewhat showy-looking cavalry regiment, but a damned fine one."

"Sir Robert was wounded at Waterloo and almost lost his leg," Lucy added as Robert poured their guest another substantial glass of port. "Our physician, Dr. Fletcher, recommended he convalesce here in Bath to recuperate from his fever and regain his strength after complications in his recovery."

"My fool of a physician believes I need to rebalance my humors or some such nonsense." Sir William snorted. "Never had a day's illness in my life until I turned seventy. I fell down the steps in my house and banged my head, and you'd think the world had ended the caterwauling that ensued from my womenfolk. At least that numbskull has stopped bleeding me, and I can't complain that I haven't enjoyed floating up to my neck in that nice hot spring water in the baths."

He finished his port and set the glass on the side table with a definite thump. "Well, I should be going. I'll send my butler around with a dinner invitation in the next few days, and I'd be obliged if you'd accept it. I'm sick and tired of staring at my own family's faces, I'll tell you that."

Sir William heaved himself out of his chair with some difficulty and accepted his footman's proffered arm. "A pleasure to meet you, my lady."

"Indeed, sir. Thank you so much for coming." Lucy curtsied as Robert walked with their guest into the hallway.

He returned relatively quickly having allowed Foley to offer his help rather than risk the stairs himself and sat down by the fire.

"What an extraordinary old gentleman," Robert remarked.

"He was certainly forthright," Lucy agreed.

"I liked that." Robert stoppered the port decanter. "He reminded me of my grandfather. I didn't expect to meet anyone in Bath who might enliven the experience, but it appears that I was mistaken."

"Perhaps you should ask Dr. Fletcher to speak to his physician so that you can join Sir William at his treatments," Lucy suggested.

"I might just do that." Robert retrieved his newspaper. "Have you any plans for the remainder of the day?"

"I shall see if Anna and Penelope wish to

accompany me on a walk to get our bearings in this particular location."

"In other words, you intend to go shopping." Robert smiled at her. He was looking remarkably relaxed, making Lucy glad that the unconventional Sir William had decided to call on them.

"If we come across any interesting shops, we might be tempted inside," Lucy acknowledged. "There is very little to admire or purchase in Kurland St. Mary."

"Thank goodness, or you might bankrupt me."

"I have almost a year's worth of my pin money saved, so I doubt I shall need to call on you to finance my excesses," Lucy pointed out.

Robert lowered the paper. "You are remarkably financially prudent."

"Unless I take up gambling . . ."

"And expect me to tow you out of the river tick?" He chuckled. "I'd do it just for the pleasure of watching you attempt to explain yourself."

Satisfied that her husband was in a far better humor than she had anticipated, Lucy rose to her feet.

"I must go and speak to Cook about the new arrivals for luncheon and check that Anna is settled."

"What about Mrs. Fletcher?" Robert asked.

"I shall leave *Penelope's* comfort and well-being in the capable hands of her husband," Lucy said firmly.

Chapter 3

꧁✥꧂

Despite the fact that Bath was no longer a fashionable place, Lucy found it remarkably charming. There were excellent shops in Bond Street and Milsom Street that rivaled those in London and offered her opportunities to purchase all kinds of fripperies from milliners, glove makers, mantua makers, and haberdashers. Due to the excellent allowance Robert gave her she no longer had to turn her gowns or scrimp and save to buy a new one.

Still delighted by his recent marriage and acquisition of his new wife's extensive fortune, the rector had given Anna a handsome gift of money to bring with her to Bath, so the two sisters were able to enjoy the excitement of their new purchases together. Penelope's budget was somewhat limited, but she made sure to give her opinion about everything Lucy and Anna bought—oftentimes with herself in mind.

Knowing that Penelope was only staying for as long as Dr. Fletcher was made putting up with her much easier for Lucy, who did have some sympathy for Penelope's straitened circumstances.

"That blue would suit you very well, Lucy," Penelope stated.

"It's not really a good color for me." Lucy turned to Penelope. They were in their favorite haberdashery looking at dress lengths of fabric.

Penelope shrugged. "Then if the gown didn't suit you when it was made up, you could always give it to me."

Behind Lucy, Anna concealed a snort. It wasn't the first time Penelope had made that suggestion.

"The blue might look well on me." Anna fingered the fine fabric.

"With your pale complexion?" Penelope shook her head. "I doubt it."

"I think I prefer the rose-patterned muslin." Lucy showed it to Anna. "What do you think?"

"I like it," Anna said in support of her sister. "Buy a length and we can take it to Madame McIntosh to make it into a day gown for you."

Penelope raised her chin and walked away to the other side of the shop to look at some hat trimmings. Lucy hesitated beside the ice blue satin.

"Leave it," Anna whispered to her. "You've already bought her two things, and she can't fit into her regular gowns anyway at the moment."

"I do have some sympathy for her," Lucy admitted. "She was supposed to marry Robert at one point, and all his fortune would've been hers."

"She *chose* not to marry him, and he has done much better with you. Penelope would have made him very miserable," Anna said firmly. "Let her pout."

The bell above the door tinkled, and a new group of people entered the shop. Lucy went to the counter to pay for her purchases and to give them the address for delivery. She engaged the girl in conversation while the fabric and trimming were wrapped in brown paper.

When she turned back toward the door Anna was standing with a group of people including a tall man in the uniform of the Royal Navy. Something about Anna's stillness caught Lucy's attention, and she moved swiftly toward her sister.

The naval officer saw her first and quickly stepped back with a bow, as a flustered Anna put her hand on Lucy's arm.

"Lucy, this is Captain Harry Akers and his family," Anna said. "Mrs. Akers, may I present you to my sister, Lady Kurland?"

A small, rounded woman with a pleasant face curtsied to Lucy.

"Good morning, Lady Kurland. It is a pleasure to meet you. I believe my son made the acquaintance of your sister while he was in London."

Lucy smiled. "How lovely. Do you reside in Bath or are you visiting this fine town as we are?"

"We live out in the countryside, my lady, and came to buy clothing and other necessities for my daughter Rosemary's upcoming wedding."

The third member of the family was blushing, so Lucy assumed she was the bride-to-be.

"A wedding is always a joyous occasion in any family. I wish you much happiness," Lucy said kindly.

"Thank you, my, my lady," Rosemary stuttered, and curtsied again.

Lucy glanced over at Anna, who was conversing quietly with the young captain.

"Perhaps you might consider joining us for tea one day, Mrs. Akers? I'm sure my sister would be delighted to renew her acquaintance with you all."

"That's very kind of you, my lady."

"We are staying at number twelve Queen's Square. Do you know it?" Lucy asked.

"Indeed." Mrs. Akers nodded. "It is a fine address, and very easy to find."

"Then may I hope to see you and your family very soon?" Lucy said. "We intend to invest in a subscription to the Assembly Rooms, so we might also encounter you there, or in the Pump Room."

"Indeed, my father is quite elderly, and we often accompany him to the Pump Rooms so that he can take the waters and meet with his various acquaintances," Mrs. Akers said. "My son is awaiting a new command from the navy so we are delighted to have his company as well."

As Lucy stored this interesting information away in her head, Penelope came over with Lucy's wrapped parcel and raised her eyebrows.

"Lucy, if we wish to visit Godwin's Circulating Library before it closes, we really should be on our way."

Mrs. Akers smiled at them both. "Then we will not detain you. It was a pleasure to meet you, Lady Kurland."

She moved away with her daughter, and Anna rejoined them, her color still somewhat heightened.

"I . . . was not expecting to see Captain Akers here in Bath."

"Did he not mention that his family lived near here?" Lucy allowed Penelope to precede her out of the shop door so she could speak to Anna. "His mother said he is waiting for new orders."

"Yes, that's what Harry, I mean Captain Akers, said," Anna replied. "His last command was scuttled by a storm with the loss of many lives." She pressed her gloved hand to her bosom. "He only survived by the Grace of God."

Lucy waited for a carriage to pass before she crossed the street. "I invited his mother to call on us in Queen's Square."

"That was very kind of you." Anna hesitated. "Although I'm not sure what purpose you have in doing so. I have already made my feelings very clear to Captain Akers."

"Feelings about what?" Penelope interjected. "Have you met this man *before,* Anna? Did your father's family in London *allow* such a thing?"

Lucy met Anna's gaze. "Perhaps we should talk about this matter when we have more privacy?"

Anna nodded as they entered the bookshop and were engulfed in the smell of ink, old parchment, and leather. Despite Anna's reservations, Lucy knew her sister well enough to judge that whether she admitted it or not, her feelings were still engaged with the young man. Whatever came of the matter, Lucy intended to ensure that Anna was given every opportunity to follow her emotions to a logical and natural conclusion.

When they returned to the house, Robert was absent with Dr. Fletcher, so Lucy ordered tea to be served in the drawing room and settled down to read the local newspaper. When Foley appeared in the doorway with a silver salver containing two visiting cards she told him to bring the visitors up.

"Lady Benson and Mr. Arden Hall, my lady."

Foley stepped back to allow the visitors to enter, and Lucy tried not to stare. She'd expected

Sir William's wife to be quite elderly, but the woman in front of her was a fragile, ethereal beauty who looked far younger than Lucy.

"Lady Benson?" Lucy went forward to greet her guests. "It is a pleasure to meet you."

Lady Benson's lip trembled. "Sir William insisted I come." She waved a languid hand at the tall youth by her side, who was in danger of being strangled by the height of his own collar. "This is my son Arden."

"My lady." Arden Hall bowed elaborately but looked even more reluctant to be there than his mother, which was quite a feat. "A pleasure."

Lady Benson sank into a chair as if she no longer had the energy to stand upright. Her gown was composed of several layers of thin muslin that clearly displayed the lines of her body and her generous bosom. Her very expensive shawl was artfully slipping from her shoulders in a way that Lucy envied but had no intention of emulating.

"May I offer you some refreshment?" Lucy inquired.

Arden glanced at his mother. "A glass of brandy would be nice, and I suspect Mother would like some tea."

Lady Benson pressed a hand to her brow. She wasn't wearing a bonnet, but had pinned a lace cap to her silver blond hair. "I have a headache. A tisane would be better."

"I'm not sure if Lady Kurland has such a thing, Mama." Arden laughed. "Pray excuse my mother. She believes the entire world should serve her needs."

There was a note of disrespect in his voice that made Lucy sit up straight. "As I sometimes suffer from headaches myself, sir, I can only appreciate how your mother feels." She addressed Lady Benson. "Perhaps you would be better off at home in bed, ma'am?"

"I've spent most of the day in bed," Lady Benson sighed. "But William *insisted* that I get up and pay my respects to you." She shuddered. "He actually raised his voice to me!"

Lucy stood and went over to the door. "Then consider your duty done, my lady. It was a pleasure to meet you, and your son." She opened the door. "Perhaps when you are feeling more the thing you can visit me again."

Lady Benson rose from her chair, her tragic expression visibly brightening. "And you will tell Sir William that I did as he commanded?"

"Of course, ma'am." Lucy nodded. "I'm sure he wouldn't wish you to suffer."

"You might be surprised about that," she sighed. "He *lives* to humiliate me."

Arden Hall took hold of his mother's arm and guided her toward the door. "My mother is quite correct, Lady Kurland. We all live in fear of the old man." He nodded to her as he went past.

"Thank you for receiving us, and good day."

"Oh!" Lady Benson pressed her fingers on Lucy's wrist. "My husband asked me to invite you to dinner on Friday. Is that convenient?"

"I believe so," Lucy said cautiously. "I will consult with Sir Robert and send you a message if we can attend."

"Thank you for your kindness." Lady Benson's smile was almost tragic.

"And please don't tell my husband that I almost forgot to invite you after all."

Lucy watched the odd couple descend into the hallway and tried to make sense of their somewhat unconventional visit. The current Lady Benson was obviously not the first wife of Sir William. She also had children from a previous marriage, which meant she wasn't as young as she looked.

Was Sir William really a tyrant who had forced his wife out of her sickbed merely to pay a call on her new neighbors, or was Lady Benson exaggerating somewhat? Lucy already knew whose side she was on but attempted to give the lady the benefit of the doubt.

She sat down in her favorite chair that overlooked the square and finished drinking her tea. Lady Benson was a very beautiful woman. Had Sir William fallen in love with her charms and then discovered she wasn't quite what he expected? Lucy would have to see them together to make any sense of the state of their marriage, but she already had her doubts.

"Good afternoon, my dear."

She turned as Robert limped into the room, and went over to him. He looked rather tired and smelled strange. She sniffed his coat.

"What have you been rolling in?"

He snorted. "You'll have to ask Patrick. He insisted I was slathered in hot mud today and wrapped up like a mummy from one of those Egyptian tombs."

Lucy pressed her mouth against his lapel to stifle her laughter.

"Oh, dear."

He put a finger under her chin so she had to look up at him. "It was quite the scene. I suspect Patrick was hoping they'd cover my mouth and stop me from expressing my opinion of such a ridiculous waste of time."

"Perhaps you should take *another* bath," Lucy suggested.

Robert walked over to the couch. "The thing is . . . I actually quite enjoyed it by the end. The heat from the mud seeped into my bones and had a remarkably invigorating effect on me."

"Really?" Lucy stared at him wide-eyed. "I'm so pleased that you derived some benefit from such an outlandish treatment and are willing to admit it."

"Indeed." Robert pointed at the teapot. "Is

there any tea left? I am rather thirsty. Patrick told me to drink lots of hot spring water, but I've had enough of that foul-smelling brew for one day."

Lucy poured him a cup of tea and resigned herself to the strange aroma surrounding her husband. If it were helping him, she would willingly put up with it, and it was no worse than when he visited the pigsty at Kurland St. Mary home farm.

"I had visitors today," she remarked as she handed him the cup. "Lady Benson and her son."

"Was she as forthright as her husband?" Robert inquired as he thanked her for the tea.

"No, she wasn't what I expected at all." Lucy fought a smile. "She was extremely beautiful, much younger than Sir William, and insisted that her husband had made her get up from her sickbed merely to pay a call on me to invite us to dinner."

Robert paused, his cup halfway to his mouth. "She sounds quite odd."

"The son who accompanied her was from her first marriage, and not Sir William's."

"Was he pleasant?" Robert inquired.

"No, he was as unconventional and rude as his mother. She invited us to dine with them on Friday."

"Then we should definitely go." Robert finished his tea in one long swallow. "It sounds as if they might be quite entertaining."

Lucy had to agree. She drank her own tea and placed the cup back on the tray.

"We also met the family of a naval officer Anna was acquainted with in London. I invited them to call on us. If they *do* come, I would very much like to further our acquaintance with them."

"Are you meddling again, Lucy?" Robert raised an eyebrow.

"Hardly." Lucy met his amused gaze. "Anna mentioned this man to me last year. I got the impression that she had started to care for him before he left to carry out his duties."

"Ah, so you are meddling, but with the best of intentions."

"Or attempting to help my sister find a man who will love and cherish her for the rest of her life." Lucy held his gaze. "What is wrong with that?"

"Nothing, my dear. Just remember that Anna is old enough to make her own decisions."

"I am well aware of that." Lucy nodded. "I would never force her to do anything she disliked."

Robert leaned forward to kiss her cheek. "I know, but sometimes you can be a little managing of those you love."

"With the best of intentions," Lucy stoutly defended herself.

"Agreed, but you also told me that Anna is somewhat reluctant to be married at all." He looked into her eye. "I can't fault your desire to make sure she is happy, but I still urge caution."

"I will do my best not to interfere," she promised, even though her interventions were usually quite successful. "But I will not stop their acquaintance from progressing if they appear to be getting along."

"Fair enough. I trust your good sense." He nodded. "With all these new friends I have so much to look forward to I can barely contain my excitement."

Foley cleared his throat in the doorway. "Excuse me, Sir Robert and my lady. You have another visitor."

"Good Lord." Robert held out his hand for the calling card and read the name aloud. "Mr. *Edward* Benson."

He raised his eyebrows at Lucy. "Send him up, Foley. It appears that our interesting day is not yet over, my dear."

The man whom Foley ushered in bore a passing resemblance to Sir William and wore the sober uniform of a successful businessman.

He bowed to Robert.

"Sir Robert Kurland? It is a pleasure to make your acquaintance, sir. My father speaks very highly of you."

His accent held a hint of the north but was overlaid by years of attending a public school that had refined his vowels.

Robert stood and held out his hand for Lucy to rise. "Good afternoon, sir. May I introduce you to my wife, Lady Kurland? She just spent a delightful few minutes this morning meeting Lady Benson and her son."

Edward frowned. "So I heard, which is why I hastened over here myself to correct any unfortunate impression my stepmother might have left with you."

Robert concealed a smile. "As I did not have the pleasure of meeting Lady Benson myself, and my wife only mentioned she had called to ask us for dinner, I cannot comment on this matter."

"My stepmother can be a little . . . *eccentric* sometimes," Edward said gruffly. "But the invitation comes directly from my father and is sincerely meant."

"And we intend to honor that summons and will present ourselves at your abode at the appointed hour with great anticipation," Robert added, and gestured at the couch. "Will you stay for some refreshment?"

"I fear I must depart. My father is waiting to speak to me." Edward bowed stiffly again. "It was a pleasure to meet you, Sir Robert, and you, Lady Kurland. I look forward to furthering our acquaintance at dinner on Friday."

He turned and left, leaving Robert staring at his wife.

"Well, that was unexpected," Robert said.

"Did Sir William send him to repair his fences? What on earth did Lady Benson tell him occurred here?"

"I have no idea and the whole family is giving me a headache." Lucy pressed a hand to her forehead. "I will retire for a nap, and maybe when I wake up some sort of order will have been restored in this society."

Robert frowned. He was so busy worrying about his own health that he forgot his wife had been ill herself the previous year.

"Are you all right?" he asked bluntly.

"I'm fine." She smiled at him. "I'm worn out from shepherding Penelope and Anna around the shops in Milsom Street. I'll be perfectly capable after I've had a nap."

He went over to take her hands, searching her face.

"Are you sure?"

"Yes, I would tell you if I was feeling unwell." She frowned. "In truth I have no idea why I suddenly feel tired, but a restorative nap makes everything better." She patted his cheek. "Perhaps you might consult with Dr. Fletcher and ask him if you can take a bath to get rid of all that mud? I'd rather it didn't end up on my bedsheets."

He shuddered. "I'll ask him. Now go and rest, and I will see you at dinner."

Chapter 4

Robert stood up as Lucy entered the drawing room. Despite his initial skepticism, after two weeks of treatment at the baths he was feeling much improved. He'd also enjoyed spending time with Sir William, who had somewhat similar views to his about the state of the country, and the nature of politics and politicians. Sir William had no compunction in sharing his opinions in the most forthright manner, which, much to Robert's amusement, had soon scared off other listeners.

"You look very nice this evening, my dear." Robert considered Lucy's gown in his favorite blue.

"Thank you." She smoothed down the silk. "It is new." She touched her hair. "Anna did my hair for me. Do you like it?"

He studied the profusion of ringlets. In truth he preferred it when Lucy simply braided her long hair in a coronet on top of her head, but he had been married long enough to know not to disappoint her.

"You look lovely. Is your sister ready to accompany us to the Bensons?"

"Yes, she is just coming." Lucy came over and straightened the folds of Robert's cravat. "You look very handsome this evening."

"I do not," he demurred. "I have it on the best authority that fierce-looking gentlemen such as myself only appear dashing when wearing uniform."

"Did Penelope tell you that?" Lucy asked.

Robert grimaced. "Seeing as how quickly she wished to get out of our engagement once I was wounded and retired from the hussars, you might imagine so."

"Her loss was my gain," Lucy said.

"Yes, but somehow we have also gained *her*."

Lucy chuckled. "That has more to do with your doctor's choice of a wife than anything we did. Has Dr. Fletcher found you a new physician in Bath yet, or is he content to leave your care in the hands of Sir William's man?"

"He hasn't said. I will ask him for his opinion tomorrow." Robert picked up his cane.

"He doesn't intend to join us?" Lucy asked with a frown.

"Seeing as he has just arrived back from Kurland St. Mary, he intends to spend a quiet night at the theater with his wife."

Lucy fought a smile and Robert held up his

finger. "I know those two hopes seem somewhat incompatible."

"Robert, you are impossible . . ." Lucy reached for his hand just as Anna came through the door.

She also wore blue, but her gown was patterned with flowers, and free of the fancy Honiton lace that edged the bodice and sleeves of Lucy's gown. Even Robert had to admit that it didn't matter what Anna Harrington wore when one's gaze was inevitably drawn to her beautiful face. Unlike Penelope, who had also been an acknowledged beauty, Anna's loveliness went far beyond the perfection of her person.

"Lucy, you forgot your shawl." Anna carefully draped a paisley shawl around her sister's shoulders. "I know we are only going next door, but I don't want you to catch a chill." She smiled at Robert. "And how are you feeling today, sir? You look much better."

"As I am now capable of getting down the stairs without assistance, I am obviously improving." Robert held the door open for his ladies to precede him. "Who would've thought that floating up to one's neck in a murky pool of yellowish boiling water with a group of complete strangers would make a man healthier?"

Anna's laughter floated back to him as he carefully navigated his way down the steep staircase. He was enjoying himself far more than he had anticipated in Bath and wasn't ashamed to admit it. In truth, he felt better than he had in years.

It took them all of two minutes to knock on the Bensons' door and be ushered through into the warmth. Robert hadn't yet met Lady Benson. He'd only gotten to know Sir William at the baths and was looking forward to finally meeting the rest of the Benson family. He found the climb up the stairs slightly more laborious than the one down, and was the last to arrive in the drawing room where Sir William was holding court.

Robert's gaze was immediately drawn to the willowy young woman languishing at Sir William's side. From Lucy's description he realized that the beauty must be his elderly host's wife, and not one of his children. Behind her chair were two young men barely old enough to shave, and gathered protectively around Sir William were three older men who all had his distinctive nose.

The stark division between the two sides was obvious to even the most casual observer. Sir William stood with some difficulty and held out his hand to Lucy.

"Good evening, Lady Kurland. May I present you to my wife, Miranda, my sons, Edward, Augustus, and Peregrine?"

While Lucy curtsied, and made Anna known to Sir William, Robert noted the disgruntled expressions of the two younger men who hadn't merited an introduction.

"Sir Robert." Lady Benson didn't get up and offered him her limp hand. "A pleasure indeed. May I introduce my two sons to you as my husband did not see fit to do so himself?" She waved at the boys. "Please make your bow to Sir Robert, Arden and Brandon."

"Ah, a lover of Shakespeare I see." Robert bowed in return.

"It was an affectation of my first husband's." Lady Benson shuddered. "I had no say in the matter at all."

She turned to view Anna, who was almost surrounded by the three older Benson sons. "Is this your sister, Sir Robert? She is very beautiful."

"Anna is my wife's sister," Robert replied.

Lady Benson tittered. "Yet you chose to marry the *other* one. How . . . unusual."

Robert met her gaze. "My wife's value is far more than just a pretty face, my lady. Beauty fades, but character and goodness remain."

Lady Benson touched her cheek as if checking *she* was still beautiful. "Indeed. A lesson for us all." She stood and tapped Sir William on the shoulder. "Shall we dine?"

"When I haven't even had a chance to speak to Sir Robert or offer anyone refreshment?" Sir William frowned at her. "There is no need for such haste, my dear."

Lady Benson sighed and sat down again. "As you wish."

She made no effort to speak to Anna or Lucy, and instead spoke exclusively to her sons, who looked as if they'd rather be anywhere than at a family dinner.

"Good evening, Sir Robert." The shortest of the Bensons bowed to Robert. He wore the plain black garb favored by clerics. "I am the Reverend Augustus Benson. I oversee several parishes just outside of Bath."

"It is a pleasure to meet you, sir." Robert inclined his head. "Do you reside in Bath or at one of your properties?"

"I have a curate who ministers to the souls of my parishioners. I prefer to spend my time here where I can gain valuable benefactors for my congregation and godly work." Augustus paused. "Do you support your local church, Sir Robert?"

"Seeing as I am married to the eldest daughter of our rector in Kurland St. Mary, you might say that I do."

Augustus raised his eyebrows. "Lady Kurland and Miss Harrington's father is in holy orders?"

Robert paused. "Well, sometimes I'm not so sure about the *holy,* but he does live in the rectory and take the odd service when he has no other choice."

Now Augustus was staring at him in horror, and Robert remembered that his dislike of some of the practices of the church was not universal.

"Mr. Harrington is a good man," Robert said firmly. "He was educated at Cambridge, I believe, and is the younger brother of an earl."

"Indeed!" Augustus cast a speculative glance back at Anna, who was smiling up at Edward Benson. "I must further my acquaintance with your wife's sister. Finding a partner who is familiar with the task of running a vicarage is remarkably difficult. We probably have a lot in common."

Robert went over to reintroduce himself to Edward and met the youngest Benson, who looked nothing like his brothers but had a distinct look of Sir William.

Eventually, the butler came in and loudly cleared his throat. "Dinner is served. Please proceed into the dining room."

Unlike the house the Kurlands were renting the drawing room led straight into the dining room, and the master bedrooms were on the floor above. Sir William insisted that Robert and Lucy sit on either side of him as the rest of the family, with Anna on the arm of Edward, filed into the other seats.

Sir William bowed his head and said grace, and then the footmen left the guests to serve themselves. There was no shortage of rich food, which perhaps explained why Sir William had failed to reduce his considerable weight or improve his health during his sojourn in Bath.

• • •

Robert looked across the table at his wife and winked, and Lucy raised her eyebrows. Her husband appeared to be enjoying himself immensely, whereas she was still attempting to navigate the somewhat peculiar family around her. Peregrine, the youngest of the Benson sons, sat beside Lucy and immediately poured them both a glass of wine.

"Drink up, my lady. You'll need it," he murmured. "My father's been consuming port all day as if it will go out of fashion. I suspect we're all going to be in for a tongue-lashing tonight. It's his favorite blood sport."

Lucy blinked at him, but he continued to smile. He was the only member of the Benson family with dark coloring, and was the most outrageously fashionable and handsome. His hair was lavishly curled and smelled strongly of pomade, giving him the look of an erstwhile poet.

Lucy took a cautious sip of her wine. "Thank you."

"You are most welcome." Peregrine continued to regard her. "Your husband has made a remarkably good impression on my father."

"I believe they have much in common," Lucy replied.

"One wouldn't think it to look at them, but I suspect you are correct. Sir Robert is something of an anomaly for his class, is he not?"

"My husband is a man with forthright opinions," Lucy agreed. "Some of which are not in step with the current political climate."

"He's just like my father then. No wonder they get along." Peregrine picked up a platter. "Would you care for some goose, my lady?"

The meal progressed without further incident, but Lucy was aware that Peregrine was correct as to the level of his father's alcohol consumption and growing anger.

"You." Sir William pointed his finger down the table at Arden, one of Lady Benson's sons. "I had a note from my tailor this morning that you haven't paid his bill in six months."

Arden shrugged. "So what? Throw it in the fire, that's what I do. Bloody tradesmen shouldn't be bothering you with it."

"That 'tradesman' has to pay his own bills and feed his family," Sir William barked. "I pay you an allowance. Why aren't you paying your bills in a timely manner?"

"Here we go," Peregrine murmured in Lucy's ear, and finished his whole glass of wine in one swallow. "This won't end well."

Arden raised his chin. "The allowance you pay me is far less than that you give Edward, Augustus, and Peregrine."

"They are sons of my blood. You are merely—"

"An inconvenience that you put up with so that you could marry my mother?" Arden didn't back down. "We understand our position in this family all too well, sir, never doubt it."

Sir William leaned forward, one hand clenched around his glass of port. "If you're that ungrateful, whelp, perhaps you'd do better with no money at all."

"Please leave the boy alone, Sir William," Lady Benson intervened. "You will make me ill."

The glare Sir William cast his wife made Lucy wish she could think of a way to politely extricate *her* family from the table. The only person who seemed to be enjoying himself was Peregrine.

"Perhaps Lady Benson has a point," murmured Augustus. "One must show Christian charity to one's family, eh sir?"

"Christian charity?" Sir William rounded on his second son, who sank into his chair like a deflated pudding. "For those lazy do-nothings who suck off the cow's teat and wouldn't know one end of a shovel from the other? Your affairs, Augustus, are in no better order than that young rapscallion's!"

The angrier Sir William got the more pronounced his northern accent became.

"And that goes for all of you." Sir William's contemptuous gaze swept the table. "I've never seen a bunch of more bacon-brained useless ne'er-do-wells in my life."

"Steady on, Father," Edward murmured. "I work for you."

"And you ignore my advice at every turn!" Sir William snapped. "With your ridiculous ideas to cut up my peace and ruin my business . . ." He took another slurp of port, which Lucy thought was perhaps unwise. "I grew up without a sixpence to scratch my arse with! None of you would survive a day down the pit. *None* of you."

Peregrine cleared his throat. "That's remarkably unfair, Father. Your hard work and determination created enough wealth to bring your sons up to be *gentlemen*. Wasn't that the whole point? Why berate us for becoming what you wanted us to be?"

Lucy held her breath as Sir William turned toward Peregrine. He was breathing heavily like an enraged bull and his complexion was purple. Peregrine didn't flinch from the contact and looked more relaxed than ever.

"Aye. More fool me," Sir William grumbled. "I thought to better myself, and what do I have to show for it? Three caper-witted sons, and two . . ." He glared down at the end of the table where Lady Benson sat flanked by her sons. "Two ungrateful fools. Mark me well I'll rewrite my will and disinherit the lot of you!"

Lady Benson rose to her feet, her voice trembling. "I think I've heard enough for one evening, Sir William. I will retire with the ladies and hope that you manage to mend your manners before you appear in my drawing room!"

Lucy and Anna hurried to leave the room behind Lady Benson, who was moving at some speed. To Lucy's mortification, Robert appeared to be enjoying the fracas immensely. When they reached the drawing room, their hostess collapsed onto the couch and covered her eyes with the back of her hand.

"Oh, the *mortification!* I am quite undone!"

Lucy went to her side. "Shall I send for your maid, my lady?"

"Yes, because I am set to swoon away at the discourtesy shown to me by my own husband." She shuddered. "My nerves are shredded! My composure *ruined!*" She laid her head back on the arm of the couch. "While you are finding my maid, ask her to find Dr. Mantel. He will soothe me, I *know* it!"

Anna went to ring the bell while Lucy patted the distraught lady's hand and murmured reassurances. It wasn't the first time she had dealt with a woman of such dramatic tendencies, and she doubted it would be the last. She did have some sympathy with Lady Benson. Sir William had behaved very badly indeed. If Robert had berated his family in such a way in front of guests, Lucy would have considered walking out herself, or something even more shocking.

The door opened, and a young woman rushed in and curtsied to Lady Benson.

"Do you want your smelling salts, Lady Miranda?"

"Why didn't you bring them *with* you, Dotty?" the lady complained, her high-pitched whining setting Lucy's teeth on edge. It crossed her mind that if Lady Benson became hysterical she would not object to being the person forced to administer a timely slap. "Why do you all *torment* me so?"

"Now, now, Lady Benson." Lucy turned as a well-dressed man came into the drawing room and knelt by the distraught hostess. "What is all this? Have I not implored you to rest and not allow such irritation to your delicate spirits?"

Lady Benson dabbed a lace handkerchief over her face and clutched at his sleeve. "My dear Dr. Mantel, how *kind* you are, how *sensible* of the horrors of my situation."

The doctor patted her hand. "You must not worry yourself, my lady. I shall ask Cook to brew you one of my special tisanes, and Dotty will bring your smelling salts to you directly."

Lady Benson gave another shudder and raised her piteous face to the doctor's. "Thank you, sir. You are the only person who thinks of my comfort."

The maid reappeared with the smelling salts grasped in her hand, and with the doctor's gentle encouragement, Lady Benson applied herself to inhaling the noxious fumes.

Dr. Mantel came over to Lucy and bowed. "I do beg your pardon for such an unusual introduction, but I must assume you are Lady Kurland?"

"Indeed I am." Lucy curtsied. "And this is my sister, Miss Anna Harrington."

"It is a pleasure to meet you both." The doctor moved closer to Lucy and lowered his voice. "I must apologize for Lady Benson's condition. She has somewhat fragile nerves."

"So I observed," Lucy replied. "Although I must say in her defense that Sir William was not being particularly pleasant to his family over the dinner table."

Dr. Mantel sighed. "He is a difficult man, but also an admirable one in many ways. I have tried to curtail his excesses. I fear to no avail."

"He was threatening to disinherit everyone," Lady Benson spoke out, her voice trembling. "He seems to think we are all parasites."

"Surely not you, my lady?" Dr. Mantel turned back to her and took the smelling salts away. "You are a devoted wife to him."

"Indeed, I do my best." Lady Benson nodded. "But sometimes it is hard, especially when he treats my beloved sons so harshly."

As if she had conjured them with her words, the two young men strode into the drawing room, identical scowls on their faces.

"We're going out," Arden snapped. "The old man is drunk, and we're sick and tired of sitting there listening to him ranting."

Lady Benson pressed her hand to her fine bosom and implored them, "Please don't leave. He will not like it. He—"

"Devil take him," Arden interrupted her. "The old fool. The sooner he dies, the better for all of us."

Dr. Mantel cleared his throat. "Now boys . . ."

Brandon swung around toward him. "No one asked for your opinion, Doctor. Why don't you go back to fawning around the man who pays your wages instead of sniffing around our mother?"

Lady Benson pointed a wavering hand at the door. "Don't speak to Dr. Mantel like that! He is the only person in this household who understands me!"

"Mother's right." Arden elbowed his younger brother. "That was uncalled for, Brandon. Apologize."

"If I must," Brandon grumbled. "I agree that the old man is the problem. If only he wasn't so tightfisted with his money." He nodded at his mother. "He told us to go to the devil, so perhaps we will oblige him. If only there was some way to cut up a lark in this boring town."

Arden bowed. "Good night, Mother. We will see you in the morning."

Before Lady Benson could issue another plea

they were gone, leaving their mother weeping, and Dr. Mantel looking very embarrassed.

"I think I should escort Lady Benson to her bedchamber," the doctor murmured. "She is quite overwrought, and is in no state to deal with Sir William."

"I quite agree, sir." Lucy smiled at him, aware that he had been put in a very difficult position. "Would you like me to accompany Lady Benson?"

"That is very kind of you, my lady, but Dotty and I will manage the task between us." He attempted a smile. "I'm sure her ladyship wouldn't want to ruin your evening."

Lucy and Anna watched as Lady Benson was tenderly escorted out of the room leaning heavily on the doctor's arm, and disappeared upstairs.

"Well," Anna said. "This evening has certainly proved far more entertaining than I anticipated it would be." She glanced around the room. "Do you think we will be served with tea, or should I ring the bell?"

Lucy sat beside the fire. "Ring the bell. I suspect we'll be here for a while before I can prize my husband away from such a spectacle."

Chapter 5

Robert shivered as the wind curled around the stone columns and attacked him from all sides. His bones were aching, and he had to pay attention to his footing on the slippery surfaces. It was also possible that he had drunk rather too much port the previous evening when they'd dined at the Benson residence. He turned to Patrick, who was accompanying him to the King's Bath.

"Why do we have to come so blasted early?"

"Because there are fewer people around for you to intimidate?"

"I hardly look intimidating when I'm up to my neck in boiling water," Robert grumbled. "At least you haven't made me wear one of those awful mop hats."

His doctor had the audacity to grin at him. "At least admit that my treatments have been helpful to you."

"Indeed they have." Robert paused at the end of the dark corridor that led toward the King's Bath. They had passed a few brave souls wrapped up in cloaks and mufflers, but the baths were remarkably quiet today. He could already smell sulfur rising in the steam like a welcome to the entrance to hell. "I will have to consider a way to import such a miraculous invention as hot spring water into Kurland Hall."

"If the Romans could manage it, I'm sure you will, too, Sir Robert," Patrick joked. "Now, who's leaving the baths in such a hurry?"

Footsteps echoed down the hallway coming toward them. Robert had to awkwardly step to the side as a large cloaked figure rushed past him without as much as an "excuse me."

With a curse, Robert righted himself, and they continued into the baths where Dr. Mantel was just emerging from one of the inner rooms clutching a parcel wrapped in brown paper and string.

"Good morning, Sir Robert, Dr. Fletcher. I am surprised to see you on such a cold day." He chuckled. "It took all my powers of persuasion to get Sir William out of his warm bed and into the baths today. Only the promise of some conversation with your good self, Sir Robert, persuaded him to rise at all."

Robert looked idly over at the bath, but it was a gloomy morning, and it was hard to see exactly who was currently in the steaming hot water.

Dr. Mantel bowed. "I must go and attend to Sir William. I will tell him that you have arrived."

He strolled closer to the baths and then spun around, his face stricken. "Dr. Fletcher! I can't see Sir William in the water, and I can't swim, and—"

Patrick was already moving toward the almost deserted bath. By the time Robert caught up his friend was stripping off his coat and boots and jumping into the steaming hot water. There was nothing bobbing on the surface except a linen cap and a small wooden tray containing a natural sponge.

Robert grasped hold of one of the pillars surrounding the bath to stop himself from slipping and looked in vain for one of the attendants. There was another splash in the water as Patrick dived down and emerged with a body in his arms that he towed toward the side of the bath.

Somewhere a lady started screaming, the sound echoing in the cavern as Patrick hauled out Sir William's body and arranged him on his side.

"Check his mouth," Patrick shouted. "Make sure he can breathe."

As Dr. Mantel appeared to be frozen in shock, Robert awkwardly got down on his knees and made certain Sir William's tongue was in the right place, and that there was nothing untoward in his mouth. Patrick thumped vigorously on the old man's back, but Sir William was no longer breathing.

"Is he dead?" Dr. Mantel asked anxiously.

"I fear he is." Patrick sat back, laid the body on its back, and gently closed Sir William's bulging eyes. "Did you see what occurred?"

"No, dammit, I left to speak to one of the vendors about purchasing a new pumice stone before he even entered the water, and when I came back—" Dr. Mantel shuddered. "I couldn't see Sir William at all. My *God* . . . I will never forgive myself."

"Having observed Sir William over the past weeks, I suspect he suffered some form of heart failure or a stroke and simply slipped beneath the surface of the water," Patrick said.

"Yes! I would agree with that possibility," Dr. Mantel said, nodding. "What a terrible tragedy. Lady Benson will never forgive me for not having taken sufficient care of her beloved husband."

"If he indeed died from failure of the heart or a stroke then there was little you could've done about it even if you'd been in the water with him," Patrick pointed out. "I'm certain you warned Sir William that eating and drinking in excess would cause him problems."

"I did warn him." Dr. Mantel sighed. "But he rarely listened to my advice."

"A common problem for physicians the world over," Patrick agreed.

Robert rose carefully to his feet. His knee was already complaining at the hardness of the stone, and the dampness of his once pristine clothing.

"Would you like me to send one of the attendants to fetch the magistrate?" Robert asked. He looked around the almost deserted space. "It appears that the rest of the patrons have decided to flee and not indulge in a dip in the baths today."

A familiar figure came rushing up to them and bowed. "Gentlemen, as the proprietor of these baths, I understand that a tragedy has befallen Sir William Benson. I offer my condolences and offer whatever help you need."

"Thank you, Mr. Abernathy." Robert bowed in return. "Perhaps you might consider closing the baths to the public until we can remove Sir William's body to his house?"

"I've already done that, Sir Robert, and ordered a carriage to transport the body back to Queen's Square." Mr. Abernathy bowed again.

"I'll travel with him, Sir Robert," Patrick said. He was shivering as he put his coat on over his wet clothes. "Mayhap you can walk back with Dr. Mantel and help him deliver the sad news to the Benson family?"

"Yes, of course," Robert said, his gaze fixing on a trickle of red that appeared to be coming from the body. He leaned in and murmured in his friend's ear, "Dr. Fletcher, why would Sir William be bleeding?"

As Dr. Mantel turned away to speak to Mr. Abernathy, Patrick gently probed the deceased's body and then looked up at Robert.

"Perhaps Sir William didn't drown or suffer heart failure." He held up his bloodstained fingers. "It's possible that someone wanted to make certain he never got out of the baths again."

Robert held Patrick's gaze. "Please do not speak of this to anyone else yet."

Patrick raised his eyebrows. "If you insist."

"I'll explain when we get back to Queen's Square." Robert straightened up. "If anyone was a likely candidate to be murdered, it was Sir William Benson."

Robert took an involuntary step back as Lady Benson started screeching like a demented banshee and then collapsed to the floor of the breakfast parlor. He supposed he should have caught her, but Edward Benson had been closer and hadn't moved an inch.

It was Edward who addressed him now, his face pale.

"My father is *dead?*"

"Yes." Robert saw no need to sweeten the news. He'd written many letters to the families of his men who had died in battle, and believed a short, heartfelt response was better received than a lot of balderdash. "My physician, Dr. Fletcher, attempted to revive Sir William when he retrieved him from under the water, but to no avail."

"Dear God." Edward sat back in his chair as if unaware that his stepmother was still lying prone on the Turkish rug while her maid and Dr. Mantel attended to her. "He's been ill for quite some time, but I never really thought he'd die. He was something of a force of nature."

"Indeed. I enjoyed his company immensely." Robert bowed. "I offer your entire family my condolences." He noted that none of the other Bensons or Lady Benson's sons were at the breakfast table at such an early hour. "If there is anything Lady Kurland or I can do to help, please do not hesitate to call upon us."

"That's very good of you, Sir Robert," Edward said. "And thank you for bringing us this sad news."

Lady Benson was carried out by one of the footmen moaning piteously, and Robert stepped out of the way.

"I should be going. Dr. Fletcher will accompany the body back to this house. He should be here very shortly."

Belatedly Edward remembered his manners. "Would you like to await him here? Can I offer you a drink or some breakfast?"

Robert hesitated. "I *would* like to wait until Sir William's body reaches this house so that I might pay my last respects, but I do not require any sustenance, thank you."

In truth, he would rather like a large brandy, but at nine o'clock in the morning that was asking rather too much of his hosts. He also wanted to speak to Patrick before any of the Benson family began to ask questions as to what exactly had befallen their father.

A commotion on the stairs drew his attention to the door as Lady Benson's two young sons came into the room. From the disordered state of their dress they had been out all night.

Edward shot to his feet, his expression darkening. "Where in God's name have you two been?"

Arden, who was propping up his younger brother, belched loudly. "Out. What is it to you?" He glanced around the breakfast room. "Where's my mother?"

"She's upstairs in her room after receiving the most devastating news," Edward said somberly. "Sir William is dead."

For a moment there was silence, and then the brothers burst into whoops and hugged each other. Robert's lip curled in distaste. If he'd had the two of them under his command in his regiment he would've taught them a few lessons about respecting the dead.

"You're pitching the gammon," Brandon said when he finally stopped laughing. "Sir William is an immortal monster."

Robert intervened. "I can confirm that Sir William is indeed deceased. May I also suggest that you show a little respect!"

Arden faced him. "Why should we? It's the

best thing that's happened since Mother married that old fool. I'm glad he drowned." He grinned at his brother. "Now we'll be *rich!*"

"Get out," Edward said, and pointed at the door. "Go to your rooms and reflect upon your appalling behavior in front of our guest, and your complete disregard for your stepfather."

"We'll go," Arden sneered. "But only because we need our sleep." He half bowed to Robert. "Good riddance, Sir Robert."

Edward turned to Robert as the pair lurched back into the hall. "I do apologize."

"There's no need. Their contempt for Sir William was on display when we came to dinner," Robert said. "I'm not surprised that they are full of vicious glee at his demise."

The butler appeared in the doorway. "Dr. Fletcher is here, Mr. Benson, shall I send him up?"

"Direct him up the stairs to Sir William's bedchamber. I have already alerted his valet." Edward went toward the door. "Shall we attend them there, Sir Robert?"

Lucy jumped up from her seat by the window as Robert appeared in the drawing room accompanied by Dr. Fletcher.

"What on earth is going on next door?' Lucy asked. "There has been a veritable procession of people and vehicles arriving all morning."

Dr. Fletcher bowed to her. "Sir William is dead."

Lucy gasped and turned to Robert, who nodded. "Sir William was in the King's Bath and apparently drowned." He hesitated. "Do you suppose you could ring the bell and ask Foley to bring up the brandy?"

After Lucy had settled Robert and Dr. Fletcher in their chairs and persuaded her husband to eat a few mouthfuls of toasted muffin to accompany his rather large brandy she sat opposite them.

"I assume you went to tell the Benson family the sad news?"

"Yes, I accompanied Dr. Mantel, who was very concerned that he would be held responsible for the tragedy."

"Why would he think that?" Lucy wrinkled her nose.

"Because he left his patient in the baths and went to speak to one of the vendors, meaning he wasn't there to see Sir William sink beneath the surface," Dr. Fletcher explained.

"Why didn't anyone else help Sir William?" Lucy wondered.

"That's an excellent question," Robert said. "To be fair, there were very few people *in* the bath at that point in the morning, and most of them are either ill or elderly. It's also possible that they didn't notice what had happened through the steam and the darkness."

"Or they chose to ignore it," Lucy sniffed. "It always amazes me how blind people become when they simply do not choose to see what is happening right in front of their noses."

"Sir William was a very large man," Dr. Fletcher added. "I doubt any of them *could* have got him out of the water. It took all my strength."

"Well, thank goodness you were there." Lucy smiled at him. "Were you able to establish why he died? Considering his somewhat choleric disposition I wouldn't be surprised if he'd had a stroke or suffered heart failure."

Robert and Dr. Fletcher exchanged a long, lingering glance, and Lucy sat up straighter.

"Is there something amiss?"

"There might be," Robert replied. "Dr. Fletcher had the opportunity to examine the body properly before he returned it to the Bensons, and things might not be as simple as they appear."

"In what way?" Lucy turned to the doctor.

Dr. Fletcher grimaced. "Just below his ribs there was a wound that looked as if he had been stabbed upward toward his heart."

Lucy covered her mouth and met Robert's gaze. "Oh, *dear*. Did you mention it to the Bensons?"

"Not yet." Dr. Fletcher looked inquiringly at his employer. "Sir Robert asked me not to say anything."

"Which was very well done of you," Lucy said approvingly at her husband. "If none of the

Benson family believe there is anything suspicious about the death, then we can question them without fear."

"With all due respect, my lady," Dr. Fletcher asked slowly, "question them about what?"

"About which one of them murdered Sir William?" Lucy raised her eyebrows. "It seems quite obvious to me."

After Dr. Fletcher left to inform his wife that his departure would be delayed for at least another day, Lucy remained with Robert in the drawing room while he recounted what had gone on at the Bensons on his early morning call. Lucy listened wide-eyed as he described the behavior of the younger boys and tutted in disapproval.

"I suppose they think that now Sir William is dead they can behave in whatever manner they wish."

"Indeed," Robert said. "One can only hope that Sir William had the forethought not to give them any money in his will. That should wipe the smiles off their faces. Their contempt for him was *appalling*."

"And Lady Benson swooned at your feet?"

Robert shuddered. "Literally. I felt as if I'd been pushed onto the stage of some overdramatic melodrama."

"You do agree that Sir William's death might not be due to natural causes?" Lucy asked.

"Yes, I do." Robert paused. "I liked the man immensely, and if there has been any foul play I intend to ensure that it is brought to light."

His determination to do the right thing resonated on his face, making Lucy quite relieved that for once she wasn't going to have to cajole him into joining her in investigating a possible murder.

"I think we should start by talking to everyone who was at the baths this morning," Lucy said. "You probably knew some of the other bathers. If they are residing in Bath they might frequent the Pump Room, and you can point them out to me."

"I'm not sure I'd recognize most of them with their wigs on and below the neck, but I'll do my best," Robert agreed. "We should also speak to the attendants at the baths." He frowned. "I noticed that there didn't appear to be anyone near the actual bath when the incident occurred, and that most of the torches had either not been lit, or had blown out because of the wind."

"If someone came in after Sir William, and before you got there, it's possible they might have deliberately extinguished the torches to make it darker," Lucy said. "It would certainly have made their task easier."

"As we approached the baths some fool came rushing out and almost knocked me over in his haste to leave," Robert added. "One has to wonder if *he* had anything to do with it."

"Did you recognize the man?"

"Unfortunately not. I was too busy trying not to fall over." Robert finished his glass of brandy. "If you wish, we can walk over to the baths right now. I feel quite unsettled, and I would prefer not to sit around worrying."

Lucy cast him a doubtful glance. "Are you quite certain? Would you prefer to rent a chair?"

"I'll be fine, my dear. Don't mollycoddle me."

"As you wish."

Lucy swept him a curtsey and went to put on her pelisse and bonnet. Her husband was a remarkably stubborn man who did not always take her advice. After three years of marriage she'd learned not to insist that he did, and tried very hard not to remind him when she was proven right.

When she came down into the hall Robert was already awaiting her, his cane in one hand and his hat in the other. He looked her up and down as if she were one of his regiment on a parade ground.

"That is a very fine bonnet, my dear."

"Thank you. It was just delivered from Milsom Street this morning." Lucy smiled at him, aware that he was attempting to make up for his earlier snappishness. "It is also remarkably warm."

"Then we should proceed." He put on his hat and offered her his arm. "Is your sister to accompany us?"

"She has already gone ahead to do some

shopping and then intends to go to the Pump Room with Penelope."

"Then we can meet up with them there after we've concluded our business at the baths."

It was only a ten-minute walk from the square to the baths, and it was mainly flat, which made it much easier for Robert. Lucy made no effort to rush, pausing to admire the architecture and to study the Theatre Royal as they went by. They threaded their way through Westgate Street past Upper Borough Walls and ended up in Stall Street.

As they entered the baths, an attendant came out to greet them.

"Good morning, Sir Robert. I regret to inform you that the baths are currently closed due to an unfortunate incident early this morning."

"I am well aware of that. Sir William was a friend of mine, and I was here with him this morning," Robert responded. "I wish to speak to Mr. Abernathy if he is available."

"I shall see if I can find him for you, sir." The man bowed.

"Were you here this morning?" Lucy asked just before the servant turned away.

"Indeed I was, my lady."

"Were you positioned close to the baths?"

"We were quite shorthanded, and what with the wind blowing so hard most of us were trying to keep warm in the back." He grimaced. "I don't think anyone saw Sir William go under the surface. If we had, someone would've gone in for him."

"Has such a thing happened before?" Robert asked.

"Yes sir, with the nature of our clientele being somewhat frail or elderly, people often fall asleep in the baths, or are overcome with the heat of the water, or the fumes. Mr. Abernathy has taught us all to keep an eye out, sir."

"But obviously not today," Robert observed. "Thank you for your insight. Perhaps you might find Mr. Abernathy for me now?"

"Yes, Sir Robert, certainly, sir."

"It sounds as if this morning was particularly appropriate for a murder," Robert mused as the servant sped off. "Not enough staff, light, nor any interest in ensuring their patrons were kept alive."

Lucy shivered as the wind howled down the stone corridor. "I can hardly blame them for not wanting to stay out in this weather. How on earth do you stand it?"

Robert patted her gloved hand. "When you get into the water, you forget about the cold. It is quite blissful."

Robert walked farther into the complex, and Lucy inhaled the noxious odors emanating from the bath. She had no intention of ever disrobing in front of complete strangers and finding out if his words were true. Steam rose from the dark surface and even at this time of the day with the sun at its brightest, there wasn't much light within the cavernous space. She could quite understand how someone might not notice a body slipping beneath the surface.

She reached Robert's side and pointed at a woman sitting by the wall with a basket beside her. "Shall we speak to her while we wait for Mr. Abernathy?"

Robert walked over to the woman and tipped his hat. "Good morning, ma'am. Were you intending to bathe today?"

"Not likely." The grin Robert received revealed the woman had half her teeth missing. "I come here to sell my perfumes and soaps to the bathers, but I won't be making much money unless that skinflint Abernathy reopens the place."

"Are you here every day, Mrs. . . . ?" Lucy asked.

"Mistress Peck and aye, ma'am. I was here at the crack of dawn when the large gentleman was fished out of the bath like a stranded whale." She cackled. "What a sight. He was a kind gentleman though. Often gave me a few pennies when he passed by."

"Did you see him come in this morning?"

"He arrived with that fancy doctor of his, and another man. I only noticed *them* because they were arguing something rotten."

"Sir William and the doctor?" Robert asked.

"The other one. He was as tall as Sir William, and had a look of him."

"Did you happen to catch what they were arguing about?" Lucy asked.

Mistress Peck looked at Lucy. "You're asking a lot of questions for someone who ain't even bothered to inquire about purchasing my wares."

Lucy obligingly chose a bar of soap. Robert dug into his pocket, produced a half crown, and placed it in the woman's grimy hand. "Perhaps you might continue to humor my wife."

"Indeed I will." Mistress Peck tucked the coin in the purse hanging from her waist. "They was arguing about money, and the old man's will. Then the doctor went off to talk to someone, the old man changed to get in the baths, and the other one eventually went off in a huff."

"Did you see his face clearly?" Robert asked.

"No, he was all bundled up against the cold."

"Would you recognize him again?"

"I doubt it. There was nothing in particular about him. He just looked like a gentleman." Mistress Peck looked past them and raised her voice. "Oi! Mr. Abernathy, are you going to open up those blasted baths? Some of us have a living to make!"

Mr. Abernathy winced as he ignored the woman and came toward Robert and Lucy.

"I do apologize for keeping you waiting. As you might imagine, I have had a rather busy morning."

"I appreciate you finding the time to speak to us, Mr. Abernathy." Robert hesitated. "Sir William was a rather particular friend of mine, and I am attempting to aid his family at this difficult time."

"I am sure that they appreciate your efforts, Sir Robert. Have you come to collect his belongings? I have them in my office. Please come this way."

Lucy exchanged a startled glance with Robert and then meekly followed along behind. They could deliver the items back to the Bensons after they had taken a look at them.

Mr. Abernathy spoke to one of the men huddled around the brazier outside his office and ushered Robert and Lucy inside. When they were seated, he stood behind his desk and shook his head.

"This is a bad business, and a very sad day for the Benson family."

"Indeed." Robert inclined his head.

"I know that Sir William was not in good health, but death is always a shock, isn't it?"

"Especially when it happens on your premises, Mr. Abernathy, and under your watch," Robert stated.

"Well, my dear sir," Mr. Abernathy protested, "I cannot *possibly* be held responsible for everything that happens in the baths. The type of people who come here, the sick, the old, and the infirm, are fully cognizant of the risk they take exposing their persons to such an environment. They do it on the advice of their physicians, mind. *Not* mine. I merely supply a service."

"Then you don't believe your staff were negligent this morning?"

Mr. Abernathy's eyes widened. "Of course not, Sir Robert. My staff is beyond reproach."

"I understand that you tell them to watch out for those in the waters."

"Indeed I do." Mr. Abernathy bowed.

"Yet no one noticed Sir William was no longer visible above the water?"

"I hesitate to speak ill of the dead, but on the one occasion when Sir William *did* fall asleep in the baths, and was awakened by one of my staff, his vocal displeasure at such treatment was such that I ordered my staff not to concern themselves overmuch with him. Sir William also had his own physician accompanying him."

"But Dr. Mantel was apparently dealing with another issue away from the actual bath?"

"That is correct. At the fatal moment, Dr. Mantel was engaged in a financial transaction with one of the vendors, and arrived back when it was too late to save his employer."

"So you think it was Sir William's own fault." Robert nodded.

"It was an unfortunate accident," Mr. Abernathy said firmly. "Sir William could have dropped dead in the street just prior to his bath, or died in his carriage going home." He raised his eyes heavenward. "Who am I to judge when our Lord will take a man of great age and in ill health?"

Despite his impertinent questioning, Robert was fairly certain that Mr. Abernathy hadn't deliberately allowed someone to pay him off so that Sir William would die in the baths. But Robert wouldn't discount him as a suspect quite yet.

A knock on the door revealed a servant carrying a pile of clothing topped by a pair of boots and stockings secured by string.

"Sir William Benson's apparel, sir."

Lucy came forward to receive the pile. "Thank you. I shall deliver these garments to Lady Benson immediately." She smiled at the man. "Are you the person who helps bathers undress?"

"I can do that, ma'am, but I also keep an eye on their things while they're in the bath. There are all kinds of folks wandering in and out of here so it stops thieving hands."

Lucy nodded, her expression sympathetic. She was much better at getting answers from people than Robert would ever be. For some reason he tended to frighten people. "Did anyone ever try to steal Sir William's clothes?"

"No, ma'am, because he always paid me extra

well to keep them safe. He was a kind gentleman in his way."

"Indeed." Lucy smiled at him. "Thank you."

A few minutes later they walked out of the baths into the ever-increasing wind, and Robert came to a reluctant decision.

"It is too cold for me to walk back, and you cannot carry that unwieldy mass of clothing through the streets. It will be picked off by the beggars."

Lucy looked up at him. "We won't need to walk. We are meeting Anna and Penelope at the Pump Room and can take the carriage back with them."

"Ah, I had forgotten." He frowned. "The lack of interest in Sir William's death Mr. Abernathy displayed and his inability to accept any blame have rather stuck in my craw."

"Do you think he had something to do with it?"

"Mr. Abernathy? I suppose he could have agreed to look the other way while someone drowned Sir William, but it seems unlikely when there is a whole collection of Bensons who seem delighted that the head of the family has died, and would be eager to dispose of him themselves."

"One of the Bensons could have paid him," Lucy suggested.

"That is true." He looked down at her. "I just remembered something odd."

"What?"

"When I told Lady Benson's sons that Sir William had died I'm fairly certain that one of them mentioned he had drowned."

"And?"

"I didn't specify exactly how Sir William *had* died, so how did they know? They were out all night. They could easily have hidden in the baths, drowned the old man, and slipped out again in the confusion while nobody noticed."

"Wouldn't you have seen them?"

"I saw that one man rushing out. Perhaps they split up. Or maybe it was only one of them who did the deed." He sighed. "Now I come to think about it, we don't even know how long Sir William *was* under the water before Dr. Mantel raised the alarm. It could've been for quite some considerable time."

"Which means that the boys could've killed him, and gone before you even got there or anyone noticed." Lucy shivered. "What a disaster."

He took her arm and continued walking toward the Pump Room. He had no desire to socialize with the town's elite, but was willing to sacrifice his principles for the sake of being warm.

"I wonder if anyone at the baths would recognize Lady Benson's sons?" Lucy mused. "I could ask Anna to sketch their faces."

"It is possible that they accompanied Sir William and their mother at some point in time,"

Robert said. "We can always go back and ask when Mr. Abernathy isn't present."

He held open the door to the Pump Room, releasing the hum of lively conversation and the faint smell of the hot spring water available from the fountain. Robert beckoned to the footman standing to attention by the inner door.

"Will you take charge of these belongings and put them in a secure place until my carriage arrives?"

"Yes, sir." The footman bowed and took the bundle of clothes.

"Thank you." Robert offered Lucy his arm again. "Then I suppose we should go on in and face the masses."

Chapter 6

Lucy was escorted up the stairs of the house and directly into the bedchamber of Lady Benson. The curtains were closed, and the air was thick with the sickly, overpowering scents of perfume and laudanum. She and Robert had looked through Sir William's garments and found nothing of interest. He hadn't been robbed, which indicated that whoever had wanted to end his life hadn't been after his purse.

Or at least not after his actual coin . . .

"My dear Lady Benson, how are you?" Lucy asked.

Lucy sat down on the chair beside the bed and smiled sympathetically at the new widow who was lying back on a mound of pillows, her long blond hair around her shoulders, and her expression tragic.

"Oh! Lady Kurland, how kind of you to call in my hour of need." Lady Benson reached out and grabbed Lucy's hand in a surprisingly strong grip. "I cannot believe Sir William is dead."

"It is indeed a tragedy," Lucy agreed.

"It certainly is for me," Lady Benson said. "How am I going to *cope* when we are so far away from home?"

"I'm sure Mr. Edward Benson will deal with everything for you," Lucy said gently.

Lady Benson sniffed. "If I leave things up to him I can guarantee I will be tossed out in the gutter with nothing but the clothes on my back!"

"Surely you jest?" Lucy countered. "He seems to be an admirable gentleman."

"Then you do not know him at all. Even my sainted husband distrusted him at the end. He was losing money hand over fist, and Sir William was about to take back control of his companies."

"Was Mr. Edward Benson aware of this?" Lucy asked.

"Indeed. They argued about it all the time," she sighed. "And now I am at Edward's mercy, and he hates my sons as well."

Lucy resolutely kept what she thought of the young men to herself. She was far more interested in what Lady Benson was intent on confiding in her.

"I'm also certain that Augustus and Peregrine would never allow their older brother to mistreat you," Lucy stated. "Augustus *is* a man of the cloth."

"There is nothing spiritual about that man whatsoever!" Lady Benson declared. "And as for Peregrine, who fancies himself a playwright and lives off his father just like the rest of them . . ."

She fell back against her pillows and pressed her fist to her breast. "I am surrounded by those who wish *ill* on me."

Lucy pointed to the parcel she had brought with her. "Sir Robert and I collected your husband's clothes from the baths. I thought you might want them."

To her astonishment, Lady Benson sat bolt upright and reached out her hand. "Give them to me!"

Lucy put the neatly folded clothes on the bed and watched incredulously as Lady Benson took out each garment, searched every pocket, and felt along every seam.

"Nothing . . ." she murmured. "There is nothing here."

"I'm not quite sure what you are expecting to find, my lady, but—"

Lady Benson interrupted Lucy. "I should have known it. He is far too clever for that."

"Were you looking for something important?" Lucy inquired.

"No." Lady Benson suddenly looked exhausted again. "It was foolish of me."

Lucy stood and surveyed the now tangled mass of clothing. "Would you like me to fold the clothes for you?"

"Take them through to Mr. Tompkins, Sir William's valet. He will know what to do with them." Lady Benson closed her eyes and lay back down, one hand shielding her face. "Good day, Lady Kurland."

Realizing she had been dismissed, Lucy gathered up the clothing, and rather than use the connecting door into the dressing room went through to the hallway and then into the second bedroom. An elderly man who reminded her of Foley was busy emptying out a chest of drawers.

"Good afternoon, Mr. Tompkins," Lucy said. "I'm Lady Kurland. I brought Sir William's clothes back from the baths for Lady Benson. She asked me to bring them through to you."

"Thank you, my lady. You can put them on the bed." He studied her carefully. "Your husband is Sir Robert Kurland, aye? Sir William thought the world of him."

"And Sir Robert reciprocated his regard."

Mr. Tompkins gestured at the open drawers and chests. "I'll pack up his trunks, and send them back home to Yorkshire. Mr. Edward can decide what to do with everything then, and what to do with me."

He had a strong Yorkshire accent that reminded Lucy vividly of his employer.

"Have you been Sir William's valet for a long time?"

"We were boys together, my lady. Grew up in the same village and ran away to make our fortunes. Sir William did all right for himself, and offered me a job when I had nowhere else to turn. I've been his valet for fifty years now."

"That is a remarkably long career, Mr. Tompkins," Lucy said. "I can only commend such excellent service."

"Sir William was worth it," the old man said gruffly. He appeared to be the only member of the Benson household who was genuinely grieving for the old man. "He's always been a hard man, but also a fair one, and with this lot of vultures circling him recently who can blame him? I don't know why he didn't pop off even sooner."

"I *had* noticed that there was some conflict between Sir William and certain members of his family," Lucy said diplomatically.

Mr. Tompkins snorted. "He wasn't very happy with any of them. The last conversation we had before he set off for the baths was about amending his will again."

"Indeed?"

"He liked to carry it around with him and rewrite it whenever someone displeased him. I was often called to be one of the witnesses." Mr. Tompkins smiled. "It put the fear of God into the lot of them."

"I should imagine it would," Lucy agreed. "I assume Sir William has a solicitor who will deal with his affairs?"

"Yes, my lady. I believe Mr. Edward has already sent for the man. Depending on the weather he should be here within the week." Mr. Tompkins bowed. "Thank you for bringing the clothes, my lady. That was Sir William's favorite waistcoat, and I believe he would want to be buried in it."

"Then his wish can now be granted." Lucy turned toward the door. "Do the family plan to take his body back to Yorkshire or will he be buried here?"

"Definitely Yorkshire, my lady." Mr. Tompkins grinned. "He'd haunt us all if we tried to bury him in the south."

Deep in thought, Lucy made her way down the stairs to the hallway. Lady Benson believed that the Benson brothers were against her. She had also suggested that Sir William's displeasure had embraced his entire family, a fact bolstered by Mr. Tompkins's claim about the old man's will.

"Ah! Lady Kurland!"

Lucy looked down to see Mr. Peregrine Benson standing at the bottom of the stairs. He wore an immaculate black coat but was smiling up at her as if he didn't have a care in the world.

"Were you visiting the recently widowed Lady Benson?" he inquired as he offered her his hand and bent over hers. "Did she manage to conceal her glee?"

Lucy frowned at him. "She was inconsolable."

"I'll wager she was. Edward won't put up with any of her nonsense, I can tell you that."

"So she imagined." Lucy paused and looked

up at his face. "Do you think he will treat her badly?"

His expression hardened. "She deserves to be left without a penny, but I doubt the old man would be that hard on her. We'll see what happens when the solicitor reads the will, won't we?"

"Why don't you like her?" Lucy asked bluntly.

"Because attempting to seduce the son of your current husband is remarkably bad form, wouldn't you say?" He raised an eyebrow. "She is amoral, and her sons are not fit to appear in polite company."

Before Lucy could even attempt to reply to his outrageous comments, the front door opened, and Edward and Augustus Benson came in speaking in hushed tones. They too wore black, but without the fashionable flair of their younger brother.

"Lady Kurland." Edward doffed his hat. "I must commend you and Sir Robert for your tireless attentions in our time of need."

Lucy curtsied. "It is our duty to help our fellow man, sir, and Sir Robert was very pleased to have made the acquaintance of an old friend of his grandfather's."

"Indeed, Lady Kurland." Augustus nodded eagerly. "You show nothing but Christian kindness."

Behind her, Lucy thought she heard Peregrine snort, but chose to ignore him. "Well, I must be on my way. Sir Robert will be wondering what has become of me." She nodded at the three brothers, noting that none of them seemed particularly troubled by grief. "Good morning, gentlemen."

Edward hastened to open the door for her and bowed low as she passed him by. Within a minute, Foley was opening her own front door, and she went up the stairs to her drawing room where she heard voices. Anna, Penelope, and Captain Akers's family were sitting there having tea. There was no sign of Robert.

Lucy untied her bonnet and went forward to greet her unexpected guests.

"I do apologize for my absence. I hope my dear sister has entertained you adequately."

"Miss Harrington has been all that is gracious." Captain Akers couldn't hide the warmth in his eyes as he gazed at Anna. "She assured us that you would return shortly, and she was correct."

Anna blushed. "Your high opinion of me is remarkably flattering." She turned to Lucy. "I merely ordered tea, and hoped."

Lucy allowed Penelope to pour her a cup of tea, aware that no one in the Benson household had thought to extend such civility toward her.

Lucy addressed Mrs. Akers. "I was visiting Lady Benson in the house next door."

"Oh yes, we heard about Sir William's death." Mrs. Akers sighed. "He was an elderly man who from all reports lived a full and productive life. May he rest in peace."

"Amen to that," Anna murmured. "Did you know the Bensons, Mrs. Akers?"

"We met the family in the Assembly Rooms. Sir William was very pleasant." Mrs. Akers paused. "I regret to say that his wife did not choose to pursue an acquaintance with us."

Penelope sniffed. "I have no idea why. She was certainly not from the higher echelons of society herself. In truth I found her remarkably dull, and not as beautiful as everyone suggested."

Mrs. Akers blinked at Penelope and then looked back at Lucy. "Regardless it is still hard to be widowed at such a young age."

Penelope rearranged her shawl over her rounded belly. "I suspect she will do very well for herself. My mother often told me to marry a much older man who would die quickly, but I chose Dr. Fletcher, who will probably outlive *me* when I die in childbirth."

"I doubt Dr. Fletcher would allow that to happen, Penelope," Lucy said robustly. "You are the most precious of his patients." She raised her eyebrows. "And don't you have to pack? I believe Dr. Fletcher said you were leaving tomorrow."

"Dr. Fletcher is *indeed* leaving for a week or so, but I will be staying." Penelope raised her chin. "You cannot possibly expect me to expose myself in my present condition to the indignities of travel *again?*"

Lucy met Anna's amused gaze. "Of course not, Penelope. You are most welcome to stay." She turned to Mrs. Akers. "Now, how are the arrangements for your daughter's wedding progressing?"

Just before the Akers family rose to leave, Robert and Dr. Fletcher arrived, meaning that their departure was delayed quite considerably. Lucy even considered inviting them to stay and dine, but was unsure whether Cook would be able to feed them. Before Lucy could put her offer to the test Mrs. Akers revealed that she had to get home anyway, and Lucy issued an invitation for a later date.

Anna walked down with the visitors while Robert helped himself to the remains of the tea. Dr. Fletcher returned to his packing with his wife accompanying him.

"Captain Akers seems like a fine upstanding fellow," Robert remarked. "And his family are very decent folk."

"Yes, they are." Lucy came to sit opposite him. "Did you notice how often he looked at Anna?"

"With all due respect, my dear, most men look at Anna. She is remarkably beautiful." He paused to drink his tea. "The thing *I* noticed was that Anna was looking back."

"Exactly." Lucy nodded. "She met Captain

Akers in London, and favored his suit until he asked her to marry him, and she retreated."

"Ah, that explains it then." Robert took the last scone and spread cream and jam on it. "Mayhap she has changed her mind and intends to wed him."

"I hope she has." Lucy gripped her hands together. "Having met him, I truly believe he is the right man for her."

Robert gave her a look. "You shouldn't be meddling."

"Someone has to," Lucy replied. "Anna needs a home and a family of her own."

"In your opinion." Robert held her gaze. "From what you have told me, Anna isn't interested in any marriage that involves the prospect of children."

"I *know* that, but—"

"Then it would be cruel to push her toward something she is mortally afraid of, wouldn't it? I know you love your sister, Lucy, but this has to be her decision."

Lucy drew herself upright. "I am aware of that. I simply meant that I would make sure Anna is given every opportunity to socialize with the gentleman and his family in the hopes that she changes her mind."

"I sincerely doubt that she will, but I will hold you to your promise not to interfere." Robert finished off his tea. "I will also do my part to engage the young man in conversation, and ascertain his worth and intentions toward Anna."

"Thank you." Lucy set her cup back on the tray with something of a bang. Robert's plain speaking was sometimes hard to stomach. "I know I can always rely on your good sense in such matters. Did you go to the baths today?"

"I did, and I spoke to some of the people who usually frequent the King's Bath at that early hour. Even those who were actually in the water were quite unaware that anything was amiss until they heard about Sir William's death afterward."

"So all we know at this point is that someone ran out of the baths at some speed when you were approaching them."

"A person no one can actually identify, and who might have nothing to do with the matter at all." Robert grimaced. "Although I have considered your idea that one of the Benson family perhaps paid someone to kill Sir William. It would be a far less risky strategy."

"I agree, but if that is the case, how will we ever find out which member of the family it was?" Lucy asked.

"I thought we should start from the other end of the tangle." Robert looked at her. "The entire family will remain here until the will is read, so we have the opportunity to observe their behavior and question them."

"Sir William's valet, Mr. Tompkins, said that

the family solicitor is on his way from Yorkshire to deal with his late client's affairs," Lucy said. "He also implied that his employer liked to amend his will whenever someone displeased him."

"So I gathered." Robert half smiled. "Sir William spent much of his time in the baths railing against his family, and threatening to disinherit them."

"*Lady* Benson told me that Sir William was at odds with Edward for mismanaging the business. Did he mention anything about that to you?"

"Indeed he did. I suspect there was some truth in his grievances, but I also know that it is hard to pass one's business into another's keeping without secretly thinking they will make a mull of it." Robert set down his cup and plate. "Every time I received a promotion in the hussars I believed the man who replaced me would never be as good to my men as I was."

"You should speak to Mr. Tompkins," Lucy said. "He already holds you in high regard. He has been with Sir William for fifty years so he probably knows more of his secrets than anyone."

"I'll send Foley over to speak to him first." Robert nodded. "He might be more willing to confide in a fellow servant than he would be in me."

"What an excellent idea." Lucy smiled warmly at her husband. "And I will continue to visit

Lady Benson. She is remarkably indiscreet about her late husband's family, and solely concerned about her own fate."

"I can't say that surprises me. Sir William admitted that he'd married in haste and was bitterly repenting his choice at his leisure."

"Lady Benson is afraid Edward will ensure that she doesn't receive a penny from the will," Lucy said. "And Peregrine, the youngest son, suggested that Lady Benson had behaved in a most *problematic* manner with him."

"Really?" Robert raised an eyebrow. "Well then, one might assume that Peregrine is the only member of the family who was hoping his father would stay alive forever."

Lucy rose to light one of the lamps and make sure the coal fire was burning brightly. "Sir William didn't approve of Peregrine's artistic career or of Augustus. In truth, he disliked them all."

"I agree, but if one of them did kill him, why *now?* What particular thing has happened in the past week or so to bring the situation to the boiling point?" Robert stood and paced the room, his gaze focused on the floor as he walked.

"Well, there was that dinner party we attended," Lucy reminded him. "Lady Benson's sons were even heard actually *wishing* Sir William would die, and lo and behold, the next day, he *is* dead. In my opinion they are still the most likely culprits.

They hated Sir William, they are unlikely to receive much from his will, and they want their mother to be in control of her own money so they can leech off her instead."

"They are certainly of the age that act irresponsibly and think later," Robert agreed. "And their disgust for Sir William was very obvious." He swung around to face Lucy. "Perhaps I *will* ask Anna to sketch their faces so I can show them around the baths, and see if anyone recognizes them."

"I think that is an excellent notion," Lucy agreed. "And let's not forget that they were also out all night, and could easily have waited at the baths for Sir William to arrive, and murdered him."

Robert walked over to the door and opened it. "It is a puzzle. I will go and speak to Foley, and see if I can engage his help in this matter. I know he will be discreet."

His wife waved him onward, and he left the room. Had he been too sharp with her about her plans for her sister's happiness? She certainly hadn't taken his intervention well, but she did have a habit of thinking she knew best for the people she loved. The fact that she was often correct in her assumptions didn't mean that she always was.

Robert was fond of Anna Harrington, and

would certainly do his part to make sure that any gentleman who wanted to marry her was thoroughly investigated before being allowed to proceed. Having met the perfectly respectable and eligible Captain Akers he suspected that Anna's aversion to marriage ran far deeper than perhaps Lucy realized. She was of a much more robust nature than her retiring sister and perhaps unable to fully comprehend Anna's frailty.

Robert opened the door into the bedchamber and discovered Foley folding his shirts and cravats.

"Ah, Foley. Just the man I was looking for."

Foley turned toward his employer and bowed. "Who else would be in here at this time of day?"

"Silas? My valet?" Robert pointed at the lengths of linen. "It's usually his job to attend to such matters."

"He doesn't do it right," Foley said stubbornly. "I sent him down to the kitchen to run an iron over your best coat while I set things to rights."

Robert was fairly certain that Silas would have a different opinion on the matter. He was equally devoted to Robert and perfectly capable of performing his duties.

"Have you met Mr. Tompkins from next door?" Robert asked as he settled into a chair beside the fire. "Sir William Benson's valet."

"Indeed I have, sir. He is a very fine gentleman indeed. Devastated by Sir William's death, devastated."

"Is he the chatty type?"

"Not at all, sir. Loyal to a fault, and as close-mouthed as a clam."

"Do you think you might be able to prize some information out of him anyway?"

Foley turned to look fully at Robert. "Information as to what, sir?"

"His master." Robert sat forward, his hands clasped between his knees. "I'm not convinced that Sir William died of natural causes. In truth, I suspect someone in his family decided to murder him."

Foley didn't immediately speak, and Robert looked up at him.

"Did you hear what I said?"

"I did, sir," Foley said slowly. "From my discussions with Mr. Tompkins I had gleaned that all was not well with the Benson family, and that he himself wasn't surprised that Sir William died so abruptly. Do you wish me to seek his confidence, sir? To see if he has any idea who might have done the deed?"

"That's exactly what I need, Foley," Robert said. "But you will have to be both careful and discreet, and only share what you learn with me or Lady Kurland. I don't want you putting yourself in harm's way."

Foley's eyes gleamed and he looked positively

thrilled. "I'll be careful, sir, don't you worry about me. I suspect that under his dour exterior, Mr. Tompkins is dying to share his views on this matter with someone. He is from the north, and they do believe in plain speaking."

"Then can I leave the matter in your capable hands?" Robert rose from his seat as Silas came into the room carrying the newly ironed coat. "Good evening, Silas. I see Foley has been keeping you busy."

"Yes, Sir Robert."

The exasperated look the younger man gave the butler didn't escape Robert's notice, but he didn't remark upon it. Foley was the oldest member of the Kurland household and was treated with great respect by everyone even when he turned to meddling. Silas knew that Robert valued his work regardless.

"There will only be Lady Kurland, Miss Harrington, Mrs. Fletcher, and myself for dinner this evening, Foley. Perhaps you might tell Cook."

"Yes, Sir Robert." Foley bowed and positively skipped out of the room leaving Silas and Robert alone.

Robert pointed at the coat. "You can put that away. I don't intend to go out."

Silas put the freshly ironed coat in the cupboard and turned back to the pile of folded cravats on the bed. "Now I'll have to refold all this lot again," he murmured.

Robert clapped him on the shoulder. "I really don't care how they are folded as long as they are put away before Lady Kurland asks me why they are cluttering up the bed."

"I'll have the whole lot cleared up before dinner, sir."

"Good man," Robert said. "I know I can rely on you."

Chapter 7

Lucy sipped her tea and attempted to make conversation with Augustus Benson while she waited for Lady Benson to put in an appearance. The vicar wasn't looking well, his jowly face haggard, and he kept forgetting what he was saying. Well used to the clergy, Lucy simply smiled and attempted to make him believe that every word he uttered was perfection. She'd discovered years ago that a little flattery went a long way with a cleric.

"Do you intend to hold a memorial service for Sir William before you return to Yorkshire?" Lucy asked. "I am sure that there are many people in Bath who hold him in high esteem, and might wish to offer you their condolences in person."

"I'm not sure, Lady Kurland."

Lucy raised her eyebrows. "Not sure that your father was held in high esteem, Mr. Benson, or that you will hold a service?"

The vicar swallowed hard. "I await the orders of my older brother and the family solicitor, my dear Lady Kurland. Obviously, I am more than happy to hold a service for my own *father*."

"Do you have the living on any of the churches within Bath, sir?" Lucy asked. "Or would we need to travel farther afield for such a service?"

"Unfortunately, my lady. My parishes are too far away, and too small to merit the attention of Bath society. Any ceremony would have to be held in a more fitting location."

"What he means is, that he's too busy bleeding his parishes dry to allow anyone to see the state they are in," Peregrine spoke from the doorway. "He's got one drunken curate managing five localities. Church services are nonexistent, and his parishioners are currently petitioning the bishop of Bath and Wells to have him removed."

Augustus shot to his feet, his face now flushed red with fury. "I'll ask you to refrain from commenting on something you know nothing about!"

Peregrine's smile was that of a cat that'd just trapped a mouse. "I know a lot more than you think, Brother. And so did Father."

"He knew nothing of these slanderous and totally false accusations against me unless you told him."

"I didn't need to tell him a thing," Peregrine drawled. "He wasn't stupid, Augustus. Just because he didn't speak like a gentleman didn't mean he wasn't fully aware of what was going on." Peregrine sauntered farther into the room. "In fact I heard him shouting at you the day

122

before he died about this very matter. The whole *house* heard him, so why are you attempting to deny it now?"

Lucy stayed very still. Both men appeared to have forgotten she was there, and she was quite willing to go along with their lack of attention.

"You are wrong," Augustus insisted. "We *never* argued. It must have been someone else you overheard, like one of Miranda's young sons."

"I heard them being read the riot act many times, but this was definitely you, Brother dear. I saw you emerge from his study, and goodness me did you look angry." Peregrine paused. "In fact, the last thing you said to him was a threat, wasn't it? That you'd be damned if he ruined your reputation, and you'd see him in hell first. Fine words for a man of the cloth."

"Why you—" Augustus's hands curled into fists, and he stepped close to his younger, taller brother.

Peregrine didn't even flinch, his gaze steady as he looked down at Augustus. "You are an abysmal human being, and I wish to God that you weren't my brother."

"And you are so much better?" Augustus snapped. "What with your *sinful* London ways, and your unmitigated depths of depravity? Do you think our father approved of *that?*"

Peregrine's smile disappeared. "No, he didn't, and he told me so in no uncertain terms."

Augustus shook his head. "But it's always been easier for you, hasn't it? The youngest son, the baby of the family, until Lady Miranda's boys came along to put your nose out of joint."

Peregrine's lip curled. "My father never liked them."

"A situation which you deliberately engineered by turning him against them because you were jealous," Augustus insisted. "You couldn't *bear* not being the favored child, could you?"

Peregrine glanced briefly down at Lucy, making her jump. "I do apologize, Lady Kurland. I didn't see you there." He bowed deeply. "Perhaps we should cease this discussion immediately, Augustus."

Augustus swiveled around to stare at Lucy, his horrified expression so ludicrous that Lucy almost wanted to laugh.

"My goodness! I do apologize for my brother, Lady Kurland. He is prone to both exaggeration and fiction. I'm certain he will reassure you himself that his remarks were meant in jest, and not to be taken seriously at all."

Peregrine raised an eyebrow. "I also apologize, Lady Kurland, but I stand by every word I uttered."

Augustus gave Peregrine one last thunderous glare and left the room, slamming the door behind him. Peregrine took his brother's vacated seat and helped himself to the brandy the butler had left on the side table. Lucy considered him, noting his hands were shaking, and that he wasn't as calm as he was pretending to be. Was it possible that some of his brother's comments had hit home as well? Had a jealous Peregrine deliberately soured the relationship between his father and the two newest additions to the family?

It was an interesting thought. Lucy would have a lot to discuss with Robert when he returned from the baths later in the day.

"I *do* apologize, Lady Kurland." Peregrine met her gaze full on. "You came to visit us out of the goodness of your heart, and ended up in the middle of a ghastly family scene."

"It is of no matter." Lucy shrugged. "My father is the rector of our parish. I have seen many family squabbles after an unexpected death. People do not always behave as you might think they will in times of crisis."

Peregrine let out his breath. "I can only agree with that. Edward is proving to be most indecisive, Lady Miranda is prostrate in bed, and I'm attempting to discover where the devil Mr. Carstairs, our solicitor, has gotten to."

"I understood that he was on his way to Bath from Halifax?"

"Indeed he is, but the weather has apparently delayed him." Peregrine finished his brandy. "To be perfectly honest, Lady Kurland, I can't wait to be rid of the lot of them so that I can go back to London."

"You could depart regardless, I suppose?" Lucy offered tentatively.

"And leave my father's body in the hands of this bunch of incompetents? If it were up to Miranda, Sir William would be robbed of everything and thrown into the river with the fishes. She is one of the most mercenary women I have ever met."

"I find that difficult to believe." Lucy wrinkled her nose. "She seems rather too dependent on others."

"She certainly *appears* that way, but you must remember that she snared herself a golden calf, and expects to receive the lion's share of his immense fortune to do with as she pleases." Peregrine finished his brandy and stood up. "Pray excuse me, Lady Kurland. I have to go to the local posting house, and see if I have received any reply to my latest letter."

He glanced down at Lucy. "Will you be all right by yourself? Are you expecting Miranda to come down?"

"I was told that she would be with me within half an hour," Lucy said.

"Good luck with that." Peregrine winked at her, his equilibrium apparently restored, and strolled out of the door.

Lucy contemplated her rapidly cooling tea. Should she go? She certainly had enough fascinating anecdotes to keep Robert enthralled until well past dinner. Just as she placed her cup back on the tray, the door opened, and Lady Benson appeared draped in black lace, supported by Dr. Mantel on one side and her maid on the other.

"Lady Kurland, I am so sorry I took so long to come down to you. I felt a little faint when I first attempted to rise, and Dotty took fright, and insisted I waited for Dr. Mantel to assure me that I was well enough to risk my health on the stairs."

Lucy curtsied. "If you truly feel that bad, ma'am, perhaps you should return to bed? I would hate to be the cause of any lapse in your well-being."

She thought Dr. Mantel's lips twitched at her honeyed words, but she might have been mistaken.

"No, my good doctor says it is important for me to rise from my bed, or at least make the attempt." Lady Benson sank gratefully down onto the couch. Her maid took up position behind the chair, smelling salts in hand. "But it is so hard to be positive, Lady Kurland, when all around me are threats to my livelihood, and that of my sons."

"Threats, my lady?" Lucy asked. "Who would do such a thing to such a recent widow?"

Lady Benson glanced fearfully around the room as if she suspected there were untold enemies hidden behind the curtains. "They all wish me ill."

"*They?*"

"I believe Lady Benson is referring to her step-sons," Dr. Mantel intervened.

"I'm certain that as her physician you are not *encouraging* her to doubt Sir William's family?" Lucy countered.

"Of course not, my lady." To his credit, Dr. Mantel looked appalled at the very idea. "My only job is to make certain that Lady Benson is well enough to represent herself when the family solicitor arrives."

"I have asked Dr. Mantel to accompany me to any meeting regarding Sir William's estate, but he insists that it is not his place," Lady Benson said.

"I will be close by, my lady. I can assure you of that." The doctor patted Lady Benson's black lace–mittened hand. "You are stronger than you think, and are a devoted mother and have your boys to fight for."

"That is true. I cannot allow Edward to deprive my beloved sons of their rightful inheritance."

Lucy forbore mentioning that the disbursal of the assets would be at the late Sir William's behest, and that Edward would merely be the executor of his father's wishes. From her own observations Lucy had a shrewd suspicion that Sir William might not have left the boys a penny.

"Mr. Peregrine Benson told me that he is

attempting to find out what has befallen Sir William's solicitor, and why he hasn't arrived yet," Lucy said.

"Peregrine hates me," Lady Benson wailed. "He probably wishes to get to Mr. Carstairs and bribe him to destroy my husband's real wishes."

Dr. Mantel cleared his throat. "I doubt Mr. Peregrine would do that, my lady, or that Mr. Carstairs would take a bribe. He is a fine, upstanding gentleman."

"I'm certain that everything will soon be resolved, Lady Benson," Lucy murmured reassuringly. "Sir William did not strike me as the kind of man who would leave his affairs in disorder."

"Exactly, Lady Kurland." Dr. Mantel bowed.

The butler entered the drawing room and bowed to Lady Benson.

"Would you like some fresh tea, my lady?"

"That would be lovely, thank you."

Lady Benson sighed and eased her head back against the couch. "It has been a very tiring day. I sorted out my wardrobe and put away all my beautiful gowns. I will have to call on my dressmaker. I only own this one gown in black because it does not suit me. I fear I will have to wear this color for *months* if not for years."

Lucy couldn't think of an appropriate reply and said nothing. She would drink yet another cup of tea and then escape back to her own house next door. Lady Benson's self-absorption was remarkably wearing.

Arden Hall came into the drawing room and bowed to Lucy and his mother.

"Good afternoon, Mother. I'm impressed that you managed to get out of your bed today."

Lady Benson pouted. "I am not well."

Arden sat down and crossed one leg over the other. "You should be feeling a lot better seeing as you don't have to put up with the attentions of the old man anymore."

Dr. Mantel opened his mouth as if to chastise the young man and then apparently thought better of it.

"He's dead, Mother dear," Arden sneered. "You hated him while he was alive, so why pretend to mourn him now?"

"How can you say that?" Lady Benson gasped, and sat up, her hand pressed to her bosom. "I loved him *excessively!*"

"You loved his money," Arden continued. "And you certainly loved being Lady Benson, but come on, Mater, you can be honest now. You couldn't stand him!"

Again Lucy wondered if she had perhaps become invisible or whether the Bensons had no ability to keep their dirty family secrets firmly in the closet where they belonged. It certainly made her task of ascertaining the truth easier than she had anticipated.

"I think you are being unfair to your mother and to your stepfather," Dr. Mantel said. "Their marriage is their business, and they are the only people who know what truly went on in it."

"Good Lord, Doctor. My mother loves to spread her woes around. She told Brandon and me how things were," Arden protested. "In truth, there were times when I had to forcibly restrain my younger brother from confronting Sir William and doing him bodily harm!"

"Brandon is rather hotheaded," Lady Benson acknowledged. "And there was that unfortunate incident at school when they sent him down for fighting."

"Fighting?" Arden's crack of laughter made Lucy wince. "That was the least of his crimes. The final straw was when he attempted to beat one of the schoolmasters with his own chair. But don't worry, ma'am. I have him well in hand now."

Dr. Mantel cleared his throat and glanced over at Lucy. "And how is Sir Robert enjoying the baths these days?"

"He is recovering nicely." Lucy smiled. "Although I believe he misses Sir William's company. He insists that everyone else there is either a fool or an invalid."

"Yet he is an invalid himself?" Lady Benson nodded. "He does seem quite young to be so afflicted."

"He is hardly *afflicted,* Lady Benson. Sir Robert held the rank of major, fought with the Tenth Hussars against the French, and was wounded at the battle of Waterloo." Lucy raised an eyebrow. "He was knighted by the prince regent for his gallantry on that day."

"Really?" Arden turned to Lucy, his face for once free of malice. "How absolutely splendid. I've always wanted to go into the military."

"Do not speak of such things." Lady Benson clutched her throat. "Do you wish to kill your own *mother?*"

Arden's expression clouded over again. "I'll leave that sort of thing to Brandon." He shot to his feet. "I'm going out."

After Arden left banging the door behind him Dr. Mantel spoke. "Actually, I think a military career might be the making of him."

Lucy nodded. "Sir Robert would agree with you."

"Maybe if Arden does receive a bequest from Sir William, he could use it to purchase a commission in a good regiment."

Lady Benson glared at her physician. "It is hardly your place to suggest such a thing— especially when I am so recently widowed, and fearful of being abandoned by everyone I know and love."

Dr. Mantel bowed. "I do apologize, my lady. You are quite right."

"I have a few errands to run before dinner so I must depart." Lucy rose from her seat and curtsied to her hostess. "Thank you so much for the tea. I do hope you feel better soon, Lady Benson."

"Good day, Lady Kurland."

Her hostess waved a vague good-bye and leaned back against the couch as if unable to support the weight of her head any longer.

Dr. Mantel walked Lucy down the stairs to the front door.

"Thank you for coming, my lady." He hesitated. "You might not realize it, but Lady Benson really does appreciate your visits. She knows almost no one in Bath, and is feeling rather isolated and unsure."

"I can imagine." Lucy smiled at him, aware that his status put him in a very delicate position with the family who employed his services.

"If Sir Robert gets a chance to speak to Arden about obtaining a commission—without his mother noticing—it might help him form a better plan for his future than raising hell," Dr. Mantel suggested.

"I'll certainly mention it to my husband, but I must warn you that Sir Robert hasn't been impressed by Arden's or Brandon's demeanor, and might be reluctant to involve himself further."

"I understand." Dr. Mantel sighed. "The

boys have, perhaps, been overindulged by their mother."

Lucy decided not to comment on that. "Do you intend to stay with the family now that your principal patient is deceased, Dr. Mantel? Or will you remain in Bath and set up practice here?" Lucy asked.

"I intend to return to Yorkshire with Lady Benson, and make sure she is comfortably settled. After that I am not sure." He smiled and bowed. "It is most kind of you to be concerned for my welfare, my lady. I truly appreciate it."

On that note, Lucy took her leave and went out into the street. She chose the path that led back into town as she had a book to return to the lending library on Milsom Street. It was sunny outside, but not warm, and she walked quickly, her thoughts on the afternoon's encounter. There was certainly a lot of information to consider. She couldn't imagine living in a household that laid bare every emotion to the world, but it certainly helped her attempts to decide which one of the Bensons had the most reason to murder Sir William.

Robert stared at Lucy as she recounted her earlier visit to the Bensons over dinner. Penelope had retired to bed and Anna was out visiting Captain Akers's family.

"Good Lord." Robert only realized his dinner

had gone cold when he attempted to eat some more lamb. "What an *extraordinary* tale."

"I know." Lucy picked up her fork. "At times I felt as if I had been relegated to a seat in the audience of a play, but I didn't complain too loudly. It was quite educational to hear them all at one another's throats."

"What are your conclusions so far?"

"Well, my suspicions of Miranda's sons still stand, but I would speculate that Brandon was the perpetrator, and that Arden is covering up for him. This also might explain why only one man appeared to be running away from the baths that morning,"

Robert nodded. "Agreed. Anything else?"

"Augustus is obviously in some trouble," Lucy mused. "I thought I might pay a visit to the bishop's residence, and see if I can ascertain exactly what is going on."

"Do you think they will talk to you?"

"Of course they will." Lucy raised her eyebrows. "I am the daughter of a rector who also happens to be a well-known scholar, and is the son of an earl. If anyone knows how to charm their way into a clerical household, it is I."

Robert couldn't argue with her reasoning. "What do you think Augustus meant about Peregrine's 'sinful' ways?"

Lucy wrinkled her nose. "I thought I'd leave that part up to you. I was also interested in his claim that Peregrine deliberately set his father against Miranda's sons because he was jealous of them."

"Why did that concern you?" Robert asked.

"Because maybe Peregrine *knew* they had been included in Sir William's will, and he was so incensed that he decided to murder his father."

"Leaving the boys still in the will," Robert pointed out.

"Maybe Peregrine thought he could change the will somehow," Lucy suggested. "All I know is that he wasn't as calm and unconcerned about everything Augustus said as he claimed to be." She cut into a potato speckled with parsley. "Did you find out anything more at the baths today?"

"Only that both Arden and Brandon have been seen there before, but that no one could definitely say that they were there on the morning in question." Robert grimaced. "To be honest, I am more interested in finding out what is going on with Sir William's business, and whether his claims that Edward was destroying it are true."

"And how do you intend to proceed with that?" Lucy asked.

"I've written to my cousin Oliver. He knows the Benson family and their business, and will probably have an opinion about them both."

"Then we are progressing—albeit slowly." Lucy sighed. "Sometimes I wonder why we get mixed up in these matters at all."

"Because this time Sir William deserves justice." Robert held her gaze through the candlelight. "I am more convinced than ever that he died before his time. I intend to bring his murder or murderers before a judge to pay for their crime."

"Our most likely candidates are still the two boys," Lucy said. "I can't quite see Augustus murdering his father in broad daylight, can you?"

"We know from experience that murderers often do the unexpected, and spring from the most unlikely of places," Robert reminded her.

"That is true, although I still doubt that a cleric, who tend to be well-known figures, would risk jumping into the baths to drown his father." Lucy drank some of her wine and grimaced. "This tastes remarkably metallic."

"It tastes fine to me." Robert finished his glass. "And if Augustus did jump into the baths he wouldn't have been wearing his clerical attire at the time, would he? He would've been wearing the same ridiculous outfit as the rest of us."

"Which lends the wearers a certain anonymity, especially if they cover up their hair," Lucy murmured. "I hadn't thought of that."

"Augustus could've drowned his father, and then joined the other bathers on the far side of the baths, and exited with them being none the wiser there was a murderer in their midst," Robert pointed out.

"As could any of our suspects." Lucy sighed. "Do you still wish to accompany me to the theater this evening, or would you rather stay in?"

"I'd prefer to go out. If I stay here worrying about the Bensons, I will be pacing the carpet all evening, and you will probably wish me to the devil."

"Probably." She smiled at him. "But I do understand your concerns."

He reached across the table, took her hand, and kissed her fingers. "I really must thank you again for insisting I came to Bath. I am feeling so much better."

"So I can see. Apparently, you needed nothing more than taking the waters and solving an unexplained death to set you to rights."

Robert chuckled. "And a wife who understands me and allows me to follow my passions."

She blushed very prettily and looked down at her plate. "I should go and change."

"If you must." He studied her muslin dress. "You look perfectly nice just as you are."

"Flatterer." Lucy rose to her feet and Robert followed suit. "I'll be as quick as I can."

Chapter 8

I t is such a pleasure to meet the daughter of the Honorable Mr. Ambrose Harrington—a man whose theological work I have long admired."

Lucy smiled at the retired archbishop's wife and her two daughters as they offered her tea. Her note to the bishop's Bath residence had resulted in an invitation to call and she had immediately acted on it. She had no real interest in seeing the bishop himself, who was fortunately in Wells, having learned long ago that the female members of clerical families and their staff generally held any secrets.

"My father is a very well-educated man, Mrs. Lemmings, with interests that span a variety of topics including those dear to the Church of England."

In truth her father was far more invested in hunting and horse racing than anything spiritual. The theology of the church did appeal to him in an intellectual manner, which meant he was quite prepared to pontificate and argue about it with the best scholars in the land, and often wrote articles for scholastic journals.

"How wonderful," the oldest Miss Lemmings breathed. "I cannot imagine how it must have felt to hear him speak in person every day."

Lucy made a mental note to remind her father to visit Bath at the earliest opportunity.

"I often helped him with his sermons and translated passages from the original Greek and Latin," Lucy said.

"He allowed you to learn those heathen languages?" Mrs. Lemmings raised her eyebrows. "My dearly deceased husband did not consider them suitable for our daughters."

"I was lucky that my father never barred me from learning anything I wished to know." Lucy smiled. "He often said that I was far too intelligent to be trapped in a woman's body."

Mrs. Lemmings nodded as if this made perfect sense to her. "Does Mr. Harrington not have sons?"

"My brother Anthony is currently abroad with the prince regent's Tenth Hussars, and my younger twin brothers are away at school." She didn't mention her older brother, Tom, who had died during the war, because it was still not a matter she was prepared to subject to public scrutiny.

"Lucky man," Mrs. Lemmings commented. "Sadly, I only had daughters."

Lucy noticed Cora, the youngest Miss Lemmings, rolling her eyes at her sister as if she'd heard that particular lament rather too often.

"Daughters are a blessing," Lucy said firmly. "They are always so supportive."

"Do you have children of your own, Lady Kurland?"

"Not yet," Lucy said. "But I have only been married for three years. It is something I would dearly love."

"You married quite late, then?" Miss Lemmings asked, and then blushed a fiery red. "Not that is it any of my business, but—"

"Yes. After my mother's early death I was convinced that it was my destiny to stay and keep house for my father, and younger brothers and sisters. As it turned out, Sir Robert, who is the major landowner in Kurland St. Mary, asked me to marry him. I was very happy to accept his proposal."

"What a wonderful story," whispered Miss Cora. "You give us all such hope."

Lucy smiled at the sisters. "Perhaps while I am staying in Bath you and Miss Lemmings might care to join us for tea, or even accompany us to the Assembly Rooms? My sister Anna would love to meet you."

"That would be most acceptable. We have secure lodgings here at the bishop's residence, but are somewhat cut off from the outside world." Mrs. Lemmings inclined her head making the bows on her lace cap tremble. "Since my husband's demise I simply cannot abide society. I fear that the girls' chances of making a good match are fading away along with their looks."

"One should never give up hope," Lucy answered. "I'm certain your daughters behave themselves impeccably in society, and that any man would be lucky to have them."

Her retort earned her beaming smiles from the two girls, and a doubtful look from her hostess.

"Have you ever been to the King's Bath?" Lucy asked Mrs. Lemmings. "My husband has been taking treatments there."

"My late husband enjoyed the hot springs very much, Lady Kurland, but I never cared for them."

"I wonder did he ever meet a Sir William Benson at the baths?" Lucy scrutinized all three faces. "He was recently taken ill at the baths and unfortunately died."

"I heard of this." Mrs. Lemmings pressed a hand to her heart. "The poor, dear man. I do remember the name. Was he involved with the church?"

"I believe his son Augustus is the vicar of several parishes in the local area," Lucy offered. "Perhaps you know of him?"

"Augustus Benson?" Miss Lemmings shuddered. "We all know about *him.* He has been on the lookout for a wife for years."

"I understand that his parishes are not wealthy so perhaps he feels he needs a helpmate to manage his finances, and tend to his flock," Lucy suggested.

Mrs. Lemmings rose to her feet. "Will you excuse me for one moment, Lady Kurland? I want to ask Cook to bring up some of her fruitcake. I am quite certain you will enjoy it."

The moment the door closed behind their mother, Miss Lemmings turned to Lucy. "Augustus Benson is a horrible man. No woman would ever marry him because even within clerical circles it is known that he uses all his income to gamble on the horses."

"As in horse racing?" Lucy asked. "Dear me."

"Rumor has it that he is in great debt," Miss Cora Lemmings whispered. "And desperately seeking a means to repay his creditors before he loses *everything*."

"Then I will make certain that any advances he makes toward my sister are nipped swiftly in the bud." Lucy put down her cup. "Having met Sir William, I assumed that his son would be an excellent man of character."

"Sir William has two other sons," Miss Cora piped up.

Lucy noticed that for a couple that did not go out much in Bath society the sisters were extremely well informed.

Cora continued. "The oldest is rather staid, but the younger one—Mr. *Peregrine* Benson—is as handsome as Byron."

Miss Lemmings nodded in agreement. "We saw him once in Milsom Street with Sir William's wife, and he was most courteous toward us."

"I have met Mr. Peregrine Benson, and he is indeed a very charming gentleman, although his current lack of employment in a respectable occupation does make me doubt his prospects as a suitable husband for my sister." Lucy looked at Miss Lemmings. "He is an artist, I believe?"

"And a poet and a playwright."

"Indeed." Lucy looked up as Mrs. Lemmings returned with a plateful of cake. "How delightful, ma'am. I love a good piece of cake."

Lucy placed a hand over her stomach and smiled at Robert. They were sitting in the drawing room of their house enjoying a late cup of tea before they dressed for dinner. "I'm not sure what was *in* that fruit cake Mrs. Lemmings asked me to sample, but it feels like it was full of lead."

"Are you suggesting that you deserve credit for forcing down cake?"

"Indeed I am, but it was worth it because it seems widely known that Augustus Benson is in debt, and not the kind of debt that he can wiggle out of, but gambling debts of honor. No wonder he wanted money from Sir William."

"So you think Peregrine was right about Augustus arguing with his father just before he died?" Robert asked.

"It would certainly make sense if he desperately needed money, and was denied," Lucy said. "I still find it difficult to believe that a man of the cloth would do such a thing."

"That is because you were brought up to venerate such men," Robert stated. "I don't blame you for being deceived."

"Well, thank you for that. How did *you* get on today?" Lucy inquired. "Did you hear back from your cousin?"

"Not yet, but I did find out there are rumors that Peregrine Benson's private life is not as it should be."

"As in how?"

Robert smiled at her. "Unnatural vices, my dear."

"Whatever does that mean?" Lucy asked with a frown.

"That he preferred the 'company' of men."

"Oh. I expect Sir William wouldn't have liked that at *all*."

"If he didn't, he certainly didn't mention it to me, which in retrospect seems odd considering how honest he was about every other problem within his family."

"He didn't tell you that Augustus was gambling away the church roof fund, either."

"True." Robert sighed, and stretched out his legs. "Did you really ask all those females to join us for dinner every night?"

"Not every night." She hesitated. "I felt sorry for the girls because their mother was so immersed in her mourning that she had little time for them."

He reached out a hand to her. "And you of all people know how hard it is for a proper clergyman's daughter to meet a good man."

"I was luckier than most," she reminded him, returning the clasp on her fingers. "Miss Lemmings said I gave her hope."

"If Miss Lemmings is half the woman you are, my dear, she will have no difficulty attracting a husband. I am more than willing to vouch to any gentleman as to the value of a wife brought up in a clerical household."

She blushed very prettily as she withdrew her hand and rose to her feet.

"Cat got your tongue?" Robert inquired as he stood as well and looked down at her.

She cupped his jaw. "It is nice to see you in such good humor."

He bent his head and kissed her on the lips. "I am feeling much better." He kissed her again. "Much, *much* better." He took her hand. "Now, come along."

She didn't move. "It is still too early to dress for dinner."

"I know." He winked at her. "But I suspect we can find something far more pleasurable to do together while we wait."

"Robert . . ."

"And think of the benefits, my love. We'll already be undressed when Betty and Silas come and find us."

"Sir Robert, might I have a word with you?" Foley inquired.

"Of course, come in."

Robert nodded at Silas, who had just finished helping him undress after the visit to the theater. "Thank you, Silas. That will be all."

"Good night, sir."

Silas left, and Foley came in, and stood beside the fireplace, his hands joined behind his back.

"What is it, Foley?"

"As instructed, I have been speaking to Mr. Tompkins on a regular basis, and he has confided in me a great deal."

"Excellent." Robert gestured at the chair behind Foley. "Sit down."

"Oh, I couldn't do that, Sir Robert. It wouldn't be seemly," Foley protested.

"Sit *down,* you old fool." Robert took the other chair. "I promise I won't tell anyone."

"As you wish, sir." Foley sat gingerly on the edge of the chair. "Mr. Tompkins wanted me to give you something."

"And what would that be?"

"His master's correspondence."

"Ah. But won't the Bensons notice it's missing?"

"Mr. Tompkins says that his master always kept everything in his bedchamber so that no one else could see it or read it." Foley sniffed. "Sir William was remarkably suspicious of his own family, and very private in his business dealings."

"Possibly with some justification seeing as he is dead," Robert pointed out.

"That's exactly what Mr. Tompkins said, sir. He believes that *someone* was coming into Sir William's bedchamber when neither of them were present, and going through his papers."

"Did he have any idea *which* Benson?" Robert asked. "There are rather a lot of them."

"Mr. Tompkins didn't say, but he *did* want you to read the letters and decide for yourself what's been going on, sir."

"How much of his business did Sir William discuss with Mr. Tompkins?" Sir Robert asked.

"Almost everything, sir. They have been friends since childhood. I think Sir William trusted him more than anyone else in his life."

"Including his own sons?" Robert asked.

"From what Mr. Tompkins said, Sir William wasn't very happy with any of them. If you are agreeable to reading the letters, sir, he says it will all become clear."

"Then I suppose the best thing is to take a look at them, and hope that the Bensons don't notice their absence," Robert said. "If Lady Kurland and I share the task, we can probably get through them quickly enough that no one will even be aware that they went missing."

Foley stood and bowed. "Then I'll ask Mr. Tompkins to hand them over."

"Thank you, and good work, Foley. I appreciate it."

"Thank you, sir." Foley hesitated. "The more I've listened to Mr. Tompkins talk, the more I've come to agree with you that Sir William did not die in peace. I'd be delighted to think that I'd played some small part in bringing his murderer to justice."

"Splendid, Foley." Robert nodded. "After I read the letters I might need to speak to Mr. Tompkins in person. Do you think he would be agreeable to that?"

"Indeed he would, sir. Remember, he already holds you in high esteem. I'd like to think that if someone murdered *you,* sir, I'd make sure justice prevailed on your account, too." Foley turned toward the door. "I hear Lady Kurland coming up the stairs so I shall leave you in peace. Good night, Sir Robert. Sleep well."

"Lucy, I need to speak to you." Penelope came and sat opposite Lucy at the breakfast table. "Goodness me, no wonder you are looking so pale and wan, you hardly have anything on your plate!"

"I'm just not very hungry this morning," Lucy admitted. "For some reason everything in Bath tastes odd to me. It's quite disconcerting." She munched determinedly on her dry toast. "What do you wish to speak to me about?"

Penelope glanced around the deserted room and lowered her voice. "Anna."

"What about her?"

"She is spending a lot of time with Captain Akers and his family."

"And?" Lucy glanced up inquiringly. "They are very pleasant. I have no objection to her being in their company."

"But he is hardly a peer of the realm now, is he?" Penelope pointed out. "And Anna is the granddaughter of an *earl*."

"As am I. Do you think I should have aimed higher than Sir Robert?"

"With your average looks, and a great deal of luck, you did very well for yourself, Lucy, we all know that. But you cannot compare yourself with Anna. She is a diamond of the first water!"

"And she had a London Season, and decided that none of the titled gentlemen who courted her would do," Lucy said firmly. "If she wants to spend time in Captain Akers's company that is perfectly acceptable to me, and to Sir Robert."

Penelope placed her hands over her growing stomach. "As you wish. I really do not have the energy to argue with you when I've been kept awake all night by this baby kicking me in the ribs."

Lucy studied the mound of Penelope's belly as the pattern on her muslin gown shivered like a blancmange. It was really quite extraordinary.

"When does Dr. Fletcher think the baby will be born?" Lucy asked, hoping to redirect her guest's concerns away from Anna and back to herself where they usually resided. "It can't be much longer, surely?"

"Another three months I believe." Penelope grimaced. "I can't reach my toes or even see them anymore."

"Well, hopefully, by the time you are due you will be safely home in Kurland St. Mary with your sister, and your husband to support you," Lucy said. "Do you hope for a daughter or a son?"

"A son, *obviously.*" Penelope raised her eyebrows. "We both know that the males in any family retain *all* the advantages. And you in particular, Lucy, must know that you have a duty to provide Sir Robert with a male heir to inherit his title."

"I'm doing my best," Lucy replied. "When Sir Robert is fully recovered and we return home I'm sure things will develop naturally between us."

"One can only hope that you are right, my dear Lucy," Penelope agreed. "From everything I have heard, Mr. Paul Kurland is quite beyond the pale."

"Good morning, my dear. Good morning, Mrs. Fletcher."

Robert came into the dining room with an unfamiliar leather box tucked under his arm. Lucy was pleased to see that he wasn't even carrying his cane let alone using it.

"When you have finished your breakfast, Lucy, perhaps you might spare me a moment of your time in the library?" Robert addressed her directly.

"Of course. I'm just about finished."

He bowed. "Then I will see you in a minute."

"Sir Robert?" With some difficulty Penelope turned in her chair to look at her host. "What do you know about Captain Akers and his family? Are they respectable?"

Robert exchanged an inquiring glance with Lucy over the top of Penelope's head. "I have inquired about the family extensively, and they are well-liked, financially solvent property owners."

"But not of the peerage."

"I doubt it, why?"

"Because Anna could do much better for herself," Penelope said firmly.

"Anna is an intelligent young woman who is perfectly capable of making a decision about the man she wishes to marry by herself. I will support her in that," Robert said.

"Oh well." Penelope started eating her second plate of food. "Don't say I didn't warn you."

Lucy rose to her feet. "Perhaps I *will* come with you now, Robert." She smiled at Penelope as she went past her. "Anna intends to take her books back to the circulating library this morning if you wish to accompany her."

"Then I will have to go, too." Penelope nodded. "We can't leave her unchaperoned."

"Betty will accompany her."

"Betty is hardly a *chaperone*," Penelope responded. "I will go. I've nothing else to do."

Lucy escaped into the hall and followed Robert into the library where he held out a chair for her at the desk.

"When is that woman leaving?" Robert inquired as he unlocked the leather box.

"That *woman* is waiting for her husband to return to Bath. I can hardly order her to leave in her current condition, can I?"

"Why not? I'll even pay for the damned carriage. She has a terrible habit of sticking her nose in where it's not wanted, and I do not appreciate being lectured in my own house!"

"This isn't your house," Lucy reminded him.

"Don't be pedantic." He glared at her. "She is a nuisance. The only reason I put up with her is because my best friend happens to have been besotted enough to marry the woman."

"She is quite beautiful." Lucy glanced over at him as he started emptying the box. "You obviously thought so at some point seeing as you asked her to marry you."

"As you well know, that was her mother's

doing," Robert grumbled. "The pair of them tied me up, and made it impossible to escape without losing my reputation, and damaging hers."

"Yet you managed it eventually."

"Thank God." He handed her a bundle of letters. "These belong to Sir William. Perhaps we should both stop talking, and start reading."

A while later, Lucy raised her head and stared at her husband, who was reading intently, his brow furrowed in concentration.

"Sir William certainly has a way with words."

"He is blunt and uncomplimentary about everything. At least he had the forethought to copy most of his replies. It saves us a lot of time puzzling out what he must have said." Robert let out his breath. "There is so much to consider in these letters that I don't know where to start!"

Lucy found a clean piece of paper. "Let's make a list. What have you read about so far?"

Robert put on his spectacles again. "Edward Benson's complete lack of understanding of how to run a business, and a refusal by Sir William to pay Augustus Benson's gambling debts. How about you?"

"Something far worse." Lucy handed Robert a letter. "This is from an 'anonymous well-wisher' in London."

He read through the letter and winced. "Well-wisher? Let's call this what it is, my dear girl, an attempt to extort money from Sir William to protect Peregrine's reputation. One does have to wonder what the man gets up to in London and why he is apparently so indiscreet." He looked at Lucy over the top of the letter. "Is there a reply to this?"

"From Sir William?" She leafed through her pile of letters. "There is a copy of his reply, which consists of one line telling the blackmailer to go to the devil, publish, and be damned." She looked at Robert. "This letter is dated just before Sir William died."

"Then one can assume that Sir William had discussed the matter with Peregrine." Robert grimaced. "I thought he at least was not a suspect, but this paints things in a very different light, doesn't it? If Peregrine thought he was about to be exposed as a sodomite he might have been willing to murder his parent to get enough money to pay *off* the blackmailer."

Lucy showed Robert Peregrine's last letter to his father. "Did you notice there is some kind of word and numbers game at the bottom of the page?"

"Yes, I've noticed that on all their letters to each other." He sighed. "I wish I could ask Peregrine what it meant, but that would mean admitting I'd been reading his private correspondence with his father, and he'd probably call me out."

"Peregrine does seem to be somewhat hot-headed." Lucy considered the letter. "But it also indicates that despite everything he and his father had a good relationship."

"Because they shared puzzles between them?"

"Yes," Lucy said definitely. "Even when Sir William is absolutely furious with Peregrine, and you can see it often in their correspondence, he never fails to continue their game."

Lucy wrote Peregrine on her list and put the pen down. "Is that everything so far? Shall we continue? I'll ask Foley to bring us some tea."

"Good Lord."

Lucy stared at Robert, who was looking down at one of the letters as if it were about to bite him.

"What is it?"

"Sir William believed that Lady Miranda was having an *affair!*"

"With whom?" Lucy asked.

"Someone close to the family, apparently. Peregrine, maybe?" Robert squinted at the closely written script. "This is a reply from his solicitor, Mr. Carstairs, who advises his client to think *very carefully* before altering his will so dramatically." Robert shook his head. "I wonder what Sir William was going to do?"

"I have no idea," Lucy said. "But I cannot wait to hear what Mr. Carstairs has to say when he finally arrives and reveals the secrets of Sir William's will."

Chapter 9

"Lady Kurland! How nice to see you out and about."

Lucy turned to find Peregrine Benson smiling down at her. She'd gone to Milsom Street to purchase a new ribbon to trim an old bonnet and was now considering whether to join her sister at the Pump Room for tea. She was feeling rather more tired than she had anticipated and longing for a nap.

"Good afternoon, Mr. Benson." She curtsied. "I was just about to return home."

"Then it would be my pleasure to accompany you." He bowed and offered her his arm. "I am finished with my business in town myself."

Lucy placed her gloved hand on his sleeve and they set off. "Did you ever locate your father's solicitor, Mr. Benson?"

"Indeed, that is what I have been attending to this morning. The poor man thought he would never get here." He chuckled. "He is safely ensconced in one of the bedrooms at the White Hart Inn and will visit the family tomorrow."

"I am glad to hear that he arrived safely," Lucy replied. "Your stepmother was very worried about him."

"She's worried about the will, my lady, not about the man," Peregrine observed as they crossed the cobbled street, and went back toward the center of town. "Although, in my humble opinion, she should be worried about the contents of the will. My father was not the kind of man who appreciated being lied to."

"Did Lady Benson lie to him?"

"When she encountered my father in London, she pretended to be acquainted with an old friend of his, and he took her at her word. Unfortunately, my father happened to *meet* this old friend just before he left for Bath and the man had no knowledge of Miranda at all."

"Oh dear," Lucy murmured. "I wonder why she did that?"

"Because she knew an old fool when she saw one?" Peregrine's smile wasn't pleasant. "She flattered him, and he fell for her tricks."

"With all due respect to Sir William, Mr. Benson, your father is hardly the first older man to fall in love with a beautiful young woman."

"Ain't that the truth, Lady Kurland." He hesitated. "I think my father was regretting his decision well before he left for Bath. Miranda spent his money like water and lavished it on her spoiled brats, which led to a lot of disagreements."

"I can imagine." Lucy stepped off the high curb, lifting her skirts out of the way of the muddy water gushing down the hill. "Lady Benson does seem to be devoted to her sons." She paused, wondering how much he knew. "If your stepmother didn't have a previous acquaintance with a friend of Sir William's, I wonder why she pretended that she did?"

"Probably because she didn't want him to know where she really came from."

Lucy looked inquiringly up at her companion and gratifyingly he continued talking.

"She was on the stage."

"Oh."

"And not even in a decent reputable London theater, but in a small touring company that made little money. I found that out from some of my acquaintances in London." Peregrine snorted. "No wonder she wanted to marry my father."

"One can see that such a marriage would definitely be advantageous for her," Lucy said.

"And her sons," Peregrine added. "The last conversation I had with my father was on the subject of Arden and Brandon. He was considering cutting them from his will entirely."

"One can see why. They are remarkably disrespectful to his memory, and to their mother," Lucy said. "Sir William told my husband that he was unhappy with *all* the members of his family. Did that include you? Your brother seemed to suggest there was some 'friction' between you and your father."

Peregrine glanced down at her. "You're a very observant woman, Lady Kurland."

"Thank you." Lucy chose to accept his rather pointed comment as a compliment. "Sometimes, one can't help but notice the conflicts in other people's families."

"Especially when they enact them right in front of you." Peregrine sighed. "I'd forgotten that you had to sit through Augustus and me arguing." He continued walking for a while and then started speaking again. "My father didn't approve of my life in London."

"I suspect most fathers feel the same when their sons come of age." Lucy nodded. "My own father gave my older brother many a lecture about how to behave in society while conveniently forgetting that his own behavior had been equally suspect."

Peregrine laughed. "My father grew up in poverty. His expectations of us were rather complicated. He wanted us to be gentlemen, but he abhorred the excesses and laziness of the very class he aspired to. I choose to associate with artists and playwrights, occupations he didn't consider worthwhile."

His smile turned wry. "Which is slightly amusing when you realize he was bamboozled into marrying an actress himself."

160

"Indeed," Lucy agreed. "Were you the person who first alerted your father to this fact?"

"I suppose I might have been. Once my father realized Miranda hadn't known his friend at all, he started asking questions." He shrugged. "It was something of a fortuitous chance that I found out who she really was, and was able to confirm his suspicions."

Lucy doubted there had been much evidence of chance involved but didn't dispute the point. His frankness about his father and stepmother was in direct contrast to his reluctance to speak about the breach between his father and himself. But who could blame him? Being a sodomite was still a criminal offense with harsh punishments and hardly something to be discussed with a stranger.

They turned the corner into Queen's Square, and Lucy was soon outside her front door.

"Thank you so much for accompanying me home, Mr. Benson." She smiled up at Peregrine. "It was very kind of you."

"You're most welcome, Lady Kurland." He swept off his hat and gave her a magnificent bow before climbing the steps and knocking on the door next to hers.

Lucy went inside, spoke briefly to Foley, and went upstairs to her bedchamber where Betty was folding newly laundered clothes and putting them away.

"My lady!" Betty turned to Lucy. "I wasn't

expecting you back." She took Lucy's bonnet and gloves and helped her unbutton her pelisse. "Are you feeling well?"

"I thought I might take a nap." Lucy smiled at her longtime maid, who had accompanied her from the rectory to Kurland Hall and stood by her during the last disastrous year. "I'm not sure why I am feeling so tired all the time."

"Well, these hills do wear one out." Betty hesitated. "I wasn't sure if I should mention it, my lady, but perhaps it is due to the arrival of your monthly courses?"

Lucy stared at her maid. "That's true, I haven't . . ." She stopped, her heart thumping. "I haven't bled since before Christmas."

Betty held her gaze. "That's correct, my lady."

"Oh, my goodness!" Lucy sat down on the nearest chair. "That's four *months*. I've been so busy caring for Robert and arranging this trip to Bath that I hadn't even noticed." She pressed her hands to her mouth, and took a long calming breath. "Please don't say anything to Silas or my husband."

"I wouldn't do that, my lady." Betty patted her shoulder. "I'll always keep your secrets. There's no point worrying the menfolk when there's nothing they can do to help, is there? And you know how they fret."

"Exactly." Lucy nodded, her mind still running in circles. "At some point, my condition will become obvious or it will—" She couldn't finish that sentence. After two miscarriages she was too afraid to even hope.

"Yes, my lady. But you are already further along this time." Betty smiled at her. "Now, why don't you take that nap, and I'll make sure that you aren't disturbed."

Robert glanced over at his wife, who was staring into space neglecting the book she was supposed to be reading.

"Are you thinking about our investigation?" He smiled. "You seem quite preoccupied."

She jumped and turned her attention to him. "I'm sorry, I was woolgathering. I spent some time with Peregrine Benson this morning. He suggested that *he* was the one who alerted his father to the fact that his new wife was actually an actress in a traveling theater company."

"That explains why her sons have Shakespearean names."

Lucy nodded. "I suppose they do. Peregrine allegedly frequents the company of artists and playwrights so he *might* have heard the gossip about Miranda there."

"That's quite possible," Robert agreed.

"I was also wondering whether Peregrine was blackmailing his father."

"With what?"

"The knowledge that his father's new wife

was an actress." Lucy held his gaze. "What if he told Sir William that he would keep quiet about the matter if Sir William would deal with his blackmailer?"

"That might be true, I suppose," Robert agreed. "But would Sir William care? He never saw himself as a member of the ruling classes and could marry whomever he wanted without incurring the wrath of some titled family." Robert paused. "The thing I *could* see sticking in his craw was that she lied to him. That he would not like."

"And we aren't even sure if Peregrine was the first person to break the news to Sir William," Lucy said. "The letter we read indicated that Sir William knew about it, but he doesn't reveal his source."

"Which might explain why Sir William refused to pay off Peregrine's blackmailer, giving Peregrine a very good reason to end his father's life."

"The thing is . . ." Lucy twisted her hands together in her lap. "Despite everything, I *like* Peregrine, and I cannot imagine him killing Sir William."

"Being likeable doesn't necessarily mean you aren't a murderer," Robert reminded her. "We've met some delightful people over the years who have turned out to be absolute villains."

"I know," she sighed. "I'd still prefer it to be Miranda's sons."

"Well, what about Miranda herself?" Robert

asked. "If Sir William really was planning on cutting her out of his will then she would definitely have a reason to kill him before he attended to the matter."

"No one saw her at the baths that morning, and she is quite memorable," Lucy said. "Although, I suppose she *could* have instructed her sons to take care of the matter for her."

"Yes, mayhap they are working together."

"So we are discounting Edward and Augustus as likely suspects?" Lucy asked.

"Not so fast." Robert took a letter out of his pocket and handed it over to Lucy. "I had a reply from my cousin Oliver. In his usual brusque manner he informed me that Edward Benson is a failure in business, owes more money than his father probably knew, and has a terrible reputation in his town."

"But none of that makes him a murderer," Lucy objected.

"It might if his father found out and had decided to disinherit *him*."

Lucy threw up her hands. "By the end of his life it appears that Sir William might have disinherited everyone!"

"Agreed. They are rather a bad lot, aren't they? To be fair, I doubt Augustus either had the nerve or the desire to kill his father. The church will cover up his misdeeds, and he will be allowed to go on his merry way."

"I wish that wasn't true, but I fear you are right." Lucy sighed. "There are quite a number of contemptible individuals within the clergy who neither believe in God nor have a single care for their parishioners."

"I can't argue with that," Robert said, and prudently kept his thoughts as to Lucy's father fitting that description to himself.

"Peregrine did say that the solicitor had arrived, and was coming to the house tomorrow to discuss the will." Lucy read the letter and then handed it back to Robert. "I wish I could be a fly on the wall."

"There's no need." Robert smiled at her. "I had an invitation to attend."

"*You* have? Why?" Lucy demanded.

"I have no idea, but the solicitor requested my presence. I will tell you all about it when I get back."

"Get back?" Lucy raised her eyebrows and looked quite like her old self. "I'm coming with you."

"This way, Sir Robert, Lady Kurland."

Robert followed the Bensons' butler through into the drawing room where a row of chairs had been set before a table. A man Robert had never seen before was fussing about the placement of a candle while Edward Benson tried to talk to him.

"I assume that is Mr. Carstairs," Robert murmured in Lucy's ear.

"One would hope so. He looks competent."

"Apart from getting lost on the way to Bath?" Robert replied as he ushered Lucy into a seat in the back row and sat beside her. "That does not fill me with confidence."

Peregrine and Augustus came in, shook hands with the solicitor, and took up residence in the front row next to Edward. They both looked remarkably nervous, which considering the mercurial nature of their late father was not entirely unwarranted.

The clock on the mantelpiece chimed the hour as the staff that had accompanied the Bensons down from Yorkshire filed into the back of the room. Edward stood up and checked his pocket watch.

"Where is Lady Benson?"

Dotty the maid curtsied. "She is just coming, sir. Dr. Mantel is accompanying her."

"And Brandon and Arden?"

"We're here." The two young men came in and sat directly in front of Lucy and Robert. Brandon seemed agitated, and Arden was talking to him constantly in a low murmur.

Just as Edward was about to walk out into the hall, Lady Benson appeared on Dr. Mantel's arm and was tenderly led to the front seat directly opposite the solicitor. The doctor retreated to the back of the room and stood against the wall, his patient's smelling salts in his hand.

Mr. Carstairs cleared his throat. "Perhaps we might begin."

Arden raised his hand. "Why is Sir Robert Kurland here?" He turned to Robert. "No offense, sir, but you are hardly a member of the family."

"Neither are you," Peregrine murmured.

"Now, look here—" Brandon growled and Arden grabbed hold of his brother, who had started out of his seat.

"Don't let him bother you, Brother. He's like an annoying wasp full of venom, but ultimately not worth killing."

Peregrine rolled his eyes. "Good Lord, a threat. I'm terrified."

Mr. Carstairs waited until everyone had composed themselves again, and held up a letter. "I received this from Sir William just before he died. He instructed me that he had amended his will again, and that Sir Robert was now included as one of his executors."

Robert blinked as all the Bensons now turned to stare at him. None of them looked particularly happy.

Ignoring them, Robert looked at the solicitor. "I am more than happy to assist you and the Benson family in any way."

"Didn't my father tell you he was doing this?" Edward asked.

"I had no idea," Robert said. "But I consider it an honor."

Mr. Carstairs put down the letter. "Thank you, Sir Robert. Now, if we might get on to the important matter of the will itself?" He looked around expectantly and the silence lengthened until Edward gestured to him.

"Well, get on with it, man. We're all ears."

"There must be some mistake." Mr. Carstairs frowned. "I am merely the legal presence required to read the will and explain anything to the beneficiaries that is not easily understandable."

The Bensons exchanged puzzled glances and Edward again spoke up. "We understand, but what is stopping you going ahead and reading the blasted thing?"

"I don't have it, sir," Mr. Carstairs said. "Sir William preferred to retain the document in his own keeping. He brought it to Bath."

"Then why in damnation didn't you say that yesterday?" Edward growled, and Lady Benson began to weep.

Beside Robert Lucy sat up straight. "Of course he did!" she whispered while the Bensons continued to argue with one another. "You said he was constantly amending things."

Mr. Carstairs banged on the table to restore order. "Where is the will?"

Edward stood and looked toward the back of the room. "Mr. Tompkins?"

"Yes, sir?" The old valet stepped forward.

"Were you aware of Sir William's will amongst his possessions?"

"I know he had it, Mr. Edward, but I don't know what he did with it."

"What do you mean you don't *know?*" Augustus joined in. "Was it in his possession or not?"

Mr. Tompkins didn't look impressed by the shouted question and took on a more truculent tone. "I saw it when he took it out to change something, but where he kept it, I have no idea. I'm just his valet. It's not my place to inquire what he chooses to do with his important documents now, is it?"

Edward turned back to Mr. Carstairs. "This is ridiculous! Why didn't you say immediately that you didn't have the will? We all assumed my father had sent it back to you before his death."

"Because nobody asked me, sir," Mr. Carstairs snapped. "One would assume you would know how your own father preferred to deal with such matters. He *always* insisted on keeping the will on his person."

Lucy nudged Robert. "Peregrine is enjoying this. Look at his face."

Peregrine Benson looked as if he was desperately trying not to laugh, Lady Benson was moaning and sniffing the smelling salts the doctor had offered her, and her two sons were furiously muttering to each other.

"Then I suppose we must adjourn this discussion until we have thoroughly searched the house and found the will," Edward announced. He bowed to Mr. Carstairs. "We will continue to pay for your room and board until this matter is successfully concluded."

"Thank you." Mr. Carstairs looked thoroughly put out as he stood and pushed in his chair. "I will return to my hotel. Please let me know when I can be of service."

Within seconds of his exit, the whole Benson clan erupted into a flurry of accusations, insults, and panicked questions. Poor Mr. Tompkins was bombarded with questions and grew increasingly red-faced as his character was called into question.

"We should go," Robert murmured to Lucy.

"Not yet. This is all remarkably interesting," she replied. "Edward and Augustus are furious, Peregrine seems to think it's all a big joke, and Lady Miranda and her sons are huddled together possibly plotting their next move."

"None of which is our business," Robert reminded her.

"Well, it *is* if you think one of them is a murderer," Lucy reminded him. "Poor Mr. Tompkins is being most unfairly blamed for this whole debacle."

"Perhaps not unfairly seeing as we both agree that he is the most trusted member of the Benson household, and had known Sir William since he was a child. If anyone knows where that will is, I'll wager it will be him."

"Then perhaps when this fuss dies down we can send Foley over to sympathize with him, and find out if that really is the case."

"That's an excellent suggestion." Robert smiled at her. "Shall we go?"

No one noticed them leaving, and Robert chose not to draw attention to it. He was just knocking on their front door when Lucy looked up at him.

"I just remembered something."

"What?"

"When I took the clothes back to Lady Benson she was prostrate in bed. As soon as I mentioned what I'd brought she sat up and went through every pocket as if she was searching for something."

"Perhaps her late husband's will?" Robert asked, and then frowned. "Maybe she was worried that someone had stolen it at the baths."

"But the man we spoke to there said he guarded Sir William's clothes very carefully."

"We should speak to him again. I wonder if someone was *supposed* to steal the will at the baths, kill Sir William, and amend the will as necessary?" Robert nodded as Foley opened the door, and he stepped over the threshold and into the hall. "Maybe she was just making sure it had gone."

Lucy started up the stairs untying the ribbons of her bonnet. "I hadn't thought of that. I suppose one of her sons could've have stolen it while the other murdered Sir William in the bath."

Robert followed her into their bedchamber. "Which might explain why Lady Benson wasn't enacting her usual gothic drama when the will was discovered to be missing this morning. She might be quite glad about it, especially if she arranged for it to disappear."

"She was rather quiet." Lucy sighed as she took off her bonnet and placed it on her dressing table. "This is all so confusing. What happens if they can't find the will?"

"Nothing. It leaves everything in a complete and utter muddle."

"But there must be some legal resources to deal with such a problem?"

"Indeed there are, but they aren't quick or timely. The legal arguments could go on for years."

"Which I suspect is not what Sir William would've wanted at all." She took off her pelisse. "It is a terrible tangle."

He walked over, took her hand, and kissed her fingers. "One we will endeavor to solve."

"You haven't given up then?" She looked up at him.

"Not at all. In truth, I suspect the fun is just beginning."

Chapter 10

"I forgot to mention that Foley is going to visit Mr. Tompkins this evening while we are out dining with the Akers."

Robert pinned his cravat in place with a modest silver pin, and put on his best coat while Silas fussed around him brushing the fabric.

"Good," Lucy said as she clasped her pearls around her neck. "It will be interesting to hear what he finds out."

She was wearing one of her new gowns, and hoped its bright pattern would eclipse the paleness of her face. She'd been feeling quite nauseous all day and wasn't enjoying the prospect of having to eat her dinner under the scrutiny of others. Admitting she *might* be with child seemed to have encouraged all the unpleasant symptoms she had so far ignored to appear.

"Are you ready?" Robert asked her as Silas handed him his hat and cane. "I ordered the carriage for six, and it is at the door."

"I'm quite ready." Lucy rose from her seat.

"I will go and see if Anna and Penelope have finished dressing."

"Penelope's coming?" Robert made a face. "Well, do your best to make sure she doesn't express her opinions too loudly. I don't want to scare Captain Akers off."

"You approve of him, then?"

"How could I not? He is intelligent, kind to his mother, and a naval hero."

"But do you think Anna will take him?"

"I don't know." He kissed her brow. "We shall do everything in our power to show that we approve of the match if she wishes to move forward, and then it is up to Anna."

Lucy sighed. "I know, but it is *very* hard not to meddle."

"I'm sure it is, and you have been most restrained, my love."

"I've tried." She looked up into his amused dark blue eyes. "It is not in my nature to keep my opinions to myself, and I have practically bitten through my tongue doing so."

He laughed, caressed her cheek, and went to open the door. "Come on, my lady of restraint. I am rather looking forward to my dinner."

It was the first time that Lucy had accepted an invitation to dine at the Akerses' house in the countryside as opposed to at their rented town house in Bath. She was pleasantly surprised by the size of the stone-built house and the expansive gardens around it. Robert had assured her the family was financially solvent, but seeing it with her own eyes made her worry less. Captain Akers was the oldest son, and at some point in the future, everything would belong to him.

Anna had been quiet on the drive over, her beautiful face turned to the window, her replies distracted. Despite their close bond, Lucy had no idea how her sister was now feeling about Captain Akers. Caught up in investigating Sir William's murder, and her own recent preoccupation with the possibility of reproducing, she had neglected her sister. Perhaps seeing her with the family would answer some of Lucy's questions.

They were warmly welcomed by Mr. and Mrs. Akers, several exuberant dogs, and smaller children, and were soon chatting away with the entire family. Robert was at his most gracious, which was a blessing. Even Penelope was on her best behavior, her speculative gaze calculating the family's wealth and standing, and no doubt coming up with her own notion as to their suitability. Lucy could only hope that she wouldn't voice her opinions out loud.

Dr. Fletcher was due back in Bath in a few days. Lucy knew that Robert had every intention of asking his friend to take his wife back to Kurland St. Mary when he left. Penelope could hardly complain after a month of living at the Kurlands' expense. Although Lucy did allow that she had done an excellent job of chaperoning Anna when Lucy was otherwise engaged.

Mrs. Akers drew her and Penelope into conversation leaving Captain Akers to introduce Anna to his younger siblings, who all seemed delighted to meet her. Robert was happily discussing the military with Mr. Akers without even the hint of an argument. It was all so very different from the turmoil of the Bensons that Lucy could hardly believe such civility and kindness existed anymore.

She allowed Mr. Akers to take her into dinner, and sat down at his right hand. To her relief, the food was plentiful and not too rich. With Robert safely away at the other end of the table with his hostess, she dined without fear that he would notice how little she was eating.

By the time they reached the treacle tart, apple pie, and jellies she had established an excellent rapport with Mr. Akers, and gathered that he was not averse at all to the marriage of his eldest son to Anna. In truth, he was refreshingly direct about the qualities he saw in Anna beneath her beauty, which endeared him to Lucy even more.

The ladies left the gentlemen to drink their port and made their way to the drawing room where a roaring fire and the tea tray awaited them. The Benson children were soon dispatched to bed, and the older women settled into a comfortable circle around the fire. Mrs. Akers paid particular attention to Anna, who seemed quite at ease in her company.

After drinking two cups of tea, Lucy had to ask her hostess for directions to use the facilities and was sent up to the dressing room between the two master bedrooms. As she ascended the stairs, the gentlemen left the dining room and a waft of smoke and brandy billowed out from the open doors. They headed toward the drawing room talking amongst themselves.

Lucy completed her business and returned down the stairs, pausing in the hall to get her bearings. The sound of scratching drew her attention toward one of the closed doors, and she went toward it. A piercing whine greeted her approach, and she opened the door to discover that one of the dogs had gotten locked inside the room.

She accepted his lick of gratitude and let him go past her into the hall. She paused to admire the rather large library, her gaze focusing on a stained-glass window at the far end that depicted a family crest. The motto was in Latin, and she walked over and peered as closely as she could at the etched glass in an attempt to decipher it.

"Ah! *My home is my strength and my purpose.* How lovely."

She was just about to turn around when she heard Anna's voice followed by that of Captain

Akers coming toward the library. There didn't appear to be another door, so Lucy stepped behind the bookcase closest to the wall and held her breath.

"Thank you for being willing to speak to me, Miss Harrington," Captain Akers said. "I must confess that seeing you here, in my home, has done nothing to dissuade me from my conviction that you are the woman I wish to marry."

"Oh, Harry. Your home is lovely, and so are your family," Anna replied.

"Then will you consent to be my wife?"

There was such a long silence that Lucy had to remember to breathe.

"I've already explained why I think that would be a mistake," Anna finally answered him. "And seeing you here, with your loving family all around you, just makes my inadequacies more obvious."

"Your *inadequacies?*"

"As I have already told you, I do not wish to be a mother," Anna replied. "Although that is not quite true, either, I would *love* to be a mother but I am mortally afraid of childbirth, you *know* this."

"Anna . . . as you have probably noticed, I have plenty of brothers and sisters. If you don't want children one of them can happily inherit this place."

"How can you say that when I see your rightful

pride in your family, and in your position in society? If I was selfish enough to deny you heirs what would you think of me then?"

"I've spent most of my life onboard a ship. This place is my home, but it isn't who I *am*." He sighed. "I want to marry you, Anna. I can't tell my heart whom to love."

Lucy put her hand to her mouth.

"Can you really tell me you don't love me?" Anna still didn't speak, and Captain Akers continued, the conviction in his voice strengthening. "Because I believe you do love me."

"Maybe love isn't enough," Anna whispered.

"Beside my duty and obligation to my family?"
"Yes."

"Those things are important to me but they aren't the sum of who I *am*. If I married you I'd want all of you. I can't promise that I won't get you with child. I won't lie to you about that."

"Thank you," Anna murmured.

"But I would do everything in my power to prevent it from happening." He paused. "I've traveled all over the world. There are more ways than you might imagine to prevent conception."

"But you cannot guarantee it," Anna stated. "And what if I did become pregnant, and lost my mind in terror? How quickly would you regret your choice *then?*"

"You are not your mother, Anna. Science has greatly improved since she died and I would make sure that you had the best available care in the world." There was an implacable note in his voice that surprised Lucy. "You cannot live your life in fear of something that might not happen."

"And what if it did?" Anna retorted. "What if I died?"

"Then I would be devastated, and I would forever blame myself."

"But you'd still be alive."

Then was another long silence before he answered her. "Yes. I would." He sighed. "What do you want me to say, Anna?"

"I don't know."

"Do you love me?"

"Yes." Anna said it with such reverence that Lucy bit her lip to stop herself from crying. "Of course I do. Too much to bring such harm on you."

"So you'd rather not take a chance on happiness? You'd rather allow your fears to rule you?"

"That's not fair, Harry."

"Life's not fair. I've almost lost my life at sea, and I've come to understand that one has to *grab* happiness when it appears, and hold on to it because tomorrow you might be dead anyway. Will you think about that? About denying us even a *chance* to be happy when we love each other, and cannot predict what the future will hold? We might not even be blessed with children. Wouldn't a year of happiness be worth *anything?*"

The next thing Lucy heard was the door slamming and Captain Akers uttering a curse.

"You can come out now, Lady Kurland. Anna has gone."

Lucy startled, and then stepped out from behind the bookcase. "I do beg your pardon, Captain. I had no intention of eavesdropping." Curiosity overcame her. "How did you know I was there?"

"I didn't until the last second when I stepped close enough to the mirror over the fireplace to see your reflection in it." He shoved a hand through his hair. "You must think me a rogue."

"Not at all," Lucy was quick to reassure him. "I thought you presented your case very well."

"You *did?*"

"Yes, you gave Anna something to think about." Lucy hesitated. "I cannot say whether she will allow herself to *listen,* but one can only hope."

"Thank you for that, my lady."

"If Anna chooses to confide in me, I will not divulge that I was present during your discussion."

He bowed. "You have my word that I will not mention it, either."

"Thank you." Lucy gathered her skirts. "Then I will return to the drawing room."

Both Anna and Lucy were very quiet on the drive home, and, as Robert had nothing in particular he wished to say to Penelope, the journey passed in relative silence. Robert had the sense that the Akers family had perhaps expected some announcement from their son as to his engagement. Whatever had happened between the couple, neither of them had looked particularly happy by the end of the evening.

Lucy yawned and leaned against his shoulder. "What a delightful family."

"Indeed." Ignoring Penelope's pointed look he drew Lucy even closer and wrapped an arm around her shoulders. "Mr. Akers was very knowledgeable, and agreeable, and, his children and dogs were well behaved."

He looked out of the window as the carriage drew to a stop outside their Bath residence and waited for the coachman to let down the steps.

"Thank you."

He assisted his three companions out and followed them up the steps. Lucy turned to him in the hall.

"I'm going straight to bed."

"Good night, my dear." He blew her a kiss as he handed Foley his hat and gloves. "I won't be long."

Anna went upstairs and into the drawing room. Penelope followed her.

"Well, Anna? What do you have to say for yourself?"

Anna looked up as if she were in a daze. "I beg your pardon?"

Robert came into the room just as Penelope started to speak again. He closed the door so that Lucy wouldn't hear anything that might send her back into the fray.

"The entire family was obviously expecting you to accept Captain Akers's proposal!"

"I . . . wasn't aware—"

"Good Lord, Anna! The man wants to marry you, his family are agreeable, and you refused him, didn't you?" Penelope threw up her hands. "You will end up an old maid!"

Anna turned around. "So what if I do? It is none of your concern! Go away and leave me in peace!"

Penelope recoiled in shock as Anna raised her voice.

"Well, there is no need for such rudeness. I am just trying—"

"To interfere." Anna obviously wasn't done. "You are worse than Lucy! At least I know she has my best interests at heart whereas you . . . All you care about is maneuvering for money and position!"

Penelope drew herself up like an offended golden goddess. "That is a *ridiculous* thing to say when I chose to marry Dr. Fletcher! Do you think I *wanted* to marry a nonentity? I married him because he loves me, and I love *him!*" She pointed her finger at Anna. "With your looks you could marry a duke, but Captain Akers *loves* you and that, my dear Anna, is the most important thing in the world!"

With a toss of her head, Penelope burst into tears and stormed out, leaving Robert and Anna staring helplessly at each other. To his horror, Robert realized that it fell to him to attempt to aid Lucy's sister.

With a soft sound, Anna sank into a chair. "Oh, my goodness. Now I have offended Penelope."

"That's a remarkably easy thing to do."

"But I made her *cry.*"

Robert hesitated, aware that tact and diplomacy weren't his strengths. "For once I have to agree with her."

"That love is more important than anything?" Anna scowled at him. "You almost married *Penelope!* What do you know?"

He sat down and took her shaking hand in his. "But I didn't. I married your sister because I love her."

"Captain Akers thinks I should marry him because I love *him,* and accept what happens."

"Isn't that what we all do?" Robert asked her. "Since marrying your sister I've had to face almost losing her, and it was awful, and terrible. She had to sit through Dr. Fletcher cutting into my thigh. Should I not have married her? Not enjoyed my life so much more with her at my side? I suspect both of us would prefer to spend our time together regardless of how short it might be."

"I'm not like Lucy. She is resilient."

"I think you underestimate yourself."

"I am tired of everyone saying that." Anna's face settled into a stubborn frown that reminded Robert all too forcibly of his wife.

"Then would you prefer me to be more direct?" He held her gaze. "You are allowing your fears to rule you."

"So I'm a coward?"

"Maybe you are. Good night, Anna." Robert stood up. "Whatever you choose to do know that Lucy and I will support you regardless."

He left her sitting there and went toward the stairs only to be waylaid by Foley.

"Do you have a moment, Sir Robert?"

Robert took out his pocket watch and checked the time. He reckoned Lucy would already be in bed.

"Yes, of course."

He followed Foley back down the stairs and into the small study that fronted the ground floor of the house.

"I spoke to Mr. Tompkins, sir."

"And what did he have to say for himself?"

"He said that Sir William had a hiding place for his will."

"Where?"

"That he said he didn't know, Sir Robert," Foley said.

"I find that difficult to believe, don't you?"

"Yes, sir, but he wouldn't budge on his story. He insisted that Sir William would send him out of the room every time he hid the will."

"And he never once peeked or caught him in the act?" Robert shook his head. "I wonder why Mr. Tompkins doesn't want the Benson family to know where the will is?"

"He did say, sir, that he was often the one to witness the changes to the will."

"So perhaps he is aware that several members of the Benson family might blame him for what he witnessed." Robert nodded. "I can see why he might not want to reveal what he knows until he is safely away from Bath, and the wrath of the Bensons."

"So can I, sir. He told me that he plans to pack up and leave fairly soon to alert the household back in Yorkshire as to Sir William's death, and prepare for his burial."

"I'm sure that Edward Benson already has these matters in hand."

"To be fair, sir, Mr. Tompkins doesn't have much faith in Mr. Edward," Foley said tactfully. "And seeing as the whole family is stuck here waiting on that will, he thinks someone needs to go back there in person and take charge."

"Well, see if you can press him further, and offer to help him finish packing Sir William's belongings. Maybe *you'll* find the damned will." Robert walked to the door. "Now I must go to bed. Thank you for your efforts, Foley. They are much appreciated."

"I must confess that I've enjoyed it." Foley bowed. "Good night, Sir Robert."

Robert went back up the stairs thinking about everything that had happened that night. He'd have to face Lucy in the morning, who would definitely wish to discuss the situation with Anna, and he'd have to tell her what Foley had discovered about Mr. Tompkins.

He had a suspicion that neither of his pieces of information would cheer her up and that she would have no compunction in sharing her displeasure with him.

Chapter 11

Lucy contemplated the dried toast on her plate and added a miniscule scrape of butter. Anna hadn't come down to breakfast yet, and, as Lucy was for once unsure of what to say to her, she welcomed the reprieve. She wanted to tell Anna to listen to Captain Akers, but despite her sweet exterior her sister had a stubborn streak that rivaled Lucy's own.

Hearing Robert's voice in the hallway, she quickly rearranged Penelope's discarded plate in front of her to make it look like she had enjoyed a hearty repast. Her husband might not be the most observant man in the world, but he wasn't a fool. His concern for her would make him ask questions that she wasn't yet ready to answer, and she would not lie to him.

"Good morning, my dear."

Robert smiled at her as he entered the dining room and helped himself to the covered dishes on the sideboard. The smell of warm ham and coddled eggs made Lucy clamp her lips together and try not to breathe too deeply. He took a seat beside her, which made it easier for her to avert her face and concentrate on putting marmalade on her toast.

"Good morning, Robert." She managed to eat a piece of toast and swallowed it down with the help of some tea. "Are you planning on going to the baths today?"

"No, I thought I'd wait until Dr. Fletcher comes tomorrow. Did Foley tell you about his discussion with Mr. Tompkins about the missing will?"

"He did." Lucy shook her head. "I cannot believe that Mr. Tompkins never saw where the will was hidden, can you?"

"No. I suspect he doesn't want it found for some reason." Robert cut into the ham. "I wonder if Sir William made him promise something to that effect?"

"As in, if he died under suspicious circumstances Mr. Tompkins was to hide the will, and tell no one where it was?" Lucy asked, her nausea disappearing as she considered the puzzle.

"Exactly." Robert chewed the ham thoroughly before starting on his eggs. "But he'd have to release it at *some* point."

"Would he? If he suspected one of them of murdering him wouldn't Sir William have preferred none of his children to inherit his fortune?"

"That's also a possibility. He didn't strike me as a forgiving man. What a tangle. I have a great deal of sympathy for Mr. Carstairs."

"I intend to visit Lady Benson this morning. Would you like to come with me?" Lucy asked.

"Yes, I would. I might be able to get a moment alone with Mr. Tompkins, and see if I can convince him to let me take the will into my safekeeping." Robert frowned. "I am concerned that the Bensons might turn to the law and accuse Mr. Tompkins of stealing from them in order to threaten him to disclose his knowledge."

"I could certainly see Augustus or Edward doing exactly that," Lucy agreed. "Perhaps you could use that as a good reason for Mr. Tompkins to hand over the will to a gentleman who would not be so easily cowed."

"As in me?" Robert nodded. "I will certainly make the suggestion." He glanced around the table. "Have Anna and Penelope been down yet?"

"I haven't seen Anna. Penelope was here." Lucy sighed. "She insisted that Anna had insulted her last night, but refused to explain exactly why."

"Anna did insult her." Robert poured himself a second cup of coffee and topped up Lucy's tea. "Penelope was remonstrating with your sister about not accepting Captain Akers's proposal. Anna said that Penelope was fixated on her acquiring money and wealth."

"*Anna* said that?" Lucy put down her cup.

"In truth, Anna shouted it right in Penelope's face." Robert winced. "And Penelope retorted by saying that *she* had married for love, and that she didn't regret it. Then she burst into tears and rushed out."

"*Penelope* did?" Lucy rubbed her forehead. "I feel as if I am entering some magical universe where everything is upside down."

"It was rather alarming to witness, and to find myself in complete agreement with *Penelope* of all people," Robert admitted. "I actually think Penelope was trying to help."

"Did Anna apologize to her?"

"No, because Penelope stormed out in high dudgeon. I attempted to calm your sister down, but I'm not sure if I succeeded."

Lucy stared at Robert. "You . . . *did?*"

"Anna asked my opinion." He shrugged. "I can assure you that I tried to be tactful, but I'm not sure if she listened to me."

Lucy inwardly shuddered at the thought of her husband attempting to offer advice to her sensitive sister, and was no longer surprised that Anna had declined to descend for breakfast.

"I hope Anna does think about this matter very carefully." Lucy was reluctant to share the details of the conversation she'd overheard because she suspected Robert wouldn't approve of her staying to listen to it. "I liked Captain Akers and his family very much, and I believe Anna cares for him very deeply."

"Then she needs to be brave and reach out for

her happiness." Robert wiped his mouth with his napkin. "That's what I told her."

Lucy rose and brushed the toast crumbs from her skirts. "I will go and see if she is awake before we leave for the Bensons."

"Take your time." Robert reached for the newspaper Foley had set beside his plate. "I need to read what our government has been up to since we left home. I suspect it will not be pleasant."

After failing to rouse Anna, Lucy put on her bonnet and pelisse and went back down to the drawing room where Robert was seated by the fire still reading his newspaper. Betty had suggested Lucy carry some dry bread in her reticule in case she felt nauseous when she was out. She'd never felt quite this sick during a pregnancy before and wondered what that meant. If she felt much worse, she would have to tell Robert what was going on.

He looked up at her over the top of his newspaper and folded it up.

"As I suspected the country is in a terrible state."

"Then perhaps now that you are feeling better you might consider standing for Parliament as you originally intended?" Lucy reminded him.

"I might do that." Robert put his spectacles in his pocket. "I can hardly be less competent than those buffoons running the country now."

Foley came in and handed Robert his hat and cane.

"Thank you, Foley." Robert gestured at the door. "Shall we, my dear?"

Lucy went outside, immediately climbed the steps up to the Benson house, and knocked on the door, which was opened by the butler.

"Good morning, Lady Kurland, Sir Robert."

"Good morning. I am here to see Lady Benson."

"Then please come in, my lady, and I will ascertain as to whether her ladyship has come down yet."

"Thank you." Lucy followed him up the stairs and into the drawing room where the fire had already been lit to warm the space. Robert brought up the rear. "I did send her a note yesterday to say that I would be here at eleven."

"Would you like some refreshment, my lady, sir?"

"Some tea would be most welcome." Lucy took a seat by the fire and removed her gloves. "Thank you."

Robert prowled the space, pausing to look out of the window at every turn and make a disparaging comment about the lack of view until Lucy wished he would sit down. She was just about to voice her request in a rather firmer manner when the door opened to reveal Edward and Peregrine Benson.

Edward went straight over to Robert. "It is a

pleasure to see you, sir, even in such sad circumstances."

Robert shook his hand as Peregrine bowed and winked at Lucy. "I must apologize for not staying longer at the reading of the will. My wife and I felt it inappropriate for us to linger."

Edward sighed. "It is something of a muddle, Sir Robert. As it stands, the will cannot be found, and Mr. Carstairs insists that he cannot act without that legal document in front of him."

"With all due respect," Lucy ventured. "Surely as Sir William's solicitor he would have enough knowledge from drawing up the will to know what it would contain?"

"That is a very good point, Lady Kurland, but my father did have a tendency to change his will," Edward said. "Mr. Carstairs quite rightly refuses to speculate as to how the validity of the bequests he dealt with agree with the document his client amended."

"Then one has to assume that Sir William brought the will with him to Bath," Robert commented. "Is it possible that it has just been overlooked?"

"I doubt it," Peregrine said. "My brothers and stepmother have turned this place upside down looking for the damned thing. If it is here, they haven't found it yet."

"You didn't search yourself, Mr. Benson?" Lucy asked Peregrine.

"Seeing as the last time I spoke to the old man he was threatening to disinherit me, I hope the blasted thing *never* turns up."

"Peregrine is jesting." Edward frowned at his brother. "We cannot allow matters to stand like this. It will affect confidence in our business enterprises and encourage our debtors and creditors to question our continued existence."

"Indeed." Robert inclined his head. "If you cannot find the will how do you intend to proceed?"

"Mr. Carstairs says there are ways to deal with such issues. They would be costly and involve employing the services of a barrister, but if that is what I must do to resolve this impasse, then I will do it."

"With what?" Peregrine demanded. "You don't have a feather to fly with of your own."

"If we have to we will borrow money against our expectations," Edward said stiffly. "And I must insist, Brother, that you cease embarrassing our guests by discussing our financial matters."

"I don't think they are the ones who are embarrassed, Brother, *dear.*" Peregrine's smile wasn't pleasant. "You seem to forget that Sir Robert's fortune comes from the industrialized north, and he is well aware of the financial aspects of our companies and not offended by my bluntness at all."

Edward looked appalled at the very thought of discussing trade. He opened and closed his mouth quite a few times before he managed to get a sentence out.

"As I said, this is neither the time nor the place for this discussion."

Peregrine bowed elaborately. "As you wish, Edward. I am on my way out to see Mr. Carstairs at the White Hart. Do you have anything in particular you wish me to tell him?"

"Why are you visiting Mr. Carstairs?" Edward demanded.

"I wish to make sure he remains in good health and doesn't bolt back to Yorkshire." Peregrine smiled. "He isn't very happy about this whole situation."

"One can see why," Robert murmured, and both Benson brothers turned toward him. "I've noticed that men who practice the law are generally rather finicky when due process isn't carried out to their satisfaction."

Peregrine strolled over to kiss Lucy's hand. "A pleasure to see you as always, Lady Kurland."

"Indeed." Lucy withdrew her fingers from his rather determined clasp.

The door opened, and Lady Benson came in flanked by her older son, Arden, and Dr. Mantel. She stiffened, pressed her hand to her breast, and stopped moving.

"Why are you both *here?* What has happened now?"

For a startled moment Lucy wondered if Lady

Benson was talking to her and Robert, but she realized her hostess's fearful gaze was fixed on the brothers.

Peregrine walked over and stared down at his stepmother, the naked insolence in his eyes plain to see. "Good morning, Miranda." He leaned in closer. "Still no tears for the man who gave you everything?"

"Go away," Miranda snapped. "You horrible little man."

Peregrine blew her a kiss and pushed past her, deliberately knocking Dr. Mantel to one side.

"Oh, I say," the doctor murmured as he straightened his cravat. "There really is no need for such bad behavior."

Edward bowed to his stepmother and then to Lucy and Robert. "I fear I must be going as well. I have some letters to write."

He slipped out of the room leaving Lady Benson glaring at his back. It was the most animated Lucy had ever seen her, but within seconds the anger was gone, replaced by the wide-eyed helpless look of a doe Lucy was more familiar with.

"I am so sorry, Lady Kurland," Miranda breathed. "As you can see, my stepsons treat me *abominably.*"

She sat on the couch and Arden took the seat behind her. "It is so kind of you to call to inquire as to my well-being. No one else in this house apart from Dr. Mantel gives a fig for my health or grief. My stepsons do not care about me at all and wish me to the devil."

Lucy smiled sympathetically. "It must be a very trying time for you, what with the missing will and a funeral to arrange."

"My dear Lady Kurland," Lady Benson whined, "you have no *idea* . . ."

Robert admired his wife's fortitude as she nodded along with Lady Benson's litany of complaints, slights, and concerns. Eventually, he glanced up as the tea tray was delivered along with some decanters for the men and excused himself. He doubted Lady Benson even noticed he had gone. He followed the butler out into the hall and called out to him.

"Is Mr. Tompkins here today?"

"I believe so, sir. I haven't seen him myself this morning, as he is busy packing up Sir William's belongings. Would you like me to send for him?"

"I'm more than happy to go up to Sir William's room and speak to Mr. Tompkins myself." Robert tapped his leg with his cane. "I need as much exercise as I can, and I don't wish to cause any trouble."

He headed for the staircase toward the center of the house. "I won't be a minute."

"As you wish, sir." The butler continued through the door and into the servants' area of the house.

Robert went up the stairs, pausing every so often to gauge who was up and about on the floor above. In their rented house the master bedroom was on the same floor as the drawing room, but in the Bensons', two separate bedrooms and a dressing room took up most of the second floor. He already knew Augustus had returned to his parish, Peregrine had gone out, and Edward and Arden were downstairs with the ladies. Foley had told him that Sir William's room was on the left, there was a dressing room in the center, and Lady Benson occupied the room on the right. He knocked cautiously on the left door, but there was no answer.

He eased down on the latch and peered inside, noticing the room was in complete disorder with clothes, trunks, wigs, and nether garments strewn everywhere. He frowned. Knowing Foley's love of neatness he reckoned that if Mr. Tompkins had left everything in such a state Foley would have mentioned it. Foley had also indicated that Mr. Tompkins was almost ready to leave.

Stepping more fully into the room Robert closed the door behind him and stood still. Not a single surface was clear and clothing was tossed all over the floor. Drawers and cupboards hung open as if a blizzard had passed through. Robert paused to pick up two books that hindered his path and placed them on the bed.

He stiffened as a curse came from the dressing room to his right. Robert carefully stepped through the debris, his cane at the ready, and opened that door to discover Brandon tipping the contents of a small leather case out onto the floor.

"What in God's name are you doing?" Robert demanded just as Brandon launched the case at his head. He managed to dodge the missile, but by then Brandon had clattered down the servants' stairs. Robert found the bellpull and rang it hard as he surveyed the damage around him. Brandon had obviously decided to instigate his own search for the will. . . .

But where was Mr. Tompkins? Had he already left, taking the vital will with him?

Robert turned a slow circle, his instincts and memories at war with the domestic scene around him. Something wasn't right; he could almost taste it.

The butler came into the room, his eyes widening in shock as he saw the chaos. "Sir Robert! What happened?"

Robert held up his hand. "Is Mr. Tompkins in the kitchen?"

"No, sir. No one has seen him since breakfast."

Robert's gaze was drawn to the wall of oak cupboards against the wall between the two connecting doors. He moved closer, his nose wrinkling even as his eyes saw nothing wrong. A trickle of brown matter on the carpet drew his attention. He swallowed hard, braced himself, and opened the largest of the cupboards, which ran the whole height of the wall.

"Oh, my God . . ." Behind him the butler recoiled in horror. "That's Mr. Tompkins! He's hanged himself."

Robert spoke without turning around. "Please go and fetch Mr. Edward Benson, and don't mention what you have just seen to anyone. Do you understand me?"

"Yes, sir. Of course, sir."

After a deep breath, Robert forced himself to get closer to the old man whose body hung like a sack of corn from the loop of the cravat tied around his neck and strung over the rail. The bulging eyes and purplish tone of his flesh were horrifying. He did not look as if he had gone willingly to his death. . . .

Robert wished Patrick Fletcher were with him, because he was certain his friend would be able to decipher the clues in a scientific way that aligned with Robert's instinct that Mr. Tompkins had not killed himself, but had most definitely been murdered.

Chapter 12

Edward Benson came back into the study where he'd left Robert drinking a restorative brandy.

"It appears that Brandon has disappeared. I've sent our servants out to look for him and insisted that Arden stays here."

"Good thinking."

Robert finished his brandy. It was barely midday. Since the Bensons had entered his life his drinking had increased substantially. When Lady Benson had swooned, Lucy and the maid had assisted Dr. Mantel in taking her back to her bedchamber—with the door into the dressing room securely locked so she couldn't accidentally venture in there and have another screaming fit.

Edward helped himself to a large glass of brandy. He looked rather pale, which wasn't surprising considering what was going on in his household as he sat opposite Robert.

"I hate to ask you this, Sir Robert, but what was Brandon actually doing when you surprised him in the dressing room?"

"He was emptying out a box of his stepfather's possessions. When he saw me he threw the box at my head."

"Dear God," Edward exhaled. "I was in Father's bedchamber yesterday speaking to Mr. Tompkins. The room was spotless, and everything was stored away."

"That's what my butler, Foley, told me when he came to help Mr. Tompkins finish the packing," Robert replied. "I have to suspect that Brandon decided to go through everything he could get his hands on and didn't care about the mess he was making."

"That boy has been no end of trouble," Edward groaned. "He's been expelled twice from school and has the most violent temper imaginable."

"Do you think he took his temper out on Mr. Tompkins?" Robert asked.

"God knows. It's possible." Edward shoved a hand through his thinning hair. "Mr. Tompkins was an old man, but he would've defended my father's possessions from anyone."

"Do you think Mr. Tompkins was the kind of man to kill himself?"

"No. He was devastated by my father's death but was determined to do the right thing and bring him home to be buried in Yorkshire soil." Edward grimaced. "And now we will be burying both of them."

"Then if you think Brandon might have had a

hand in Mr. Tompkins's death what do you intend to do about it?" Robert inquired.

"I think it is too late to try to pretend that Brandon isn't dangerous. If we can't locate him ourselves I intend to contact the authorities to see if they can find him. It's probably pointless to attempt to keep this within the family. There is nothing missing from Brandon's room, and he ran off without his hat and coat. At some point—unless he has a considerable amount of money in his pocket, which I doubt—he will have to come back here and face us."

"I agree." Robert placed his glass on the silver tray. "Would you object if I spoke to Arden before I leave?"

Edward frowned. "May I ask why?"

"I was a cavalry officer during the war and often dealt with junior officers and enlisted men with very little sense and a lot of overconfidence. I suspect that the key to finding Brandon is his brother."

"Then have at it. Arden will never speak to me."

Robert stood up. "I think Arden might be redeemable. A stint in a decent regiment would knock him into shape fairly quickly and give him a defined purpose in his life."

"If we ever *find* the blasted will then I will certainly consider your suggestion, although my feelings toward him and his brother are currently not very complimentary." Edward rose and bowed as Robert went toward the door.

"There is one more thing." Robert paused. "Would you object to my physician, Dr. Fletcher, seeing Mr. Tompkins's body?"

"Dr. Mantel is supervising the laying out of the body in Mr. Tompkins's bedroom on the top floor. We will need another coffin to transport him back to Yorkshire along with Sir William. Perhaps you might ask the good doctor?"

"Thank you, I will." Robert opened the door. "Now, where will I find young Arden?"

Robert followed the directions up the stairs to the next floor and discovered one of the footmen sitting outside a locked door.

"Mr. Benson said I might speak to Arden. You can lock the door behind me, and I'll knock when I'm ready to leave."

"Yes, sir." The footman unlocked the door and Robert stepped inside the room where Arden was sitting on the side of his bed. He leapt to his feet when he saw Robert and scowled.

"What's going on? Where's Brandon?"

Robert took a seat beside the fireplace. "Don't you know?"

"I heard some cock and bull story about him wrecking the old man's room and running off, but why I've been locked in here when I should be the one going after him is beyond me."

Robert remained silent until Arden stopped pacing and glared at him.

"What?"

"I went to find Mr. Tompkins but instead discovered your brother rifling through your stepfather's possessions. When he saw me he ran away. Why do you think he might have done that?"

"Run away?" Arden shrugged. "Because that's just how he is. Whenever he's caught kicking up a lark he attempts to escape the consequences."

"*Kicking up a lark?*" Robert asked. "Destroying someone's property is not amusing."

"It is if you're Brandon and you hated your stepfather." Arden kicked the corner of the bed. "If you let me out, I'll find him. I know all his favorite haunts."

"I believe Mr. Benson is planning on setting the authorities on him."

"Why would he do that?" Arden demanded. "Did Brandon *steal* anything, or just give you a bloody good fright?"

"Did you know that Brandon intended to search for the will?"

Arden blinked at him. "What?"

"The missing will," Robert repeated patiently. "What else would he have been looking for?"

"I have no idea." Arden tried to look unconcerned. "Probably money or something to pawn to pay his debts."

"He didn't tell you anything? That seems unlikely when you are so close." Robert eased back in his chair. "In fact, I don't believe you."

Arden's expression clouded over. "I don't care what you think of me, Sir Robert. You have no say in this family, and your opinion counts for nothing."

"It might if you aspired to get into a particular regiment. I have some influence in that sphere that might benefit you."

"If I tell tales on my brother," Arden objected. "What kind of honorable man would do that?"

"A man who feared that his brother had perhaps crossed a line?" Robert suggested.

Arden came to stand right over Robert. "What exactly are you trying to say? Did Brandon . . . *hurt* someone?"

"Why would you think that?"

"Because—what has happened—tell me!" Arden shouted.

"Mr. Tompkins is dead," Robert said. "I found his body in the dressing room just after your brother tried to brain me with a leather box."

Arden sank into the chair, his head bowed, his hands twisted together in front of him. Robert didn't say anything and waited for the young man to look up at him again.

"You think Brandon killed Mr. Tompkins," Arden croaked.

"It's possible," Robert agreed. "The fact that he

ran away isn't helping his case." He paused. "If you can tell me where to find him then at least he can be brought here to explain himself rather than being incarcerated in the town gaol and formally charged."

Robert tensed as Arden shot to his feet, went over to his desk, and furiously started writing. He rose to as Arden approached him with a piece of paper.

"Take this."

Robert raised an eyebrow.

"It's a list of all his favorite places to go."

"Thank you." Robert took the paper. "I will endeavor to find him and bring him home to you."

"If I came with you we would find him much more quickly."

"Alas, you will have to remain here. The thought of finding your brother and then the two of you conspiring against me and running off together doesn't sit well with me." Robert folded the note and put it in his pocket. "I will make sure that you are told when Brandon returns."

He'd reached the door before Arden spoke again.

"Sir Robert?"

"Yes?"

"Is Mr. Tompkins truly dead?"

"Unfortunately, yes. He was hanging in the closet."

Arden paled and swallowed hard. "He was always nice to me."

"He was a nice man, and a loyal employee of Sir William." Robert inclined his head. "Goodbye, Arden."

He knocked on the door and was allowed out. After thanking the footman he made his way down to the drawing room and found Lucy awaiting him. She looked rather tired, but he suspected that anyone who had to deal with Lady Benson's hysterics would look the same way.

"Are you all right?" Robert asked as she turned around and spotted him.

"Dr. Mantel finally persuaded Lady Benson to take a sleeping draught, and I was able to leave." She sighed as he took her hand in his. "She really is the most exhausting woman I have ever met."

"I wouldn't argue with that." Robert lowered his voice even though they were alone. "Let's go home where we can talk freely."

Lucy realized she hadn't eaten anything all day and hastened to send an order down to the kitchens to bring up something for her and Robert to sustain themselves with before dinner. She took a few moments to take off her bonnet, smooth her hair, and wash her face before returning to the dining room. Robert hadn't yet come back from breaking the bad news to Foley, so she was alone with her thoughts.

Robert had given her a few details about what had occurred between him and Arden. She only knew that Mr. Tompkins was dead, and was eager to hear the whole story. Unfortunately, the notion that Brandon had killed the valet in a rage was not only possible but all too likely. And if Brandon had murdered Mr. Tompkins, was it also likely that he'd murdered his stepfather as well?

Anna came in and stood by the fire warming her hands. She wore a plain high-necked gown, and her hair was pinned up in a severe fashion unlike her normal soft ringlets. She turned to Lucy and frowned.

"Where have you *been* all day, Lucy? Despite my attempts to apologize, Penelope won't speak to me and has refused to leave her room. Foley didn't know when you would be back, and I wanted to speak to you most *urgently.*"

"I was detained at the Bensons'." Lucy didn't sit down. "There was a—"

"I don't know why you bother with Lady Benson. She is an incredibly selfish woman." Anna talked over Lucy, which was most unlike her. "Her *problems* are mainly of her own making."

"And yours are not?" Lucy fought off her weariness. "What do you wish to speak to me about, Anna?"

"Captain Akers, of course. Last night he asked me to marry him again, and I turned him down."

"Oh."

"Is that all you have to say?" Anna demanded.

"What would you like me to say?" Lucy met her sister's gaze. "We have discussed this at length. The only thing that can change is you, Anna. If Captain Akers cannot persuade you to change your mind, then maybe he is not the right person for you after all."

"But I care for him very deeply," Anna whispered.

"So you said before."

Anna drew herself up. "I can see that you are not interested in discussing this properly with me, Lucy. I hoped you would *listen* to me, and—"

"I *have* listened to you, and I fully intend to support whatever decision you wish to make," Lucy said wearily. "What more do you *want?*"

"Some compassion? Some *understanding?*" Anna tossed her head. "But perhaps I should've realized you are incapable of those things."

Lucy briefly closed her eyes and held on to the back of the chair as a wave of dizziness overcame her. "Forgive me. I am rather tired. I—"

"Lucy!"

She blinked hard and managed to fumble her way around and sit before she fell down. Anna knelt in front of her and took her hands, her blue eyes filling with tears.

"I'm so sorry, I didn't mean to upset you and I should never had said such *awful* things." Anna dabbed at the tears now coursing down her cheeks. "I am turning into a *horrible* person."

Lucy offered Anna her handkerchief. "It's all right. It's just been a rather trying morning."

"Shall I fetch Robert for you?"

"No!" Lucy squeezed Anna's fingers hard. "Please don't bother him. I haven't eaten since breakfast and I'm simply hungry. As soon as I eat something I'll feel much better." She took a deep breath and managed a wobbly smile. "Can we talk later? I fear I will not be much help at the moment."

"Of course." Anna helped her up and held on to her elbow until she seemed satisfied that Lucy wasn't going to crumple into a heap. "Foley said there is food in the dining room so perhaps I'll walk you there, and you can tell me what on earth has been going on at the Bensons'."

"I fear I was rather short with Anna earlier," Lucy confessed as she sat with Robert in the dining room after her sister had gone.

"You were?" Robert raised an eyebrow. "What did she do?"

"She accused me of not supporting her." Lucy sighed. "I told her that we would accept any decision she made regarding Captain Akers. That still wasn't good enough to satisfy her."

"Your sister is rather out of sorts," Robert said tentatively.

"Yes, and I *know* I can be opinionated, but—"

215

He reached for her hand across the table. "In this instance I believe she is in the wrong, and you have been all that is reasonable. We can't force her to marry the man, and that's the end of it."

"I have to agree with you."

"Well, that is good to know." He smiled at her. "After hours of Lady Benson wailing at you I'm surprised you had any patience left for your sister at all."

Lucy made a face. "Lady Benson *is* rather trying. I don't know how Dr. Mantel puts up with her."

"She probably pays him well, or at least Sir William did." Robert hesitated. "I asked Edward Benson if Dr. Fletcher could look at Mr. Tompkins's body, and he said to ask Dr. Mantel. Do you think he would object?"

"Dr. Mantel has a very high opinion of Dr. Fletcher, so I don't see him demurring," Lucy said. "Why do you want our doctor to look at the body?"

"As an ex-military surgeon, Patrick is very good at determining the causes of violent deaths."

"How exactly *did* Mr. Tompkins die?"

Robert grimaced. "He was hanging from the railing in one of the closets."

Lucy shuddered. "Is it possible that he killed himself?"

"It's possible, but according to Edward Benson the old man was intent on bringing his master's body back to Yorkshire and taking care of his effects until there was nothing else he could do for him. He didn't look like the type of man to fall into a pit of despair to me."

"I'd agree. He seemed to be very strong-willed and stubborn."

"As are most men from Yorkshire," Robert added. "My cousin Oliver amongst them."

Lucy fiddled with her teaspoon. "Does Edward think *Brandon* killed Mr. Tompkins?"

"I assume he does, seeing as he told me that if he couldn't find Brandon by tonight he would be notifying the town authorities and asking them to apprehend the lad and take him to gaol."

"Do *you* think Brandon killed Mr. Tompkins?"

"Well, he certainly was in the right place at the right time." Robert frowned. "But as I didn't catch him in the act I can't say for certain."

"Brandon is known to be violent. He has a terrible temper and has been expelled from school," Lucy pointed out. "He might even have killed Sir William as well."

"What makes you think that?"

"Well, it stands to reason, doesn't it?" Lucy asked. "Mr. Tompkins probably knew more than he was letting on, and maybe he tried to confront Brandon and Brandon turned on him?"

"I suppose that is possible," Robert said slowly. "The sooner we can locate the young fool, the quicker the truth will out."

Chapter 13

"He suffocated." Dr. Fletcher drew the cover down to Mr. Tompkins's waist and pointed at his neck. "The cravat tightened around his neck leaving those vivid bruises until he couldn't draw breath into his lungs. It probably took a while because it wasn't done on a professional scaffold or by a skilled hangman."

Robert nodded. As military men both he and Patrick had attended their fair share of hangings, him in his capacity as an officer, and the doctor to lay out the corpse and make sure the man was really dead.

"Could Mr. Tompkins have done this to himself?"

"Yes, but look at his arms and torso." Patrick directed Robert's attention to the valet's sturdy body. "There is a considerable amount of bruising around his wrists, and his hands are badly scraped up, which indicates that whatever was happening to him he wasn't cooperating. I think he was attempting to fight someone off."

"Someone who eventually overcame him,"

Robert murmured. He'd never been comfortable around the dead. They brought back too many memories of battles fought long ago and the injuries that had almost ended his life at Waterloo.

"There's one more thing." Patrick cupped the back of Mr. Tompkins's skull. "There's some damage or swelling here as well, which suggests he got a thump on the back of his head to keep him quiet while his murderer strung him up."

"Thank you for the vivid details." Robert shuddered. "I don't suppose you can hazard a guess as to how long ago he died, can you?"

"Not with any great accuracy. Was he stiff when you cut him down?"

"No, he wasn't." Robert paused. "Does it matter?"

"Well, you said Brandon was in the room minutes before you found the body. If he'd been the one doing the killing, the body wouldn't have been stiff because rigor mortis takes a while to set in."

Patrick's extensive knowledge about the processes of death had been acquired on the battlefields of the war with Napoleon and was unparalleled in Robert's experience. His casual acceptance of the many horrors of death never ceased to simultaneously impress and appall Robert.

"Have they found him yet?" Patrick asked as he drew the sheet over the dead man's head.

"Brandon? No. I went out to look for him yesterday afternoon myself, but I couldn't find him." Robert hesitated. "If you can spare me some time this evening, I thought I might go out and search for him again."

"Bath is a large town, Sir Robert."

"I know, but I have the advantage of a list of his favorite haunts supplied to me by his brother."

"How did you get that?" Patrick asked. "Both of them seemed equally obnoxious to me, so I'm surprised the older one offered his help."

"I believe Arden has aspirations to join the military."

"Ah. And you have the connections." Patrick nodded. "It makes sense. Of course I'll come out with you."

"If your wife is agreeable, of course," Robert added hastily.

Patrick made a face. "My wife is not very happy with me as she can no longer touch her toes, sleep comfortably in her bed, or fit into any of her favorite dresses. I suspect she would be quite delighted to see the back of me for a few hours."

"Do you think you might take her home with you when you leave this time?" Robert asked nonchalantly.

He was rewarded by a knowing grin. "Is she driving you mad?"

"I would never say that, but—"

"It's all right." Patrick washed his hands. "I know she can be a little trying sometimes." He turned back to Robert. "The thing is . . . I'm concerned about how close she is to giving birth."

"I thought she had another month or two to go."

"So did I, but I think we might have miscalculated." He grimaced. "I would hate to get halfway home and then have to stop in some godforsaken inn where she'd have to give birth in a bed of straw."

Robert tried to imagine Penelope's fury if that happened, but attempted to reply diplomatically. "No woman would want that."

He was already wondering how he would break the news to Lucy that not only was Penelope staying, but that she might give birth at any moment. . . .

"Ah, good morning, gentlemen."

Robert turned as Dr. Mantel came into the room and bowed to them. The doctor wore his usual modest brown coat, breeches, and scuffed boots that in Robert's opinion needed a good polishing.

"Thank you for allowing me to view the body, Dr. Mantel." Patrick shook the doctor's hand. "It was quite instructional."

"You are most welcome." Dr. Mantel nodded. "It is always a sad day when a man takes his own life, and somewhat horrifying to view the damage he has wrought upon himself."

Robert and Patrick exchanged a quick surprised glance.

"You believe he killed himself?" Patrick asked slowly.

"He hung himself using his own cravat in a cupboard." Dr. Mantel frowned. "He was distraught because of the loss of his master and worried about his future employment. One cannot condone such actions, but one can certainly sympathize with the poor soul."

"Did no one mention to you that Brandon was discovered in the dressing room and that he fled when I discovered him?" Robert asked.

"Well yes, I heard he was *there,* but the poor boy could hardly have known . . ." It was Dr. Mantel's turn to stare at the two men. "Are you suggesting that *Brandon* had something to do with this?"

The shock on the doctor's face was evident. Robert nodded to Patrick, who took up the conversation.

"From my examination it seems that as well as the bruising around the neck there are other injuries to the body." Patrick pulled back the sheet again and Dr. Mantel flinched. "There is enough evidence of a struggle to suggest that someone manhandled Mr. Tompkins into that cupboard, knocked him half-unconscious, and then strung him up with his own cravat."

Dr. Mantel's mouth hung open. "Oh, dear

God," he said faintly. "What the devil am I going to tell Lady Miranda?"

"There's no need to say anything to her at this point," Robert intervened quickly.

"But if her son is implicated in a murder . . ." Dr. Mantel sank into the nearest chair and looked up at Robert. "She will be *inconsolable*."

"Your concern for her well-being is admirable, Doctor," Robert said. "I would suggest that knowing the strain she is under right now, *not* telling her anything would be the right thing to do."

Dr. Mantel nodded fervently. "Perhaps you are right."

"Does Lady Benson know anything about Brandon's presence in the dressing room?" Robert asked.

"I don't believe so, otherwise she would be in a state of panic that would concern me deeply. She is a *delicate* soul, Sir Robert, and has suffered greatly from the unpleasantness of the Benson sons."

"Do you think she has noticed Brandon has not returned home yet?"

"He isn't the most dutiful of boys and wouldn't necessarily seek her out on a daily basis," Dr. Mantel said. "She did ask me whether Arden was home, and to my shame I told her a slight fib that he was indisposed and not able to come to her side."

"I think you did the right thing, Doctor." Robert nodded. "If Brandon comes back tonight and explains himself, then she will be able to remain in blissful ignorance."

Dr. Mantel stood. "Then let's hope that the boy returns. I suspect he ran away because he encountered you, Sir Robert, and you scared him silly."

"I do have that effect on people sometimes," Robert admitted. "Perhaps his attempt to knock me out was merely a playful gesture on his part."

"One cannot doubt it." Dr. Mantel's smile returned, and he turned to the door. "The undertaker is coming this afternoon to measure for the coffin. I must ask one of the maids to make sure that Mr. Tompkins is dressed in his finest garb before he is sent back to Yorkshire and his final resting place."

The doctor left, and Robert and Patrick regarded each other.

"Do you want me to report my findings to Mr. Edward Benson or not?" Patrick asked bluntly.

"Perhaps we should find young Brandon first, and see what he has to say for himself."

Patrick frowned. "I would prefer Mr. Benson to see the physical evidence on the body for himself."

"Mr. Benson is already predisposed to believe that Brandon is a murderer. If you write out a statement, and I witness it, I think that will be enough to convince him." Robert glanced over at the body. "And this poor man deserves to be shut away from the madness."

Patrick nodded. "I forget that you don't like dead bodies."

"I've seen far too many of them," Robert murmured. "And they continue to haunt and follow me to this day."

"Yes, you and Lady Kurland do seem to uncover more than your fair share of fatalities." Patrick put on his coat. "Now I must go and write that letter for you and speak to my wife."

"Of course you must go and search for Brandon." Lucy looked up from her darning at Robert. "I will enjoy a quiet evening with Anna and Penelope while you and Dr. Fletcher are out."

"Thank you." Robert took the seat beside her. "There is one more thing."

"Yes?"

"It's about Penelope."

Lucy put down her work and gave him her full attention. "What about her?"

Robert met her inquiring gaze full on, thinking he might as well get it over with.

"Dr. Fletcher says she is further along in the pregnancy than he realized, and he cannot risk transporting her back to Kurland St. Mary at this point."

She stared at him for a very long time. "Oh, no."

"He is worried that she might not make it home without going into labor."

She let out her breath. "Then she will have to stay here."

Robert took her hand. "I'm sorry."

"It's hardly your fault if our doctor can't work out when his own *child* will be born, is it? Penelope might be something of a burden, but I would not wish her to suffer on my account."

Robert kissed her fingers. "You are remarkably tolerant, my love."

"That's because I have no choice. Does Dr. Fletcher intend to stay here until the baby is born, then?"

"I believe so."

"Then he can take good care of Penelope." Lucy nodded. "He can eat with her, walk with her, and accompany her on *all* her excursions."

"I'll tell him," Robert agreed. "I will make sure that he remains constantly at her side." He stood and bowed. "Well, I must be off. Wish me luck."

"Do be careful, won't you?" Lucy looked up at him, her gaze worried.

"I'll do my best, and I'll have Patrick with me at all times."

"I'll try and wait up for you."

He paused at the door. "How about we agree that I'll wake you up if something interesting has happened?"

"As you wish." She stifled a yawn behind her hand. "I must confess that all this walking around Bath does wear me out somewhat."

Robert went down into the hall where he found Patrick putting on his hat and glancing nervously up the stairs. He had the look of a man who had just faced down an enemy and was now in full retreat.

Glimpsing Penelope appearing on the landing, Robert headed for the front door where Foley awaited him. "Come on, my friend." He accepted his hat and gloves, tucked his cane under his arm, and went down the steps.

It wasn't quite dark out in the square but the lamplighters were already at work. Patrick came down the stone steps behind him and let out his breath.

"Thank goodness she can't move very fast at the moment."

Robert concealed a smile.

"She's developed this distressing habit of bursting into tears every time I say a word. I'm not sure what to do about it," Patrick confided.

"Stay mum?" Robert suggested.

"I've tried that and then she accuses me of not caring enough for her to bother to speak." Patrick sighed. "I almost wish the old Penelope was back—the one who criticized me and stood up to me at the slightest provocation."

"Don't we all," Robert said dryly. "You're supposed to be a doctor. Aren't you *used* to dealing with women with child?"

"Yes, but none of them are my wife." Patrick pulled on his gloves. "Now, where are we going to start looking for this young fool?"

"Not in the well-lit parts of town, I can assure you." Robert had already checked all the locations Arden had given him on the previous outing and had a fair idea of the route to take. "We're visiting the dilapidated inns, the whorehouses, and the gaming parlors."

Patrick patted his coat pocket. "Then it's a good thing I brought my pistol and my favorite knife."

As the evening wore on, Robert began to hate the stench of unwashed bodies, drunkenness, and despair emanating from those who frequented the lower levels of society. He'd almost had his pocket picked twice and had fended off more than one over-perfumed woman offering him her services.

They extricated themselves from yet another bawdy house and moved on down the narrow unpaved street with a clogged gutter running down the center of the cobblestones.

"Where next?" Patrick asked. He looked far less perturbed than Robert, being more used to working amongst the extremes of humanity.

"The inn on the corner." Robert pointed out the old stone building with its thatched roof and sagging doorways. "If you can call it that." Lights flickered through the shutters and a waft of ale and sweat curled around them at the entrance.

Patrick went first, and Robert followed him, ducking his head to avoid the low-hanging beams. No one looked up as they entered, which gave Robert precious seconds to look around the room. All eyes were turned to a dice game taking place at one of the crowded tables.

A roar was followed by a groan as one of the barmaids distributed tankards of ale to her customers and coins were thrown toward the dealer and dice thrower.

"There," Robert mouthed in Patrick's ear. "At the table to the right of the dealer."

"I see him."

Brandon was intent on the game and seemed unaware that he was being observed. His fumbling motions as he attempted to drink his ale made Robert suspect he was a trifle disguised.

"Let's get as close as we can on either side of him without him noticing," Robert continued. "And the second he moves, we'll take him."

"Agreed."

As Brandon was unlikely to recognize Patrick he took the longer route around the room, crossing directly in front of Brandon's gaze, but the boy gave no sign that he noticed anything. Robert went more slowly and found a position against the wall directly behind Brandon as if he was observing the game.

When the barmaid went past, he bought a pint of ale and sipped it as he watched the progression of the game. If Brandon kept drinking he'd need to piss soon, and that would offer them another opportunity to catch him.

Eventually, Brandon lurched unsteadily to his feet and attempted to climb over the bench he was sitting on. It took him a while to untangle his legs, and then he staggered off toward the rear of the inn, Robert and Patrick in pursuit. Before Robert could call out to him, two large men pushed past him and went straight toward Brandon, who was now pissing against the wall of the stables.

"Oi!"

Brandon didn't look up, and the men closed in around him.

"You owe us money."

"I don't have any," Brandon snarled as he fastened his trousers.

The larger of the two men grabbed him by the throat. "Then why was you gambling, toff?"

"Take your hands off me!"

The man laughed. "Give me my money, and I'll do whatever you want, your lordship. That's half a crown you owe me, and two shillings to my friend here."

Brandon attempted to get out of the man's grasp and ended up being slapped around the face.

"Quieten down, little man. If you ain't got the

coin, maybe you've got a nice pocket watch or tiepin that will do instead?"

"I don't have anything, you bacon-brained idiots!"

Another slap. Robert winced and cleared his throat.

"Gentlemen, may I make a suggestion?"

All three men turned to stare at him. Brandon's nose was now bleeding. Patrick stepped up beside Robert, his pistol already cocked.

"How about I pay this young man's debt to you, and in exchange you let me take him into my custody?"

"You the law?"

"Unfortunately not, but I am a connection of this man's stepfather. I feel it is my duty to restore him to the bosom of his family."

"I don't want to go home," Brandon slurred. "Everyone hates me there."

"We can discuss that on the way back," Robert said firmly. He took two half sovereigns out of his pocket. "Gentlemen? Do we have a deal?"

Within a few moments, both men grabbed the tossed coins and disappeared back into the inn. Patrick seized hold of Brandon just before he toppled over, and jerked his head in the direction of the stables.

"Let's leave through the courtyard so our new friends don't get any ideas about robbing us as we pass through the inn."

"Agreed." Robert took Brandon's other arm and nodded. "Let's go."

As they walked back toward the more civilized parts of the town, Robert considered what to do next. In truth, he was obliged to deliver Brandon back to the Bensons, but for some reason his instincts were telling him not to.

"Do you think we could get him into our town house without the Bensons noticing?" Robert asked Patrick.

"If we came up through the mews at the back of the garden, I don't see why not." Patrick paused. "Why do you want to do that?"

"I'd like to ask him a few questions before the Bensons get to him."

"While he's drunk and loquacious?"

"Exactly."

Patrick heaved a sagging Brandon back onto his feet. "Then let's see if we can get him back there before he either pukes on my boots or passes out."

Foley opened the back door and frowned at Robert.

"What on earth are you doing, Sir Robert? The servants' entrance is not a fitting way for a baronet to enter his own house."

"Needs must, Foley." Robert nodded at his disapproving butler as he and Patrick came inside with Brandon slung between them. "I'll need to borrow the butler's pantry for an hour or so."

"As you wish, sir." Foley wrinkled his nose as he held open a door off the main corridor that eventually led to the kitchen. "I assume you don't wish me to alert Lady Kurland as to your presence?"

"You assume correctly," Robert spoke over his shoulder. "I would, however, appreciate some coffee and brandy for myself and Dr. Fletcher."

"As you wish, sir." Foley closed the door and went off muttering so loudly Robert could hear him through the wooden panels.

Patrick lowered Brandon into one of the chairs, pulled up another for himself, and placed it right beside the drunken boy. He gently shook him.

"Brandon? Wake up. Sir Robert wishes to speak to you." Patrick glanced up at Robert. "You might ask Foley for a bucket in case this young fool decides to cast up his accounts."

"Good idea."

Robert waited until Foley came in with the requested beverages and had provided them with a bucket before settling himself opposite Brandon.

"Your family is very worried about you."

"Bloody hell, not you again." Brandon opened one eye. "Why do you keep turning up when you're not wanted?"

"It's a talent of mine." Robert paused. "Why were you in Sir William's bedchamber?"

"I don't have to answer your questions," Brandon growled. "You have no authority over me."

"That's true, but I was very fond of your step-father, and I consider it my duty to preserve his memory."

"What the devil does that mean?"

Robert set a cup of coffee at Brandon's elbow. "Why were you going through his possessions?"

"None of your flaming business!" Brandon suddenly sat forward, his fists clenched and his gaze fiery. Beside him Patrick tensed.

Robert regarded Brandon until the boy began to squirm in his seat. "Hurling insults at me will hardly result in us accomplishing anything, will it? You might not believe it, but I am trying to help you." When Brandon said nothing, Robert continued speaking. "I assume you were attempting to steal money to pay your gambling debts?"

"Why would you think that?"

Robert raised an eyebrow. "Because I had the opportunity to view your attempts to gamble, and you have neither the ability nor the finances for it."

"That's got nothing to do with you."

"Then you weren't looking for money." Robert contemplated the sullen boy. "Were you looking for something in particular?"

Brandon's eyes flickered and Robert pressed on.

"Was I the only person you encountered in that dressing room trying to stop you stealing your stepfather's possessions?"

"I wasn't *stealing*—I was—*looking* for something!" Brandon shouted, and shot to his feet. Patrick joined him, one hand on the boy's shoulder preventing him from leaping at Robert.

"For the will?"

"No! Dammit! You don't understand!" Brandon said. "Sir William kept a lot of things from me and Arden—things that rightfully belonged to us from our father! I was trying to get what belonged to us!"

"Such as?" Robert asked.

"None of your bloody business."

"Strange that Arden didn't mention any of this when I spoke to him last," Robert mused.

"Arden?" Brandon sat back in his chair. "What are you lying about now?"

"It's no lie." Robert held the boy's indignant gaze. "How do you think I knew where to find you?" He took out the list and showed it to Brandon. "This is your brother's handwriting, isn't it?"

"Give that to me!" Brandon attempted to snatch the list out of Robert's hand, but Patrick slammed him back in the chair and held him there by his shoulders.

"Your brother is very worried about you," Robert said. "That's why he offered to help me find you."

"Why didn't he come himself?" Brandon asked. "Is he locked up as well?"

"You are hardly locked up." Robert glanced around the room. "When we have finished our conversation, you are free to leave and take your chances with the local magistrate."

"Edward would never allow me to be taken up like a common criminal," Brandon scoffed. "He's too much of a coward and is terrified of damaging the family name."

"You're wrong there." Robert paused. "If you don't return by midnight tonight, Mr. Benson intends to allow the authorities to put you in gaol."

"For what?" Brandon had the gall to laugh. "Throwing a box at your head? They'd let me out in a second!"

"One has to assume that you haven't spoken to anyone from your family since you ran away from me?" Robert asked.

"Of course I haven't." Brandon frowned. "Why?"

Robert looked at Patrick, who nodded at him.

"Because there has been a death in the house."

"Good Lord, did Edward have heart failure because of me?" Brandon's smile was full of vindictive spite. "What an excellent lark."

"No, it wasn't Edward." Robert watched Brandon's face very closely. "It was Mr. Tompkins."

"Old Tompkins?" Brandon blinked. *"That's* why the old man wasn't there when I went into Sir William's bedroom."

"Oh, he was there," Robert said, suddenly tired of the unpleasant individual he was dealing with. "I'm surprised you didn't come across him in your very thorough search."

Brandon smiled. "Where was the old chap, then? Hiding under the bed?"

"I think you know damn well where he was." It was Robert's turn to raise his voice and use a tone he'd perfected as an officer in the cavalry. Brandon shrank back into his chair. "Seeing as you probably murdered him and put him there."

Brandon opened his mouth and then closed it again, the color draining from his face.

"I'll give you a choice," Robert said. "Run away and wait for the authorities to catch you and face murder charges, or be an honorable man, go home, and face up to the consequences of your actions."

Robert lifted his gaze to Patrick. "Perhaps you might wait with Brandon until he makes his decision. If he chooses to run, let him. If he decides to go home, make sure he gets there."

"Yes, Sir Robert." Patrick nodded. "I'll let you know what he decides."

Robert left the room very carefully, not slamming the door behind him. He was no longer a man who sought out conflict, but the sick joy on Brandon's face as he'd talked about who he hoped was dead made Robert want to throttle the boy with his bare hands.

He continued up to the drawing room where Foley had left the candles alight and paced the floor. As far as he could tell, Brandon hadn't been telling the truth about anything. He'd claimed he'd merely been taking back his own property. But what on earth could that have been? Robert paused to consider Brandon's statement. There was no one amongst the Bensons who could answer that question except Lady Miranda and Arden, and he suspected they wouldn't be very forthcoming.

What could Sir William have held on to that belonged to the boys? The only other person who would probably have known the answer was Mr. Tompkins and he was dead. Which led Robert back to his suspicion that Brandon had been found going through Sir William's things by Mr. Tompkins and that the poor valet had ended up being murdered by the young man in a fit of rage.

A light tap on the door was followed by the appearance of Patrick, who came in and bowed to Robert.

"He decided to run."

"The little fool," Robert said. "Although I can't say I'm surprised. What a thoroughly contemptible individual." He turned away from the window and sat beside the fire. "Then we need do nothing further. Let Edward Benson make the decision to ask for help from the magistrate's court in the morning, and justice will take its own path."

Patrick sat opposite him. "Do you think Brandon killed Mr. Tompkins?"

"He's big enough and has the right temperament. If he was at the baths somewhere that morning, he could easily have murdered Sir William as well. He and Arden knew Sir William had drowned before anyone else," Robert said. "I had a young officer like him in France. He enjoyed killing far too much—took pleasure in the pain and suffering of others. I eventually had to send him home after he tortured some poor prisoner to death."

Patrick shuddered. "I've seen those kinds of men as well. You can't fix them. I wonder how long it will take Brandon to fall foul of the law?"

"If he receives no help from his brother I doubt he'll last long." Robert snorted. "He couldn't even avoid amateurs like us."

"What did you think about his story of merely claiming back his own property?" Patrick asked.

"I wasn't expecting him to say that," Robert admitted. "And it does concern me, but my first thought is that he killed Mr. Tompkins in a blind rage when the old man stopped him searching."

"I could see that happening." Patrick nodded. "And Brandon was quite bruised and battered himself, wasn't he? Almost as if he'd been in a fight."

"Maybe with Mr. Tompkins." Robert scowled. "Who knows? But if Brandon *did* murder the valet, perhaps he killed the master as well."

"Did anyone see Brandon at the baths that morning?"

"No, but no one saw anything," Robert said gloomily as he shoved a hand through his hair. His leg was hurting, and he yearned to get out of his mud-splattered clothing and wash away the filth of the slums. "This business is making my head ache."

"Then perhaps you should go to bed." Patrick stood up. "Sometimes a good night's sleep will clear your thoughts."

"Indeed." Robert rose, too. "Thank you for assisting me so ably this evening."

Patrick grinned at him. "It was a pleasure. It felt just like the old times when we fought our way through the mountains of France."

Robert made sure the fire was burning down and picked up one of the candles. "Now I will take your excellent advice and make my way to bed."

Chapter 14

Y ou said you would wake me up if anything exciting happened."

Lucy regarded Robert balefully over the rim of her cup. It was early the next morning, and they were alone in the dining room where Robert had just finished telling her about his extraordinary encounter with Brandon.

"I tried." Robert folded his newspaper and placed it on the table. "You were snoring and refused to stir."

"And now I find out that you caught Brandon and let him go again!"

"As I explained, I didn't feel as if I had a choice. He isn't a child and he made his own decision to flee rather than face up to his accusers like a gentleman. I *hoped* he would do the right thing."

"I'll wager you are correct that Mr. Tompkins caught him going through Sir William's things and Brandon killed him."

"That's a distinct possibility."

"But what?" Lucy asked. "You don't look quite convinced to me."

He flicked a smile at her. "You know me too well." He hesitated. "This might sound odd, but we both know Brandon has a terrible temper."

"Agreed." Lucy nodded encouragingly.

"So if he'd killed Mr. Tompkins in a fight, don't you think he would've simply left the body on the floor and continued his search?"

"Rather than hanging Mr. Tompkins out of sight in the cupboard?" Lucy considered her husband's words. "I hadn't thought of that."

Robert sighed. "Maybe I'm thinking about it too much, but Brandon did look genuinely startled when I mentioned that it was Mr. Tompkins who had died."

"Arden did say that Brandon is something of a liar," Lucy reminded him. "The most likely explanation is still the most obvious one, that Brandon lost his temper, killed Mr. Tompkins, and hid his body in the cupboard."

She refilled her teacup and added plenty of milk. On Betty's recommendation, she'd attempted to eat porridge rather than toast this morning, and it had settled well in her stomach. Robert was busy eating his way through a plate of ham, eggs, and sausages with the occasional bite of toast and sip of coffee as he talked. The return of his appetite and the relaxation of the lines of pain on his face made her quietly happy.

"Then there is this other matter," Robert said. "Brandon said he was searching for something that belonged to him that Sir William had withheld. What do you think he meant by that?"

"He could have been talking about the will."

"He denied being there to search for the will." Robert paused. "Knowing Sir William it is quite possible that he kept information about the boys to himself. He was notoriously secretive."

"But what information could he have that merited Brandon killing Mr. Tompkins over it?" Lucy set down her cup.

"That's the question." Robert sat back.

"If one believes Brandon was speaking the truth," Lucy reminded him.

He frowned at her. "Good Lord, Lucy, you are being remarkably close-minded this morning."

"I am merely pointing out the obvious, which is what *you* usually do when I go on my own flights of fancy. The most likely explanation is that Brandon murdered both Mr. Tompkins and Sir William. *Why* he murdered them might indeed have more to do with the information he was trying to retrieve than his desire to stop the publication of the will, but until the will turns up we cannot be certain."

"I don't think it will take the authorities long to find Brandon and lock him up in the town gaol. He has no money, no acquaintance in town, and very little ability to blend into the background," Robert observed.

"Then perhaps we should wait to see what

Edward decides to charge him with." Lucy folded her napkin and placed it on the table.

She looked up to find Robert staring into space, an arrested expression on his face.

"What is it?"

"The will."

"What about it?"

"It must still be here somewhere."

"I think we can all agree about that," Lucy replied. "So what?"

"Mr. Tompkins was planning on taking the body and Sir William back to Yorkshire at the end of the week."

Lucy blinked at him. "Yes, I know."

"So maybe someone didn't *want* him taking Sir William's possessions away before they got another chance to search for the will. Killing Mr. Tompkins adds to the delay and keeps everything right here."

"But killing Mr. Tompkins also got rid of the person most likely to know where the will *is*." It was Lucy's turn to pause. "Perhaps someone hopes that the document will never be found, and the estate will be fought over in a court of law." She stared at Robert. "Now who on earth would benefit most from that?"

Robert knocked on the door of the Bensons' house, where he was admitted by the butler and led through into Edward Benson's study.

"Sir Robert Kurland, Mr. Benson."

Edward came around his desk to shake hands with Robert and offered him a seat.

"Thank you." Robert sat down. "I hope I am not disturbing your work."

"I am not able to do much at the moment." Edward grimaced. "As you might imagine, Sir Robert, the longer the will is missing, the harder it becomes to make plans for the future."

"If it is not located, do you plan to go to court?"

"I won't have any choice. The businesses cannot run without a new injection of capital to modernize our operations. My father, bless his soul, strenuously resisted change, which means we now lag behind many of our competitors."

After his correspondence with Oliver, Robert knew that Edward was speaking at least some of the truth. His lack of management skills was obviously not mentioned as a factor in his company's ills.

"It is certainly expensive when one has to turn to the courts," Robert agreed. "I have had to alter some of the inheritance requirements for my own estates since being given the baronetcy, and it cost me a pretty penny."

But he'd been willing to pay whatever it cost to safeguard his wife and potential offspring in the event his despicable cousin Paul inherited the title.

"Has Brandon returned home yet?" Robert

turned the conversation in the direction he desired.

"Unfortunately not."

Robert took out the letter Patrick had written for him. "You might wish to read this account from my doctor about the state of Mr. Tompkins's body."

He handed over the letter and waited in silence as Edward read it through.

"Dear God," Edward said faintly. "Is it possible that Brandon deliberately *killed* Mr. Tompkins in a fit of rage? I wondered perhaps if it had been an accident, that he'd said something to upset the man and caused him to give up hope, or—"

"I cannot say, Mr. Benson. I can only vouch for the honest nature and intelligence of my physician."

"Why didn't Dr. Mantel mention this?"

"With all due respect, sir, I doubt the good doctor has ever encountered a body that has been violated in such a way. Dr. Fletcher served as an army surgeon. His experience with wounded and dying soldiers is extensive."

Edward's hands were trembling as he put down the letter and met Robert's gaze. "Is this why you asked if your man could view the body?"

"I must confess that after finding Brandon in the dressing room and watching him flee, I did wonder if anything untoward had taken place." Robert cleared his throat. "I do hope you forgive me for interfering in such a private matter."

"*Forgive* you? Sir Robert, your interest and help have been invaluable." Edward selected a clean sheet of paper. "I will write to the local magistrate and ask him to apprehend Brandon on the suspicion of murdering Mr. Tompkins."

Edward's enthusiasm to lay the blame at Brandon's door didn't surprise Robert in the least. It would be most convenient for the three Benson brothers if one of their father's stepsons were blamed for everything. . . .

"He can be held at the gaol while we attempt to resolve the matter of the will."

"Still no sign of it?" Robert asked.

"No. I am thinking of having the floorboards and wainscoting removed in the bedchamber to see if the damn thing was secreted there." Edward sighed. "Mr. Carstairs is not willing to stay in Bath for much longer and is asking for instructions on how to proceed. I'm wondering whether we would be better off returning to Yorkshire and settling matters there."

"With Brandon retained in Bath Gaol?" Robert asked. "Would Lady Benson be agreeable to that?"

"Oh, Good Lord, Lady Miranda." Edward groaned. "She will not take this news well at all."

"She is certainly a very devoted mother," Robert said diplomatically. "I can't imagine her believing one of her sons is guilty of murder."

"Neither can I."

Robert stood up. "Well, I must be going. Please let me know how things turn out. Lady Kurland and I are most concerned for the continuing well-being of your family."

He bowed and went out of the door. In the hallway, he spotted Arden loitering on the stairs, obviously waiting for him.

"Good morning."

Arden came over and lowered his voice. "Did you find Brandon?"

"I did, but he refused to come home."

"Couldn't you have *made* him?" Arden asked.

"I offered him a choice as a gentleman, and he chose not to face the consequences of his actions."

"Because he's a stupid fool," Arden groaned. "Now Edward will set the watch on him, I *know* it."

"Then perhaps, seeing as you have been liberated from your room, you should find Brandon yourself and encourage him to return before he is clapped up in gaol."

Aden looked up at him. "What did he say when you found him?"

"About what exactly?"

"Did he tell you why he was in there?" Arden persisted.

"He suggested he was looking for something that affected you both."

"What an idiot! I *told* him—" Arden abruptly stopped speaking.

"Told him what?" Robert asked. "Not to destroy anything while he searched? Not to lose his temper and *kill* anyone?"

"Is that what you think he did?"

"You know I do." Robert met Arden's angry stare. "And you know your own brother, which is why you constantly stay at his side and try to prevent him from exposing his rage to the world."

Arden gulped hard.

"If you did send him into that bedchamber and he murdered Mr. Tompkins, his blood is on your hands as well as Brandon's," Robert said. "So I suggest if you find your brother, you impress upon him that he needs to turn himself in and accept the consequences."

Robert stepped back and inclined his head a frosty inch. "Good day, Arden."

Arden ran back up the stairs, and Robert turned to the front door where his hat and gloves sat on the hallstand. He picked them up, and as the butler had discreetly disappeared at the first sign of trouble, let himself out.

He didn't normally lose his temper with young men, but the brothers made his blood boil. Had Arden sent Brandon to search for something? For a moment, Robert wished that he had been a little bit more sympathetic and perhaps gleaned the answer to that important question. But it was not in his nature to accept incompetence and dishonesty easily. He left the subtler questioning to Lucy.

"It is very kind of you to call, Mr. Benson." Lucy smiled at Peregrine, who had unexpectedly appeared in her drawing room. "Sir Robert will be back shortly if you wish to speak to him."

Peregrine sat opposite Lucy and smiled back. "I'm quite content to speak to you, my lady."

"Then shall I order you some coffee? Or do you drink spirits at this time in the morning?"

"I always like a drink, Lady Kurland, and seeing as my family are currently driving me to Bedlam, a glass of brandy would be much appreciated."

Lucy gave Foley his instructions and returned to sit opposite her visitor. Anna and Penelope had repaired their relationship sufficiently to agree to go to the Pump Room together, and then on to Sidney Gardens accompanied by Dr. Fletcher for a breakfast event. The thought of attempting to eat more food under the observant eye of Dr. Fletcher had persuaded Lucy to plead tiredness and stay home.

"Has Brandon returned?" Lucy asked after Foley brought their refreshments.

"He has not, my lady. I believe Edward intends to enlist the help of the local watch in finding him."

"On what grounds?"

"I suspect Edward thinks Brandon had something to do with Mr. Tompkins's demise."

Lucy tried not to look shocked, but suspected from the smug smile on her visitor's lips that she hadn't quite managed it.

"Oh, my goodness."

"I *did* wonder why Edward allowed your Dr. Fletcher to see the body," Peregrine murmured. "It was almost as if he expected to find something was wrong."

Lucy sat up straight. "Dr. Fletcher is a very experienced physician. He was also a surgeon in the military."

"So a man who would recognize the difference between a violent death and a suicide." Peregrine nodded. "What an interesting choice for your family doctor, Lady Kurland."

Lucy sipped her tea and said nothing.

Peregrine shifted restlessly in his seat. "I suppose you've also heard that the will cannot be found."

"I was there when Mr. Carstairs asked to see the will and nobody knew where it was," Lucy reminded him.

"That's right. The solicitor asked Sir Robert to attend." Peregrine's smile wasn't kind. "I almost wish the will had been read. It would have amused me greatly if my father had left the entire company to your husband."

"I suspect such an outlandish amendment would not stand up in court," Lucy said. "Are you really disappointed that the will hasn't been found, or would you rather it was lost forever?"

"What an interesting question, Lady Kurland," Peregrine said slowly. "Why would you think I wish the will never saw the light of day?"

"I believe you mentioned that you and your father were fighting just before he died. Were you not worried that he might have disinherited *you?*"

"I didn't mention it. Augustus did, but I concede your point." Peregrine paused and let out his breath. "I don't care what's in the will, Lady Kurland."

"Even if you get nothing?" Lucy ventured.

"Even that. I *care* that my father is dead. We fought about everything, but I greatly admired and respected him." He met her skeptical gaze head-on. "Why do you think I keep talking to you about these personal family matters?"

Lucy stayed mute and Peregrine continued.

"Because I'm not stupid, Lady Kurland. I've noticed that you and Sir Robert seem to have a vested interest in proving that my *father* was murdered." He sat back, one arm draped along the top of the couch. "Will you deny it?"

"Sir Robert was very fond of your father."

"And?"

"And I cannot say anything else until I have spoken to my husband," Lucy added.

Peregrine kept talking. "If my father was murdered, and so was Mr. Tompkins, one must assume that the killer has an interest in my family."

"One might say so." Lucy decided to proceed with caution.

"In truth, one *must* say so. I can't imagine there are two separate murderers currently roaming Bath who independently decided to attack *my* family."

"It would be a remarkable coincidence."

"Then this has to be about money," Peregrine stated.

"It generally is." Lucy nodded. "And the disappearance of the will makes it all the more likely."

She half turned as the drawing room door opened and Robert appeared. He paused on the threshold, his dark blue gaze assessing Peregrine before he bowed his head.

"Mr. Benson."

"Sir Robert." Peregrine remained standing. "I was just inquiring of your lovely wife as to your interest in my father's murder."

Robert noticed that Lucy was looking rather guilty as he advanced into the room and took the seat beside hers.

255

"What makes you think your father was murdered?"

"I think you're the person who should be telling me that." Peregrine finally sat down. "Lady Kurland asks the most penetrating questions, and I can only assume that you both share my suspicions."

"My wife and I have some . . . experience in bringing murderers to justice. I was fond of your father," Robert said. "He reminded me of my own grandfather. Sir William's death seemed somewhat *convenient* to me."

"In what way?"

Robert shrugged. "He was far away from home, he was unwell, and was getting older, and he took a devilish delight in upsetting his family and tinkering with his will. At some point such behavior does tend to catch up with you."

Peregrine slowly nodded. "Thank you."

"For what?"

"For being honest with me. I was beginning to think that I was the only person who believed my father's death wasn't an act of God or a tragic accident."

"It still might have been," Robert reminded Peregrine. "Such things do happen randomly."

"Yes, but the fact that the will hasn't turned up tips the balance toward a deliberate act."

"Your father did not approve of the life you

chose to live in London," Robert remarked and Peregrine's skin flushed.

"I know. We fought about it endlessly," Peregrine said.

"But it never occurred to you to kill him?"

"Frequently, but I would never have put those thoughts into action. Just because we didn't agree about something didn't mean we couldn't coexist amicably enough." Peregrine sat forward. "I liked him, Sir Robert. When we weren't arguing we enjoyed many similar pastimes, such as word puzzles and theatrical comedies. I was the fool who took him to the theater where he met Miranda!"

"So if Sir William hadn't died, you would not have been in any financial trouble?"

"Why do you say that?"

Robert held his gaze. "Your father mentioned some . . . unhealthy gossip about you."

"Did he." Peregrine's smile disappeared leaving his face curiously blank. "I wonder whom he received that information from? One might speculate that Miranda kept at least some of her connections amongst the scum of the theatrical world. It would be just like her to spread gossip to spite me."

"One might also guess that if you introduced her to your father she would've been more grateful," Robert suggested.

"Exactly."

"If you expect us to believe that you played no part in your father's demise, is there anything you might wish to add to help us along?"

"Not that I can think of, but I am more than willing to answer any questions you might have in the future." Peregrine looked from Robert to Lucy. "Although your wife is already quite an expert at getting information out of me in the most *charming* manner."

"Lady Kurland is an exceptional woman," Robert agreed. "And quite invaluable to me."

His pronouncement caused his wife to blush and cast her gaze modestly to the floor, which amused him greatly.

Peregrine stood up. "Well, at least we understand each other now." He bowed. "I will do everything I can to help you catch this murderer—even though it is probably a member of my own family."

"If you had to take a guess at which person it was, whom would you pick?" Lucy asked.

"Brandon?" Peregrine suggested. "He seems the most likely choice, and he is already under suspicion of murdering Mr. Tompkins. And seeing as we have already agreed that it is unlikely that there are *two* murderers at large then he definitely would fit the bill."

Robert stood and escorted Peregrine down the stairs, and into Foley's hands, and then returned to the drawing room.

"What did you make of that?" he asked Lucy as he shut the door. "Do we believe him?"

Lucy bit her lip. "I'm not sure."

"I thought you'd be convinced he was speaking the truth after all those fine compliments he bestowed upon you." Robert sat next to her.

"I'd like to *think* he was telling the truth. But there are several issues that still concern me."

"Such as?"

"We know that Peregrine was fighting with Sir William, and that he was being blackmailed from the correspondence Mr. Tompkins showed us."

"Agreed." Robert nodded.

"So despite what he said, Peregrine still had a reason to want money, and Sir William's death would provide it for him."

"He said he didn't care about the money and insinuated that any rumors that had reached Sir William had come from a biased source—that is—Lady Miranda, a woman he despises."

"But we *saw* the correspondence," Lucy said. "Peregrine knew about the accusations and was arguing the matter out with his father. That hardly sounds like the actions of an innocent man." Lucy wrinkled her nose. "I wish we'd kept copies of the letters. I'd love to read them again."

"We still have the letters," Robert said. "Foley didn't manage to get them back to Mr. Tompkins before he died."

"Then I shall *reread* them." Lucy paused.

"Despite their differences their letters to each other were far warmer and full of affection than any of Sir William's other correspondence. And Peregrine did sound *quite* sincere when he stated that he missed his father more than his money."

"I have to agree with you," Robert said reluctantly. "It was the only time I have ever heard Peregrine *sound* sincere about anything."

Lucy offered Robert the brandy decanter and coffeepot, and he declined both.

"He was rather quick to pin the blame on Brandon though, wasn't he?" Robert said.

"Because Brandon is the most likely culprit," Lucy reminded him. "Had Mr. Edward Benson heard anything from the fugitive?"

"No, and after he read Dr. Fletcher's letter he wrote to the magistrate's court accusing Brandon of murdering Mr. Tompkins and asking for his imprisonment. I was quite surprised at his enthusiasm for the task." Robert sighed. "I saw Arden when I was leaving the house, and he's gone out looking for his brother. I was rather short with him."

"He probably deserved it." Lucy patted his sleeve. "One has to think that both of those boys are implicated in this murder."

"That's what I tried to suggest to Arden. As he is the older brother, and the one with a modicum of sense, if Brandon *were* searching for something then it was probably at his older brother's bidding."

"So Arden confirmed Brandon's excuse that he was looking for something more personal than the will," Lucy said. "I wonder what that could be?"

"I have no idea, and I can't think of anyone in the Benson family who would offer up that information without becoming immediately suspicious."

"There are so many things that we still don't know," Lucy complained. "The will is still missing, two men are dead, and we are no closer to discovering *why*."

"I wouldn't say that. The fact that Mr. Tompkins was killed means that someone was determined to stop him speaking out, which indicates that our first assumption that Sir William was murdered was correct."

Lucy raised her eyebrows. "And how many more members of the Benson household will have to die before we are able to identify the murderer?"

"That's a very good question." Robert grimaced.

"Maybe Brandon will confess to both murders and justice will prevail," Lucy said hopefully. "With his temper I doubt he has the ability to stay silent for long."

Chapter 15

﹏✖﹏

Lucy sat at her desk and read through the letter she had just written to Grace back in Kurland St. Mary. Unwilling to draw Robert's attention to the possibility that she might be with child she had decided to share the news with Grace and ask for her advice. As she read, her hand came to rest on the slight roundness of her belly as if seeking her own confirmation that she wasn't entirely imagining the whole thing.

She'd received a packet of letters from the rectory from both her father and Rose and intended to distribute them to the others at dinner. She'd set her own letters aside to read later with everyone else's, and would reply to them tomorrow. Unlocking her desk, she sealed the letter to Grace, added the address, and resolved to walk into town later to send it on its way.

Robert had left Sir William's correspondence on the top of her desk and she opened it again, this time carefully separating the letters into piles according to who had sent them. The first pile she read was between Sir William and Mr. Carstairs, which included much complaining about the cost of everything from the client, and a lot of explaining from the poor solicitor.

What was interesting was the advice Mr. Carstairs gave Sir William about making sure that any amendments he made to his will were legally witnessed and signed. Lucy gained the sense that Mr. Carstairs was trying to say that the volume of such changes and corrections made the will harder to interpret and might cause problems in the future.

"If we ever find it," Lucy murmured to herself. "Where on earth could it be? Could it possibly have been stolen at the baths when Sir William was murdered and already destroyed?"

Lucy made a note to herself to go back and speak to the servant who had looked after Sir William's possessions.

She returned to the letters and read through the correspondence between Peregrine and his father. Peregrine's letters were covered with excellent sketches, riddles, and Shakespearean word puzzles, and were full of lively conversation. Even when the subject matter turned hostile the letters were still crammed full of both men's personalities and respect for each other.

Lucy compared the letters to those written by Augustus and Edward, which were equally contentious, but lacked the underlying affection and exasperation bursting from the others.

Had Sir William liked the fact that Peregrine stood up to him? From what she remembered of the old man, Lucy suspected that he had. His annoyance with Peregrine sprang not from his exasperation about the lack of purpose in his life and his morals, but from the fact that he'd allowed himself to be blackmailed.

Lucy picked up the last letter Peregrine had written to his father and read it aloud.

"I don't want your money, you blathering old fool. These accusations are ridiculous and untrue! I just want you to use your influence to shut the rumors down at the source!"

In light of what Peregrine had told them yesterday Lucy considered his words afresh. Was he suggesting that if his father confronted Miranda, whom Peregrine suspected was spreading the lies, then nothing further would need to be done? Lucy read through everything once again and could find no hint of Peregrine actually asking for money. It appeared that it was Sir William who had first mentioned the matter to Peregrine. Unfortunately, even if he had written another reply to Peregrine's outraged reply, Sir William hadn't made a copy of it.

"Why *didn't* Peregrine ask for money?" Lucy wondered aloud. "Such accusations could destroy a man's reputation."

But if he'd believed the rumors came from his father's own wife then perhaps he'd felt justified in assuming they might amount to nothing. Or had he already decided that he was going to end his father's existence and solve all his problems in one desperate throw of the dice? Despite his lazy exterior, Lucy sensed that Peregrine was no coward, and that beneath his devil-may-care attitude lurked a man who hated and loved very strongly. He'd be ruthless as well—a quality that Edward and Augustus also lacked.

Lucy shivered as she turned to consider Edward Benson. He seemed far too mild and accommodating to be actively involved in a murder, but the speed at which he'd offered up Brandon to the magistrates hinted otherwise. Despite her confident prediction to Robert that Brandon was the guilty party, she was beginning to have her doubts. . . .

Augustus would not have the nerve to carry out a murder, and Lady Benson was too physically weak . . . Lucy paused and searched through the letters to find the one where Sir William was concerned that his wife might be having an affair and read it through again. Letters in hand, she went through into the drawing room where she'd left Robert reading the paper.

"I wish to ask your opinion about something."

He locked up and immediately set his newspaper to one side. "What is it?"

"In the letters to his father Peregrine insisted

that he hadn't done anything that merited him being blackmailed."

"Yes, I remember that."

"He also told *me* that Lady Miranda had attempted to lure him into entering a relationship with her," Lucy said. "So which is it?"

"Ah. You're saying that he can hardly be both a lady's man, and a man's man."

"Exactly." Lucy kept going. "What if Miranda spread rumors about him *because* he refused her advances?"

"His visceral dislike of her could certainly stem from that," Robert agreed. "But it still doesn't mean he prefers women."

"But what if he does? He is *very* passionate in his dislike of her. He also contradicted himself yesterday when he said *he* had introduced Miranda to his father when previously he suggested that she'd claimed friendship with an old friend of Sir William's to get to know him." Lucy paused to breathe.

"Peregrine said he took Sir William to a play Miranda was in. He didn't say he introduced them to each other," Robert demurred.

"That's what he implied," Lucy returned. "And it's more than likely that Sir William *did* take an interest in Miranda at that point. She *is* very beautiful."

"Maybe he did it behind Peregrine's back?" Robert suggested.

"I suppose that's possible. Peregrine might not have appreciated that, either." Lucy frowned. "Maybe he was in love with her and was furious that she chose his father over him."

Robert stared at her as if she had gone mad.

"Or what if she loved him back?" Lucy persisted. "And Peregrine conspired with Miranda to kill his own father, and this whole business between them of hating each other is just an act?"

Robert recoiled. "That's *absurd.*"

Lucy flung up her hands. "Think, Robert! Miranda and Peregrine knew each other in London. Peregrine *introduced* Miranda to Sir William. Maybe he wasn't expecting her to go off with his father, or maybe that's exactly what they planned all along!"

"All right." A frown appeared on her husband's brow. "I am beginning to see your point. But if he truly is a murderer why would he offer to help us discover *himself?*"

"Because he is arrogant enough to believe he is too clever to avoid detection. By befriending us he has already discovered that we believe his father was murdered," Lucy said. "Now he can keep an eye on what we do next to see if we uncover *more* evidence, and prevent us from exposing him as a murderer. What better place to hide than in plain sight?"

Robert held out his hand. "Give me the letters."

He read them through and then looked up at her. "You are making quite a lot out of some very tenuous connections, my dear, but I can't discount your opinion. You have proven to be right too many times in the past."

"Thank you for that at least." Lucy sat down opposite him. "I am aware that I might be grasping at straws, but I think we should at least be aware that Peregrine might not be behaving honorably toward us."

"Noted," Robert said. "And Sir William *was* suspicious that Miranda was having an affair. Maybe he wasn't prepared to pay off the black-mailers because he knew Peregrine was involved with his wife."

"Or Sir William thought that when he saw Peregrine in person, he would remind his son that he held the purse strings, and that Miranda was now his wife and that would be the end of it."

"And order Peregrine to leave well alone?" Robert nodded. "Which might have given Peregrine another reason for murdering his own father. You're right to be wary of him, my dear."

Lucy smiled at him approvingly, and he raised an eyebrow.

"What?"

"You are being remarkably open to my flights of fancy."

"Mainly because we have nothing else to go

on," Robert admitted wryly. "I have a horrible feeling that the Benson family are going to return to Yorkshire, settle the matter of the will with the courts, and all go away much richer without anyone being held to account."

"Then we shall continue to do our best to avoid that happening," Lucy said firmly. "Now I have to go out. Do you wish to accompany me?"

"I'm waiting for Dr. Fletcher to return from his shopping expedition with his wife, so we can go to the baths together." Robert's smile was wry. "I can't believe I'm saying this, but I miss the hot springs."

"It is a shame that we don't have one in Kurland St. Mary," Lucy agreed. "Although the thought of the entire village floating around in their underthings is not very appealing."

Lucy left the room to the sound of Robert's appreciative chuckle. If there was a way to replicate the benefits of the baths in her own home then she would do everything in her power to find it for her husband.

Betty helped her into her pelisse and Lucy tied the ribbons on her bonnet before they descended the stairs and went out into the square. Lucy would miss the shops and entertainment available in Bath but was starting to long for the peace and quiet of her own home. They had less than four weeks left on their lease, and she had no intention of extending it. If she were with child, she would much prefer to be close to Grace and in her own village.

After paying to have her letter sent to Grace in Kurland St. Mary, Lucy turned toward the baths and made her way toward the room set aside for changing. Luckily, she had a good memory for faces and was able to recognize the man she and Robert had spoken to on the day of Sir William's death.

He came over to speak to her, a smile on his face.

"Good afternoon, Lady Kurland. Have you decided to sample the amazing healthful benefits of the baths today?"

"I have not," Lucy replied. "I wanted to ask you about Sir William Benson."

"The poor gentleman who died." His smile disappeared, and he looked down at his boots. "Why's that, my lady?"

"I was wondering if anyone asked you to . . . look away from Sir William's belongings that last morning he was in the bath?"

"No, my lady. No one *asked* me to do that."

Aware that her time was limited, Lucy decided to be more direct.

"Did someone pay you to do so?"

He hesitated and again avoided her gaze. "I can't say."

"Can't or won't?" Lucy asked. "I do not wish to get you in trouble, but I would like to know if anyone asked you or paid you to search Sir William's clothing and retrieve something for them?"

She took out two gold sovereigns and held them out to him. If he had been paid at some point, maybe she could offer him more of the same.

His gaze fastened on the money, which was probably equivalent to a quarter of his yearly wage, and he licked his lips.

"I left Sir William's clothes unattended for a couple of minutes."

"Who asked you to do that?"

"I wasn't asked directly." He shrugged. "One of the other servants here handed me a note wrapped around some coins."

"Do you still have the note?"

"No, my lady. I threw it away." He finally looked up at her. "You probably think badly of me after me saying how much I prided myself on guarding Sir William's clothes, but my wife's expecting our third child, and we're barely able to afford our rent and food as it is."

"Did you see the person who approached Sir William's clothing?"

"No, because I walked right away and hid around the corner." He grimaced. "I was ashamed of myself."

"So you don't know if anything was taken?" Lucy asked.

"I noticed that Sir William's coat felt lighter

when I picked it up afterward, but his purse and watch were still there, so I didn't think too much of it."

"Indeed." Lucy sighed. If the will had been taken out of Sir William's pocket, she still had no idea who had done it or where the will currently was. "Well, thank you for your help." She held out the coins.

He stepped back. "I can't take your money, my lady."

Lucy met his gaze. "Why not, if you took a bribe from someone else?"

"Because I regret what I did." His mouth twisted. "I liked Sir William, and the thought that my actions might have caused him harm doesn't sit well with my conscience."

Lucy didn't press him further and let him go back to his work. She discovered Betty sitting patiently on a bench near the door of the baths, chatting to another woman, and went toward her.

"Afternoon, my lady! Back again?"

She recognized the woman she and Robert had met trying to sell her wares at the baths the morning Sir William had died.

"Good afternoon, Mistress Peck." Lucy smiled at the woman who was sitting next to Betty. "The soap you sold me was very fragrant."

"Thank you. I pride myself on the quality of my offerings." She patted the bench beside her.

"I've been talking to your maid. She says you're *Lady* Kurland."

"That's correct. My husband was honored with a baronetcy from the prince regent for his conduct at Waterloo."

"My late husband was a soldier. I did wonder if your husband was a military man, he had that ramrod spine and domineering presence."

"He can be quite formidable," Lucy acknowledged as Betty moved from the bench to stand behind her.

"He was a friend of that Sir William's."

"Yes, indeed." Lucy sighed. "The poor gentleman. He is going to be transported back to Yorkshire for burial later this week."

"I saw that man again."

"Which man?" Lucy inquired.

"The one who came in that morning with the doctor and was arguing with Sir William. He came to speak to Mr. Abernathy the other day, and this time he wasn't quite so wrapped up in his cloak and scarf." Mistress Peck chuckled. "Same beak of a nose of him as his da, but blacker hair. Handsome, too."

"That was probably Mr. Peregrine Benson, his youngest son." Lucy nodded.

"He brought the widow with him as well."

"Lady Benson?"

"Aye, the beautiful blond lady who was draped in black and clinging to his arm like climbing ivy."

"They probably came to pay their respects to Mr. Abernathy," Lucy said. "Lady Benson might have wanted to see exactly where Sir William died. Did they speak to any of the bathhouse employees?"

"Can't say I noticed them traipsing about much." Mistress Peck sniffed. "When I approached her with my basket, she flapped her hand at me like I was an annoying gnat."

Lucy studied the array of soaps and lotions and picked up several before handing the woman one of the gold sovereigns and standing up.

"Please keep the change."

Mistress Peck grinned up at her. "Thank you kindly, my lady!"

Lucy handed the soap to Betty to place in her basket, and they left the baths. She had a lot to tell Robert when she got home. . . .

Robert was just knocking on the front door when a carriage drew up in the cobbled street and Edward Benson stepped out of it. He paused when he saw Robert and doffed his hat to him.

"Sir Robert, just the man I was hoping to see."

Robert walked back down the steps to the flagstone pavement and waited as Edward paid off the driver.

"Good afternoon, Mr. Benson."

"Brandon has been apprehended and is now in Bath Gaol."

"That is excellent news," Robert replied. "Is he unhurt?"

"Apart from a few bumps and bruises when he tried to escape the watch, he is quite well. I've paid for him to have his own room so he will at least be comfortable while he awaits the magistrate's decision as to whether to proceed to trial or not."

Robert raised an eyebrow. "You are now convinced that he murdered Mr. Tompkins? For what purpose?"

"I doubt Brandon had a purpose," Edward replied. "I suspect Mr. Tompkins told him to get out of the dressing room, and Brandon simply lost his temper and killed him in a rage."

"Why do you think Brandon was in there in the first place?" Robert asked.

"Who knows? Does it even matter?" Edward asked. "A man is dead, Sir Robert. That is what we need to concentrate on now."

"How is Arden taking it?"

Edward made a face. "Very hard, as you might imagine."

"And Lady Benson?" Robert persisted.

"We haven't told her yet." Edward sighed. "I'm actually hoping I can persuade her to go back to Yorkshire with Sir William's body while I remain here and sort out this mess as best I can."

"Without her knowing her son is being held in gaol on charges of murder?" Robert murmured.

"Good luck with that. When do you hope she will leave?"

"At the end of the week. I've already booked a traveling carriage to accompany the funeral vehicle. She will be quite comfortable with her maid and Dr. Mantel in attendance."

"What about Arden?"

"He'll stay here with me. I'll impress upon him that I need him to support his brother and not upset his mother."

Edward didn't sound too convinced of his own success, but Robert didn't remark on it.

"If there is anything either Lady Kurland or myself can do to help, don't hesitate to call upon us." Robert touched his hat and turned back to his own front door. He was becoming heartily sick of the Benson family in its entirety. If it were up to him none of them would ever benefit from the hard work and industry of the murdered Sir William. They were all too full of self-interest and willing to sacrifice Brandon Hall without a qualm of conscience.

Robert threw his hat at Foley and stomped up the stairs to the drawing room where he found Anna reading a book, and no sign of his wife.

"Good afternoon, Robert." Anna looked up at him inquiringly. "Can I order you some tea?"

"No, thank you." Robert bowed. "Is Lucy home?"

"Not that I know of." Anna put down her book.

"Would you like me to go and see if she is in the kitchens?"

"Please don't disturb yourself on my account. Is Dr. Fletcher about?"

"He is out walking in the square with Penelope." Anna hesitated. "Is everything all right?"

Robert let out his breath. "I am just contemplating the vast selfishness of the majority of the population, and the fact that a good man does not necessarily have good offspring."

"Are you thinking of anyone in particular?" Anna asked tentatively.

"Just the Bensons at the moment, but my theory holds true about everyone else. Look at my cousin Paul. He is a disgraceful human being, but his parents weren't. Look at your father!"

"You do have a point," Anna agreed. "Which makes one wonder why anyone wishes to procreate at all. What if you had a child who was more like Paul than like you?"

"I suppose it is possible," Robert grudgingly agreed. "But if we all held to that rule then the humankind would cease to exist. I suspect one rolls the dice and takes one's chances."

Anna's expression grew thoughtful. "I suppose you are right."

Just as Robert was about to reply Lucy came in unbuttoning her pelisse. "Ah. Robert! Just the person I wished to speak to. I've been at the baths."

He followed her down the hall to their bed-chamber, and waited until Betty helped her change her dress and left.

She sat at her dressing table, looked in the mirror, and smoothed down her hair. "I have some interesting news to share with you."

"About the Bensons?"

"Yes, of course!" She swiveled around on her seat to stare at him. "What else?"

"Quite frankly, I am sick of the whole lot of them," Robert grumbled.

"Then you won't want to hear that someone *did* get to Sir William's clothing at the baths?"

"Who?" Robert demanded.

"Unfortunately, the servant was sent money and a note, and didn't see who it was."

"How convenient."

"He did say that Sir William's coat felt lighter when he picked it up, but his purse and watch were still there." Lucy held Robert's gaze. "It's extremely likely that someone took the will out of his pocket and that it has already been destroyed."

"Good." Robert sat back in his chair and crossed his arms over his chest. "If that's the case then the whole lot of them will have to go to court and fight it out. In my considered opinion they all deserve one another, and the pittance that will undoubtedly be left when the cannon smoke clears."

Lucy angled her head to one side and studied him. "Are you feeling quite well?"

"I just encountered Edward Benson, who informed me that Brandon has been apprehended and that he plans on getting rid of Lady Benson before she notices."

"I doubt that will work. She might be a little overdramatic, but she does care for her sons." Lucy pinned up a stray lock of hair. "How does Edward think he's going to stop Arden from telling her everything?"

"By appealing to Arden's good sense." Lucy raised her eyebrows. "Exactly. If he wants Miranda out of that house he's going to have to drug her, tie her up, and send that coach off at a gallop before she wakes up."

"Miranda was at the baths yesterday with Peregrine," Lucy said.

"What? I thought they couldn't stand the sight of each other."

Lucy's smile was a little smug for Robert's liking. "And Peregrine was the man who accompanied Sir William and Dr. Mantel to the baths on the morning he died."

"Good Lord." Robert sat back and studied his wife. "You have been busy today."

She shrugged. "I just thought it might be worth revisiting the baths and talking to the servant again. I didn't expect to meet the soap seller and be freely gifted all that extra information."

"Freely?"

"Well, it cost me a sovereign, but it was well worth it." She smiled at him. "So what do you think? Did Peregrine get the attendant to turn away while he went through Sir William's pockets, secured the will, and then ran off, almost knocking you down in his haste to leave?"

"You're forgetting the part when he kills his father," Robert objected.

"Ah, yes." She frowned. "I suppose he could still have done that, but wouldn't his clothes have been wet if he'd gotten in the bath?"

"Maybe Lady Miranda did the killing while Peregrine ran for it," Robert suggested.

"Perhaps she did."

"Don't be ridiculous, Lucy, I was jesting. She's a weak and rather feeble woman."

"She's also an actress who managed to snare a very wealthy baronet for a husband." Lucy didn't lower her gaze. "It's not the first time we have encountered a female murderer."

"You think she dressed up as an old crone, got into the baths, and stabbed Sir William when no one was looking?" Robert demanded.

"Why *not?*"

"Because your ideas are becoming more and more preposterous!"

"Well, *you* tell *me* what the answer is!" Lucy was no longer smiling. "I am merely trying to help, and you"—she swung around and presented him with her back—"are being very difficult and have given me a headache."

Robert took a deep breath as his wife fussed around with her earrings and resolutely ignored him. After a few minutes of strained silence, he got up and put a tentative hand on her shoulder.

"Forgive me? I allowed my frustration over this whole business to boil over, and I was unfair to you."

She shrugged off his hand. "I'm feeling rather tired. I don't think I'll bother to come down to dinner tonight after all. Could you ask Betty to bring me up a tray?"

With some difficulty, Robert persuaded her to look at him. "I'm *sorry.*"

To his horror, she looked as if she was about to burst into tears.

"I really do have a headache, and you are right, sometimes I do guess wrongly why someone might be a murderer." She swallowed hard. "Would you prefer it if I kept quiet?"

"No." He cupped her chin. "I would be devastated if you did that. I was merely frustrated with my own lack of ideas and took it out on you. Please forgive me."

His wife was normally far more forceful when she stood up to him, and he always enjoyed their sparring. This evening he had obviously gone too far.

"Are you sure that you don't want to come

down to dinner and share the joy of Penelope's complaining, and Anna's wistful sighs?" he coaxed.

She finally managed a smile, which relieved him greatly. "I'd rather stay up here until my headache disappears."

He kissed her fingers. "Then I will leave you in peace." He hesitated. "If I am truly forgiven."

She patted his cheek. "Yes, of course you are."

He left after one last uncertain glance back over his shoulder, and a resolution not to upset her anymore. He always thought of his wife as the kind of woman who could put up with anything, but perhaps he needed to remember that even she had her limits.

Chapter 16

❧❦

There's a Mr. Arden Hall wishing to speak to you most urgently, Sir Robert," Foley announced from the door of the study where Robert had retired to spend the rest of the evening after enduring dinner without the company of his wife.

"Then send him in."

Robert rose to his feet and waited for his unexpected guest to be shown through to the study.

"You've got to help me." Arden started speaking the moment Foley closed the door.

"With what?" Robert asked, and offered the young man a seat he didn't take.

"With Brandon. Edward thinks he *murdered* Mr. Tompkins?"

"Yes, I was aware of that."

"Then how can I stop it?" Arden asked. "I spoke to Brandon yesterday. He swears he didn't do it."

"And you believe your brother."

"He wouldn't lie to me." Arden met Robert's gaze. "Why *would* he? He knows that even if he *had* killed Mr. Tompkins I would still stand by him."

"So what did Brandon tell you that makes you so certain of his innocence?" Robert sat back down, sipped his brandy, and offered Arden a glass. "He was in the dressing room around the time Mr. Tompkins was killed. I saw him there myself."

"And Brandon told you that he was looking for something."

Mindful of his earlier disastrous attempt to throw scorn on his wife's suggestions, Robert attempted to be diplomatic.

"Brandon threw a box at my head and ran away. If he was looking for something, did he find it?"

"No, because the old man was really good at keeping things hidden." Arden frowned. "They can't even find his will. My mother is beside herself."

"What exactly do you want me to do, Arden?" Robert asked slowly.

"I want you to tell me how to get Brandon out of gaol!"

"Does he currently have a member of the legal profession representing him?"

"I believe so. Edward said he'd done everything he could to help Brandon." Arden hesitated. "If you would be willing to drop the charges—"

"Wait." Robert held up his hand. *"What?"*

"The charges against Brandon." It was Arden's turn to look at him as if he were daft.

"I didn't accuse him of anything, Edward Benson did."

Arden's mouth slowly opened and then closed without him emitting a sound. His hands fisted, and he swung around toward the door.

"The *bastard!*"

"Don't run off just yet," Robert called out in his best commanding officer voice. "If you lay a finger on Edward, I can guarantee he'll find a way to put you right in that cell beside your brother. Sit down and talk to me."

Arden's shoulders slowly lowered, and he turned around, his expression now icy cold. He took the seat Robert pointed at and accepted the glass of brandy.

"Now drink up." Robert waited until some color came back into the young man's face. "I assume you still want my help?"

"If this is on Edward, then I don't need you to do anything, thank you, sir," Arden said stiffly. "I should've known all that fake sympathy and concern was a lie."

"I think Edward truly believes that your brother killed Mr. Tompkins in a fit of rage." Robert paused. "You can't deny that Brandon has a temper."

"I know he does, but he *liked* Mr. Tompkins, we both did."

"But what if Mr. Tompkins got in the way of his search? Would that not have angered your brother?"

"Brandon said that when he got into Sir William's bedchamber there was no sign of Mr. Tompkins, so he was able to search in peace until you arrived and disturbed him. If Mr. Tompkins *had* been there, do you think Brandon would've been allowed to make such a mess without the valet raising the alarm earlier?"

Robert didn't reply, but he conceded that Arden had a point.

"So Brandon said he didn't see Mr. Tompkins at all."

Arden nodded. "Exactly. So he couldn't have killed him, could he?"

"What exactly was Brandon searching for?" Robert decided to change tack for a moment. "You insisted it wasn't the will."

Arden's lips thinned, and Robert held up a finger.

"If you want my help, then you'll have to be honest with me."

"Apparently, Sir William had some damaging information about our father," Arden said reluctantly as he shifted in his seat.

"Lady Miranda's first husband?"

"Our father, yes."

"And how did you come to know about this?"

"Because my mother was upset, and she told

us that someone had been spreading lies about her."

"To Sir William?" Robert asked.

"Yes, and that he had started to doubt her and was considering ending their marriage."

"That must have indeed been upsetting for her, and for you boys." Robert paused, trying to think how to phrase his next question. "Did Sir William tell her exactly what his concerns were?"

"Only that he had been deceived and was not happy about it." Arden frowned. "Mother said that Sir William had been collecting evidence against our father. Sir William was considering launching a legal case to declare his marriage to my mother invalid."

Robert considered Arden for a long moment. "Forgive me if this sounds harsh, but your mother didn't seem very happy in her marriage. If it was dissolved, would she not perhaps have welcomed such an outcome?"

"She didn't believe it would be possible for Sir William to simply dissolve the marriage as if it had never even taken place, and that he would have to take it through the courts. She told us that a divorce is very expensive and requires an act of Parliament or something to pass, and that the shame of being a divorced woman would kill her," Arden said. "And she said she would be poor again."

"Ah, I see her point. Did she ask you and Brandon to find the information for her after Sir William died?"

"No, of *course* not. She would never ask such a thing of us. Brandon and I decided that the documents should not be seen by Edward, Peregrine, and Augustus, and used against our mother to prevent her gaining her fair share of Sir William's fortune."

"But if Sir William hadn't actually *achieved* his aim of divorcing your mother, such information as he had gathered would no longer be useful, would it?" Robert pointed out.

"We don't know that." Arden sat forward. "What if Edward decided it *was* useful?"

Robert nodded. "One has to assume that if Sir William *did* have the documents with him he would have kept them alongside his will."

"Which cannot be found." Arden sighed. "I know you won't believe me, but when Brandon went to Sir William's bedchamber, he hoped to speak to Mr. Tompkins and beg him to let us have the information about our father."

"Which leads us back to the unpalatable fact that if Mr. Tompkins had *refused* such a request your brother's temper might have gotten the better of him, and he might have accidentally killed him."

"Brandon swore to me that he *didn't* do it," Arden repeated.

"Is it possible that he lied to you because he knew you would be disappointed in him?"

Arden met Robert's gaze. "No. We stand together. We've had no choice."

Robert sat back. "I am not sure what I can do to help you, Arden, but I will make certain that Brandon is well treated at the gaol, and that he is supplied with a competent man at law to defend him if the magistrate decides the charges are valid, and he must stand trial."

"He won't stand it for long in there," Arden said gloomily. "He's already desperate to get out. I tried to tell him to be patient, but he's not the kind of person to take advice well."

"I noticed that," Robert said dryly.

"I'm worried that he'll end up dead," Arden confessed. "That he'll try to escape or decide it is easier for him to die and get it over with, and then I'll be left here all alone."

"Do you think it would help if I went to speak to him?" Robert asked.

"Probably not. He isn't very fond of you for turning him in to Edward."

"I didn't have a choice in the matter seeing as I discovered a dead man in the cupboard." Robert paused to look Arden in the eye. "You do understand that the fact that Brandon was in the room at roughly the same time as Mr. Tompkins died might make a jury consider he was guilty?"

"I know that." Arden rubbed his forehead and suddenly looked older than his years.

"And do you also understand that if there is a trial I will probably be called in as a witness against your brother?"

"I'm not stupid, Sir Robert, and I'm not asking you to stand up there and lie for Brandon."

"That is good to know. I can, however, stress that I didn't actually see your brother *with* Mr. Tompkins at any point."

"Then you don't believe Brandon was the one who killed him?"

Robert sipped the last of his brandy before replying. "If Brandon didn't kill Mr. Tompkins, and we discount the notion that he committed suicide, who do you think *was* the murderer?"

Arden was silent for quite a while before he spoke. "I'd think it was either Edward or Peregrine."

"Why?"

"Edward isn't running the businesses very well and needs more money, and Peregrine . . ." Arden wrinkled his nose. "He likes to stir things up and make everyone unhappy just like the old man. He would consider it a big lark to upset the family like this."

"But surely Edward would *want* the will to appear rather than killing Mr. Tompkins, the only person who might know where it is?"

"Edward's the oldest son. If the will isn't found

he thinks the courts will give him control of everything."

"He might well be right." Robert sighed, and then refocused his attention on the young man sitting opposite him. "Promise me that you won't provoke Edward into a fight when you return to the house tonight."

"I'd like to plant him a facer, but I won't. I don't want to end up in gaol," Arden stated. "I *will* keep an eye on him and make certain that he doesn't try to do anything to harm Brandon's chances."

"That's an excellent idea." Robert rose and put his brandy glass back on the tray. "Now you should go home or else your poor mother will wonder what has happened to her *other* son." He went to open the door. "Has she noticed Brandon is not at home yet?"

"Dr. Mantel and I agreed not to tell her the truth. She thinks he's off at a racecourse with some friends." Arden scowled. "I don't like deceiving her, but I believe it is for the best."

"I agree. That was very wise of you." Robert waited until Arden went past him into the hallway before closing the door behind them. "Good night, Arden. I promise I will keep your confidences to myself."

Arden nodded and went toward the front door, his head down, leaving Robert staring at nothing. A moment later, he headed up the stairs and went into his bedchamber where Lucy was sitting up in bed reading a book.

"Oh good, you're still awake." Robert pulled up a chair and set it beside the bed. "I was just speaking to Arden Hall."

"About what?" Lucy removed her spectacles and set them on her bedside table. She did look tired, but not as upset as she had earlier, which relieved him greatly.

"What Brandon was searching for in Sir William's bedchamber."

"He *told* you?"

"He came to me thinking I was the one who had laid charges against his brother—a notion inspired and not corrected by Edward Benson, apparently."

"Good Lord."

"Arden said that Sir William had documents and information relating to their father, and was considering applying for a divorce from Lady Miranda. He says that Brandon was trying to get the documents back before Edward got hold of them and used them against his mother."

"I suppose his explanation has some merit," Lucy mused. "Did he say *why* Sir William was so intent on this course of action?"

"In what sense?"

"Obtaining a divorce *is* very difficult and costly. Surely one has to wonder exactly what evidence Sir William had acquired to make him think the effort was worthwhile?"

"I see what you mean. Sir William was not the kind of man to waste his money." Robert frowned. "I didn't think to ask Arden whether he knew exactly what was in the papers. I should have done so. I was more interested in why he and Brandon were so determined to suppress the information even after Sir William had died."

"And what did Arden have to say about that?"

"He was convinced that Edward would use the information to disinherit Lady Miranda."

Lucy set her book aside. "But if the evidence was gathered simply so that Sir William could obtain a divorce, then how could it be relevant to Edward now?"

"Arden said it was related to his father."

"Miranda's first husband? The one who died in mysterious circumstances?"

"Yes, and I see your point. If the papers weren't still a threat then Arden and Brandon wouldn't still be after them, would they?"

"One would assume not, especially seeing as it seems that they were willing to kill to obtain them." Lucy paused. "I wonder what Mr. Hall did? Perhaps he was a convicted felon or died in prison."

"Which might indicate that Arden wasn't quite as forthcoming with me about what was in those papers as I first imagined." Robert shoved a hand through his hair. "I knew he wasn't telling me everything, but I was so desperate to get *something* out of him that I was afraid to push too hard."

"Do we know *anything* about Miranda's first husband?"

"We don't, but Peregrine might."

"Perhaps we should ask him about that." Lucy nodded. "I'll ask him tomorrow. He is more likely to offer an answer to me than to you."

Robert sat back. "The thing is . . . I don't think Brandon did kill Mr. Tompkins."

Lucy regarded him unwaveringly but didn't speak.

"It's all tied up together, isn't it?" Robert groaned. "The will, the information about the deceased Mr. Hall, and both deaths."

"A will that might already have been stolen and destroyed," Lucy reminded him.

"And a boy in gaol soon to face charges of murder." Robert reached out and clasped his wife's hand. "We have to do something, Lucy. There is too much at stake for us to fail now."

Chapter 17

❧❦❧

"What a delightful surprise, Lady Kurland." Peregrine bowed and offered Lucy a seat in the drawing room close to the fire. "Did you come to see Lady Benson? I understand that she is out collecting her new black gowns from her mantua maker and no doubt complaining that the color doesn't complement her beauty."

"I didn't come to see Lady Benson. I came to see you."

Peregrine took the seat opposite her, his expression amused. "Then how can I help you?"

Lucy folded her hands together on her lap. "In the spirit of cooperation you suggested regarding the recent deaths in your family, I wanted to ask you a few questions."

"Please, go ahead." He waved an airy hand at her. "Always delighted to oblige a lady."

"It concerns your relationship with Lady Benson." Lucy had decided that at this point she had nothing to lose by being frank. "I am slightly confused about how she met your father."

A wary gleam entered his eyes. "Ah, that."

"You originally suggested that Lady Benson met your father when she claimed to be an acquaintance of one of his old friends. You later told me that you took your father to a play and introduced Lady Benson to him there."

"*Did* I?" He sighed. "My lamentable memory."

"So which is it?" Lucy inquired.

"It is a combination of both those things. I did take my father to see a play, Miranda happened to be in it, and she did claim to know a friend of my father's."

"When you introduced her to him?"

"I think I might have done that." He shrugged. "Does it really matter? And to be frank, Lady Kurland, I do not see what this has to do with someone murdering my father unless you are trying to build a case against my stepmother, which I am very happy to encourage."

"Do you really think she murdered him?"

He made a face. "I wish I did, but she wasn't at the baths that fateful morning."

"How would you know?" Lucy asked.

"Because I was there." He raised his eyebrows. "Didn't you know?"

It was Lucy's turn to stare. "I heard that your father and Dr. Mantel were accompanied to the baths by another man. Was that you?"

"Yes, my father was proving very obstinate over a particular matter. We were arguing over the breakfast table and continued our disagreement until the moment he stripped down in the baths. At which point, I walked out in a rage and left him and Dr. Mantel to it." He raised an eyebrow. "Anything else?"

"What exactly were you arguing about?"

"Miranda, of course. My father had something on his mind about her, and he was refusing to tell me what it was."

"You weren't arguing about your being blackmailed?"

His smile widened. "My, my, you are good at discovering the worst about people, aren't you, Lady Kurland? And yet you look so damned upright and respectable."

Lucy maintained her silence and offered him her blandest inquiring smile.

"All roads lead back to Miranda, don't they?" Peregrine sighed. "She didn't like the way I treated her sons, and invented some fantasy that I preferred to bed men to discredit me with my father. She persuaded one of her theater friends to send my father a demand for money. It was all done out of spite. I believe my father was beginning to realize that."

"Do you think he had begun to tire of Lady Benson?" Lucy asked.

"Who would not? She is a vapid and unpleasant leech." He shrugged. "There was definitely some maggot stirring in his head. He loved his secrets, and he was full of rage about something.

Unfortunately, he died before I was able to get the whole story out of him."

"That was a terrible shame," Lucy agreed. "Can you tell me anything about Mr. Hall?"

Peregrine blinked at her sudden change of subject. "Dennis Hall? The boys' father?" His irritating smile returned. "My goodness, Lady Kurland, you really are out to get Miranda!"

"Sometimes, understanding what happened in the past helps one solve a problem in the present," Lucy replied. "Was he an actor?"

"I assume so. I can't say I met the man. I believe he died in prison when the boys were small, leaving her penniless. Miranda stayed on with the same band of traveling players and brought her boys up with that community until she captured my father."

"You sound as if you knew Miranda quite well before she met your father," Lucy commented.

"Amongst other things I'm a playwright. Miranda's theater company were the first to perform one of my plays. I had to work quite closely with them to make sure they presented the words I'd written in the way I wanted."

"And that was when Miranda told you about her first husband?"

"Miranda told me nothing, Lady Kurland. I met the boys first and learned their story from the other cast members who had helped Miranda raise them."

"Yet you don't seem to care for the boys or Miranda now."

"Because she went out of her way to use me to ensnare my father," Peregrine said. "I *hate* being used."

"I suspect none of us enjoy that." Lucy hesitated. "Did you ever find out exactly what happened to Mr. Hall?"

"You'd have to ask Miranda, and I doubt you'd get an answer. She's far too sensitive about the subject."

"Did the boys remember him at all?"

"I doubt it seeing as Brandon was a babe in arms, and Arden not much older." Peregrine turned to the window. "I hear a carriage. Miranda has returned. If you don't wish to speak to her, you should probably leave now."

"I have no objection to speaking to her," Lucy replied. "In truth, she probably deserves some sympathy. Her husband is dead, her stepsons seem united against her, and one of her sons is likely to be charged with murder."

"I loathe her, but don't assume Edward and Augustus feel the same way. They are both far too concerned about the family name, and despite maybe wanting to get rid of Miranda, they would never have the balls to actually do it." Peregrine rang the bell and ordered tea.

"Seeing as Augustus is a clergyman one would hope not," Lucy said. "And Edward is the oldest, and should protect his father's widow and follow through on his wishes."

"Which he will do if he can ever find that will. He and Miranda are agreed that they will take the matter to the courts if it isn't recovered." Peregrine turned to the door. "Good morning, Dr. Mantel. How is your patient?"

Dr. Mantel looked exhausted, and Lucy felt a momentary twinge of pity for him having to deal with Lady Miranda every single day.

"Lady Benson is still quite emotional but rapidly improving. She managed a whole two hours at the dressmaker's without feeling faint." Dr. Mantel bowed to Lucy. "Good morning, Lady Kurland."

"Good morning, Dr. Mantel. I am so glad to hear that Lady Benson is feeling more the thing."

"She'd feel a lot better if this will turned up, wouldn't she?" Peregrine spoke up. "But then, wouldn't we all?"

Dr. Mantel ignored Peregrine and focused his attention on Lucy. "I will accompany her back to Yorkshire at the end of the week. I feel it is only fitting."

"Is she paying your wages now, or are you doing this out of the goodness of your heart?" Peregrine asked.

Dr. Mantel finally turned toward Peregrine. "I could hardly leave Lady Benson in distress, Mr. Benson."

"So you're working for nothing?" Peregrine laughed. "Good luck ever getting your money back. Edward is as tightfisted as my father. If the will isn't found, he'll control the purse strings, and my stepmother had better remember that."

Lady Benson entered the room and glared at Peregrine.

"Why haven't you gone back to London?"

He didn't bother to rise, but regarded her from the couch. "Why would I leave when I am enjoying myself so much?"

"Your father has *died!* How is that amusing?" Lady Benson said, her voice trembling.

"Because it's left you and my brothers in something of a quandary."

"I did nothing to deserve your derision." Lady Benson sat on the couch. "Yet you continue to insult me." She found her black lace–trimmed handkerchief and dabbed at her cheeks.

"Good Lord, woman, after all those years on the stage you are still a terrible actress," Peregrine drawled. "But then you never relied on that particular talent when you had so many others."

Lady Benson swallowed hard, and a tear trickled down her cheek. "You are a *horrible* man."

"I can't argue with that," Peregrine agreed. "If Edward keeps all the money to save his company, will you return to acting? If so you might want to take a few lessons."

Lady Benson sat up straight. "Edward has

303

recently reassured me that he will do everything in his power to make sure that I receive my widow's portion."

"Has he now?" Peregrine's expression grew thoughtful. "I wonder why he did that?"

"Because he is a better man than you will ever be," Lady Benson said fiercely. "And he intends to respect his father's wishes!"

Peregrine glanced over at Lucy, and then back at Miranda. "My father told me that he had certain . . . damaging information about your first husband. I wonder how long you would have *remained* Lady Benson if what he'd heard turned out to be true?"

Lucy focused her attention on Lady Benson, who looked visibly shocked by Peregrine's provocative comments.

"I have absolutely *no* idea what you are talking about, Peregrine." She rose from her seat and stared him down. "If such 'rumors' did reach Sir William, we all know who provided them, don't we?"

He leaned back and looked up at her. "Let's just call it tit for tat, shall we?"

She turned and marched out of the room without her usual delicacy, and was quickly followed by Dr. Mantel and her maid.

Lucy raised her eyebrows at Peregrine, who grinned at her. "Why on earth did you do that?"

"What?"

304

"Inform Lady Benson that Sir William was suspicious of her first husband?"

"Why shouldn't I tell her what she probably already knows?" He shrugged. "She's not stupid. She must have been aware that my father's affection for her had dwindled to nothing." His gaze narrowed. "Why would it bother *you?*"

Mindful that Peregrine had no knowledge that Miranda's sons were already searching for any evidence concerning their father, Lucy considered her reply carefully.

"Sir William didn't tell you he had damaging information about Mr. Hall, *I* told you that."

"And I considered what you said and connected the fact that my father was furious with Miranda with the interesting new information about Mr. Hall." He smiled. "The fact that she reacted to the suggestion so badly proves that we are on the right track."

"*We* are not, Mr. Benson. Your methods are highly irregular, and one might even say audacious."

"Says the lady who has discovered all my secrets," Peregrine retorted. "You are hardly in a position to be sanctimonious, Lady Kurland."

Lucy rose from her seat and curtsied. "I must be going."

Peregrine stood, too, and came over to take her hand and kiss her fingers. "Always a pleasure, my dear lady. Do come again."

Lucy suspected that the glare she gave him only provided him with even more amusement and ammunition, but she couldn't help herself.

"Give my regards to Sir Robert, won't you?"

"Indeed." Lucy headed for the door, aware that she'd been bested, but determined that Peregrine would not see it. She was beginning to wonder if Peregrine would eventually blurt out the truth—that he had been the one to kill his father after all. . . .

Lucy yawned discreetly behind her fan as the opera singer giving the concert in the Upper Assembly Rooms continued her rather long and mournful aria. Beside Lucy, Robert shifted in his seat as if either his leg was paining him, or he was as bored as she was.

When the singer finally drew to a close to rapturous applause the audience was invited to attend a light supper during the interval. Robert stood, offered Lucy his arm, and they strolled from the blue painted walls and five crystal chandeliers of the ballroom into the cozier but more packed Octagon Room, with its four fireplaces that were providing far too much heat in the crowded rooms.

Lucy fanned herself and then turned to Robert. "It is far too hot in here. Shall we venture into the card room or the vestibule?"

"Yes, please." He headed for the nearest exit,

politely excusing himself as they progressed. "It's like trying to herd cattle in here."

Lucy chuckled. "I have to agree with you. Perhaps we should follow the Fletchers' example and retreat to the refreshment room. Anna is with them as well."

"As if I haven't seen enough of them during the past few months." Robert patted her gloved hand. "It is quite pleasant to spend a moment alone with you and forget about the damned Bensons."

Lucy squeezed his fingers. "Then you are about to be disappointed because here comes Peregrine, Edward, and Lady Benson."

She fixed a smile on her face as the Bensons approached. "Good evening, Lady Benson. Are you enjoying the concert so far?"

"It is passable," Lady Benson said. "Despite my protestations, Dr. Mantel and Edward *insisted* that I leave the house and attempt to forget my sorrows."

"What an excellent notion," Robert agreed. "I often find that a brisk walk outside with my dogs or a change of scenery clears my head wonderfully."

Lady Benson gently shuddered presumably at the idea of that much exertion and raised her beautiful gaze to Robert. "You do not suffer as I do, Sir Robert."

"You're probably right about that." Robert bowed. "Now, I must take my wife out of this

307

crush and make sure she has something to eat. If you will excuse us?"

He smiled and very firmly led Lucy in the opposite direction.

"Peregrine was very quiet, wasn't he?" Lucy said as they moved out of earshot.

"Perhaps he's regretting sharing all his secrets with you."

"That might be it," Lucy said, frowning. "Lady Benson and Edward seem much in charity with each other, don't they?"

"I didn't notice. I was too busy hoping the widow wasn't going to perform one of her swoons and expect me to catch her." He shuddered. "I cannot bear weak women like that."

"You wouldn't catch me if I swooned?" Lucy asked.

He stopped in the doorway to smile down at her, his blue eyes glinting. "*You* are not a weak woman, and I seem to remember that in the past I have most definitely caught you when you've swooned."

She touched the lapel of his coat. "My very own hero."

"Hardly that. But I would protect you with my life." He brought her fingers to his lips and kissed them. "Shall we go and find Anna, and get her opinion of the opera singer?"

The second half of the concert proved to be much more entertaining than the first, and Lucy enjoyed it immensely. Even Robert was tapping his foot to the music at one point, and Anna was in heaven. Lucy did feel rather sorry for poor Penelope because every time she settled on her chair, the babe would start moving, making her feel most uncomfortable.

Lucy only knew this because Penelope made sure that everyone seated near them shared in her discomfort. Poor Dr. Fletcher looked rather beaten down by the end of the performance and eager to leave. As Robert had ordered a carriage to take them down the steep hill of Gay Street back to Queen's Square she suspected Dr. Fletcher's desire to flee would take far longer to achieve than he wished.

Even though they waited until most of the audience had left the ballroom, the lobby was still crowded. It had begun to rain and many of the patrons remained inside the building discussing the likelihood of the shower continuing, or whether they should risk walking home.

"Good evening, Miss Harrington." Lucy turned as Captain Akers approached Anna. "Lady Kurland, Sir Robert."

"Captain Akers." Anna curtsied, her cheeks reddening. "How are you? I haven't seen you for several days."

His smile to her was perfectly polite, but held none of its previous warmth. "I do apologize, Miss Harrington. I've been in London." He raised his gaze and scanned the crowd. "And now I must apologize again and leave you as I attempt to find my sister and her fiancé's family. I saw that it was going to rain and brought the carriage out to bring them home."

"How . . . kind and thoughtful of you," Anna said, her gaze lingering on the Captain's face. "How *very* like you."

He looked down at her for an instant and then away, as if the sight of her beautiful face was somehow too much for him to bear.

"Good-bye, Miss Harrington."

And he was gone, swallowed up in the crowd in an instant. Lucy reached out to touch Anna's arm.

"Are you all right?"

"Why wouldn't I be?" Anna's attempt at a smile was rather wobbly. "Are we going to attempt to get our cloaks?"

"Dr. Fletcher is attending to that," Robert spoke up, and then pointed at the wall nearest the exit. "Mrs. Fletcher is sitting over there. I suggest we join her."

After almost half an hour of waiting for the carriage, Robert put his pocket watch away and surveyed his party. Penelope was complaining about something, Anna still looked stricken from the encounter with her suitor, and Lucy was attempting to keep everyone's spirits up. He strolled over to the front door and looked up at the sky. The rain had stopped, and the cobbled streets weren't flooded. He knew from experience that it was only a fifteen-minute walk all downhill to their rented house.

He returned to Lucy and murmured, "I think we should give up on the carriage and walk."

"I am more than happy to do so." She fastened the clasp of her cloak in a businesslike manner. "Is it still raining?"

"No." Robert caught Patrick's eye. "We've decided to forget about the carriage and walk back. Do you wish to accompany us, or will it be too much for Mrs. Fletcher?"

Penelope stood up. "I am quite capable of walking. In fact, I am feeling quite restless and would like to go as soon as possible."

Dr. Fletcher shrugged. "As you wish, my dear—although I can order you a chair if you prefer?"

"And leave me in the hands of unknown ruffians who would take advantage of my delicate condition?" Penelope asked.

"I would, of course, walk alongside you," Dr. Fletcher reassured his wife, who didn't look impressed.

Anna rose as well. "I am also ready to walk."

"Then we will leave immediately." Robert paused at the front door to inform one of the footmen that if a carriage *did* finally turn up for

Sir Robert Kurland to send them away with a flea in their ear.

He offered Lucy and Anna an arm, and then led the way past the architectural wonder of the Circus, and down onto Gay Street, which would lead them almost directly into Queen's Square.

The streets were reasonably well lit and patrolled by the watch, so Robert wasn't too concerned about getting his ladies home safely. About halfway down Gay Street Lucy poked him in the ribs.

"Oh, dear. It's the Bensons again."

Robert immediately slowed his step and looked farther down the road where there was a huddle of people. "It looks as if Edward and Lady Benson are about to hire two chairs." He snorted. "They are almost home!"

He waited until Dr. Fletcher and his wife caught up with him before moving on. Now that they were relieved of Lady Benson, the two remaining men were moving far more quickly and seemed oblivious to their surroundings, or to the fact that Robert and his party would be obliged to follow them all the way home.

As the ground leveled out, Robert reached an intersection and paused to allow a succession of barrel-laden carts to pass by. Anna dropped back to walk with the Fletchers. By the time Robert picked his way through the puddles and filth of the cobblestones there was no sign of Peregrine or Dr. Mantel.

"Nearly home now," he murmured to Lucy. "Although I cannot wait to be really home in Kurland St. Mary. How many more weeks are we supposed to stay here?"

"Less than four," Lucy said as she smiled up at him. "And if you really hate it that much I'm sure we could leave earlier as long as you are willing to forgo the rent money."

"I'll consider it." Robert lowered his voice so that only Lucy could hear him. "I'd still like to sort out this business with the Bensons before we leave."

"I agree. It would be a shame to walk away when we are so close to solving the murders."

"Close?" He glanced down at her. "I feel as if we are as far away from finding out the truth as we were when Sir William died."

"I don't think Brandon killed anyone," Lucy stated. "I think it was Peregrine all along. He was there at the baths that morning, he hates Lady Benson and her sons, and he doesn't care about what happens to the rest of his family. He seems to think that everything is a big joke, but under that amusement lurks a far greater sense of purpose."

"Why do you think he killed Mr. Tompkins then?"

"Because Mr. Tompkins knew where Sir

313

William had hidden the will. If Peregrine had already killed his father and had the will stolen at the baths, he wouldn't want the valet telling Mr. Carstairs where it was supposed to be, and then everyone realizing it wasn't there. That would cause a whole other scandal."

"So you think Peregrine has the will?"

"I think he had it, and that he read it." Lucy hesitated. "Didn't you ever get the sense that he knew too much? That he was secretly laughing at everyone all the time while we floundered around in the dark?"

"Yes, now that you put it like that, I can definitely see it." Robert walked a bit farther before he replied, "And if it is Peregrine, what do you think we should do about it?"

"Confront him?"

"For what purpose?"

"To confirm our suspicions?"

"We can't prove anything though, can we?" Robert argued.

"But we might be able to convince Edward to withdraw the charges against Brandon," Lucy contended.

"That's a good point." Robert considered her arguments as they walked onward to their destination. "If Edward wants to attempt to deal with Peregrine then that's up to him. Do you think Peregrine destroyed the will?"

"I should imagine so." Lucy sighed. "I suppose

for him the idea that everyone will have to stand by and watch Edward sink all their money into his failing companies is somehow amusing."

"I thought you said you liked Peregrine," Robert reminded her.

"If he wasn't a murderer, his outrageous arrogance would be something to admire, but he is, and my opinion of him is not high," Lucy stated.

"So do you think he wanted Lady Benson for himself, or that the rumors about him preferring men are true?"

"I'm not sure," Lucy sighed. "Mayhap we can ask when we confront him."

A shout echoed down the street and Robert's head went up. He peered into the darkness ahead and saw some kind of struggle at the corner of Queen's Square.

"Stay here," he commanded Lucy, and headed for the melee, Patrick at his heels.

Three men surrounded Peregrine and Dr. Mantel, who were attempting to fight them off. The doctor went down with a crash onto the flagstone pavement, swiftly followed by Peregrine. Robert reached the men just in time to pull one of them off the doctor before all three ran away.

Neither Dr. Mantel nor Peregrine immediately rose to his feet, and Robert and Dr. Fletcher crouched beside the two men.

"Go to the house, Penelope, ask them to bring some light," Dr. Fletcher said in a tone that

315

indicated he had no time for his wife's nonsense. *"Quickly!"*

Anna took Penelope's hand, and the two women hurried toward the house.

Dr. Mantel struggled to sit up. His face was scratched, and one of his hands was bleeding as if he'd used it to ward off a blade.

"What in God's name *happened?*" he croaked.

"You were attacked." Robert handed the man his handkerchief. "Did they take anything from you?"

Dr. Mantel searched his pockets. "My money's gone, and my watch." He used Robert's handkerchief to wrap around his hand. "Nothing that isn't replaceable, thank God." His gaze fell on Peregrine, who was still sprawled out on the ground. "Is he all right?"

Patrick turned to give Dr. Mantel a cursory glance as his hands moved over Peregrine with practiced speed. "He's unconscious. Come over to his other side and help me locate the source of this bleeding."

Dr. Mantel crawled around Peregrine's recumbent form and stared down before gingerly placing his hand on the body. He attempted to clear his throat, and then shook his head before scrambling to his feet and backing away.

"I don't know how to *do* that. I don't know bloody *anything!*"

"Sir Robert!"

Robert looked up to see Foley approaching with two lanterns, closely followed by one of the kitchen maids and an assortment of footmen. As Dr. Mantel staggered away, his hand to his mouth as he dry heaved, Lucy took his place at Peregrine's side.

"What do you want me to do, Dr. Fletcher?"

Patrick glanced over at her. "From the look of him, he's been stabbed, but in this light, and with his dark clothing, I can't see where. You'll have to feel over him to see if you encounter blood-soaked cloth."

Lucy stripped off her gloves and set to work, not appearing to notice that her new ball gown was now covered in mud and filth from the road.

"Here." She looked up at Patrick. "Just under his shoulder. The blood is pouring out."

"Then press down as hard as you can," Patrick ordered. "And don't move."

Lucy did as she was told, aware of the wetness seeping through her silk gown and petticoats and the rancid smell of the gutters around her. Dr. Mantel had fled, and Robert had followed him to make sure he went into the Benson house.

Anna had returned and was ripping up a sheet to make bandages while Dr. Fletcher and one of the footmen attempted to cut Peregrine out of his extremely tightly fitting coat and waistcoat.

She continued to press down on the wound, her fingers growing colder and number with every second.

"Well done, Lady Kurland. This is definitely the only wound we need to worry about." Patrick was now crouched beside her. "You can let me take over now."

"Is he still alive?" Lucy asked.

"He is at the moment, but he's lost a lot of blood. Hold the lantern still, Foley." Dr. Fletcher cut off Peregrine's shirt to expose the area around the ugly wound. "When I ask you to remove your fingers do so as quickly as possible and then get out of my way."

"Yes, Dr. Fletcher."

He fashioned a wad of cloth and laid two strips of bandage under Peregrine's torso.

"Now, Lady Kurland."

Lucy let go, and blood briefly seeped out again before Patrick placed the cloth over the wound and tied the two bandages tightly over it.

"This should do until I can get him into the house and have a proper look."

Robert helped Lucy to her feet and wrapped an arm around her shoulders. Her knees were aching, and she was shivering with cold.

"Bring him into our house, please, Foley," Robert ordered.

"Not the Bensons'?" Patrick asked.

"No. I'd rather he survived the night."

Foley organized the footmen, and under Dr. Fletcher's direction they carefully picked Peregrine up and brought him into the bedchamber next to the doctor's. When everyone was back inside the house, Robert turned to Foley.

"Lock all the doors. Don't let anyone in unless I say so."

"Even the Benson family, sir?" Foley asked.

"Especially them." Robert patted Foley's shoulder. "Thank you for your quick response, and please thank the rest of the staff."

"I will, sir." Foley bowed. "I'll send up some brandy and tea to your room as soon as we get ourselves organized, sir."

Robert turned to Lucy, who had remained standing in the hall. Even as he watched her, she started to sway, her gaze fastened on her blood-stained hands.

He caught her elbow in a firm grip and held on to her. "Stand firm, my love. Let's get you upstairs."

"Yes . . ."

He was relieved that she hadn't actually swooned because he suspected his leg would have buckled if he'd tried to carry her up a flight of stairs. Betty was already in their bedchamber. She swooped on Lucy and took her through into the dressing area exclaiming about the state of her clothes and her hands. Robert let out a long breath as his heartbeat steadied and finally returned to normal.

"Shall I help you change, sir?" Silas spoke from behind him, and Robert looked down at his disheveled muddy clothing.

"Yes, please."

"You weren't hurt in the skirmish, sir, were you?" Silas asked, his expression worried, as he poured hot water into a basin and placed soap and a towel beside it.

"No, I simply did my best to help." Robert shook off his memories and the smell of blood, and unbuttoned his coat. "I don't know what you think, Silas, but I suspect my best coat will never be quite the same again."

Lucy lay in the bath until the water cooled around her. She'd used almost a whole bar of the lavender soap she'd bought at the baths trying to scrub the blood from her skin, and yet she still didn't feel clean. Feeling a man's warm blood pumping out under her fingers was an experience she hoped never to repeat.

The fact that Peregrine was still alive was a miracle. . . .

Betty helped her out of the bath and into her nightgown and dressing robe.

"Is Sir Robert still in the bedroom?" Lucy asked Betty as she braided her hair.

"He said to tell you that he's just gone to speak

to Dr. Fletcher, and then he will be back to have supper with you. Foley is just bringing that up." Betty smiled at Lucy. "How are you feeling now, my lady?"

"Much better," Lucy said, smiling in return. "It was not quite the way I expected my evening to end."

"I'm not sure that your gown can be properly cleaned, my lady." Betty laid it over her arm along with Lucy's other clothes. "But I will do my best."

"Please, don't bother." Lucy shuddered. "I don't think I could wear that dress again anyway."

"As you wish, my lady." Betty curtsied and went out of the servants' door. "Please ring for me when you wish to retire to bed."

Lucy took a seat beside the fire and thanked Foley when he brought a covered tray of food and a pot of chocolate for her. She left the food alone, poured herself a drink, and sat staring into the fire until she heard Robert come back in the room.

"Well, Peregrine isn't dead yet, but Patrick says his life is still in danger." Robert paused to kiss the top of her head before he sat down opposite her. He had a large glass of brandy in one hand and wore his favorite silk banyan.

Lucy shuddered. "Considering how much he was bleeding I'm not surprised."

"Patrick also commended your calm good

sense and had a few choice words to describe Dr. Mantel."

"He panicked quite badly, didn't he?"

"Indeed," Robert said dryly. "I made sure he went into the Benson house, and left him to it. I'll wager he'll hide in his room like the coward he proved to be and not tell anyone what happened."

"Not all physicians are used to seeing bloody wounds, Robert."

"I know, but one has to question his professional competence if he can't even act on a direct order from a fellow physician."

Lucy sipped her hot chocolate and allowed the sweet warmth to settle in her stomach.

"Does it seem odd to you that three pickpockets would venture as far as Queen's Square, which is well lit and patrolled by the watch?" Robert asked. "Because it does to me."

Lucy sighed. "I was hoping you weren't going to mention that."

"Here's the thing, Lucy. Does it strengthen the case against Peregrine—that Edward now wants to get rid of him?" Robert asked. "Or does it mean that Peregrine is innocent, and Edward is far more conniving than we thought and is attempting to get rid of all his competition?"

"I don't know," Lucy said. "Does Dr. Fletcher need someone to share the nursing of Peregrine tonight?"

Lucy's words ended on a yawn, and Robert leaned over and took the cup out of her hands.

"If he does, it will not be you. Now eat some of these buttered crumpets and let's go to bed."

Chapter 18

Lucy woke up to the sound of the scullery maid making up the fire in their bedchamber. It was still dark so she kept her eyes closed, and waited for the noise to stop and the maid to leave. She rolled onto her back, placed a protective hand over her slightly rounded stomach, and breathed out slowly. Beneath her fingers she felt a slight fluttering, as if she'd swallowed a butterfly, and went still.

After the horrible end to her night, she'd worried that she might have overexerted herself, and had feared the worst. But there had been no blood spotting and she still felt perpetually nauseous. She smiled into the darkness. Perhaps this time with God's grace she might be lucky. . . .

Determined not to dwell on her hopes and unable to go back to sleep, she considered the problem of Peregrine and the Benson murders anew. What were they missing? If Robert was correct, and Edward wanted to make sure he took complete control of the family fortune the attack on Peregrine made sense. But even if Edward got rid of Peregrine and paid off Augustus's debts to keep him quiet there still remained the problem of Lady Benson.

Unless . . .

"Robert!" Lucy rolled onto her side and shook her husband's shoulder. "Wake up!"

He opened his eyes and scowled at her. "What is it?"

"Lady Benson!"

"What?"

She'd forgotten that he was never at his most amiable first thing in the morning.

"What if Dennis Hall isn't dead?"

Robert came up on one elbow and looked down at her. "Her first husband?"

"Yes. It's so obvious!" Lucy said. "Why didn't we think about it sooner? If Sir William found out that Dennis Hall was still alive, then that would make Miranda a *bigamist,* and would give him grounds to have the marriage annulled."

"I suppose it would."

It was Lucy's turn to sit up. "If it *is* Edward who wants to control the entire Benson fortune, having that information would help him get rid of Miranda *and* her sons, wouldn't it?"

"Arden was afraid Edward would use his father against him," Robert said. "I wonder if that's what he wasn't telling me? That he knew his mother was a bigamist, and that finding those documents and destroying them would protect

326

her." He paused. "But how would Edward know about them?"

"If Sir William boasted to Peregrine that he had evidence to end his marriage, do you not think he did the same to Edward? Or Peregrine might have told him, or *somebody*."

Robert exhaled and sat back against his pillows while Lucy watched him anxiously.

"So you now think Edward is the murderer, even though we don't have any evidence that he was at the baths that morning," Robert stated.

"Maybe he paid someone to do it," Lucy said stubbornly.

"And what about the will?"

"What about it?"

"Did Edward steal it from the baths, or is it still missing?"

"I . . . hadn't thought of that." Lucy bit her lip. "But wouldn't it be in his best interests if the will never turned up anyway? If it's lost, he'll go to court and will probably be given control of the money. If he found it, and the documents about Dennis Hall, then he can keep the will hidden and use the other information to discredit Miranda."

"He *could* have killed Mr. Tompkins," Robert said slowly. "He was definitely in the house that morning, and he was very eager to place the blame on Brandon."

Lucy nodded, her hands clasped together in her lap, her long braid hanging over her shoulder.

"The thing is, my dear, we still can't *prove* anything," Robert said. "We have no witnesses who saw Edward at the baths that morning."

"Perhaps we simply haven't asked the right questions," Lucy said stoutly. "I am quite prepared to go back there and try again."

"What a mess." Robert sighed, drew Lucy against his side, and wrapped his arm around her. "And now I am wide awake and will never get back to sleep."

Lucy rubbed her cheek against his chest. "I do apologize for waking you."

"Don't be." His arm tightened around her. "If I'd had the same thought I would've woken you up, too."

An hour later, Robert was sitting with Lucy at the breakfast table eating his way through a hastily assembled meal that had apparently, according to Foley, put Cook in a right fluster seeing as they were up two hours earlier than normal. He was quite content eating what was left over from the previous evening's dinner, and as Lucy ate like a bird in the morning she was happily eating toast.

Patrick appeared in the doorway and paused when he saw them. He'd removed his coat and his shirtsleeves were rolled up to the elbow. He hadn't shaved and the white of his linen was spotted with brown flecks of dried blood. Robert beckoned him in and pulled out a chair.

"You look as if you have been up all night. Sit down and eat something before you collapse."

"Thank you." Patrick nodded at Lucy and accepted the cup of coffee she poured him. "Mr. Benson is still alive. He stopped bleeding quite quickly, which was a mercy, because sometimes a man will be drained dry and there's nothing I can do about it." He took a slurp of coffee. "I've bound up the wound, and now we just have to wait for him to regain consciousness, and hope to contain the fever that will certainly occur."

"That's good to hear." Robert handed Patrick a plate of food. "Eat."

Patrick obliged and between mouthfuls thanked Lucy for her assistance again, railed against Dr. Mantel's incompetence, and praised Betty for sitting up with Peregrine for half the night while he took some rest.

"May I visit Mr. Benson this morning?" Lucy asked.

"Of course, my lady." Patrick nodded. "Not that you'll get much sense out of him at the moment."

"Thank you." She looked at Robert. "Should I write a note to the Bensons explaining where Peregrine is, and the current state of his health?"

"No, I think I'll pay a call on Mr. Edward Benson myself," Robert said. "I'd rather the whole lot of them stayed out of my house."

Patrick set down his knife and wiped his mouth with his napkin. "I'm surprised Mr. Benson wasn't round here last night after seeing Dr. Mantel run in there in such a panic."

"Perhaps the good doctor didn't mention what happened to anyone," Robert suggested. "It certainly wouldn't reflect well on him now, would it?"

"But surely the Bensons noticed that Peregrine didn't arrive home from the Assembly Rooms?" Patrick frowned at Robert. "Unless there is yet another thing going on I am not aware of?"

"All I can tell you at this point is that if any of the Benson family do manage to convince me that they can see Peregrine, they are not to be left alone with him even for a second," Robert stated.

"Understood, Major." Patrick stood and offered Robert an impeccable salute. "Now, thank you for breakfast. I will change my clothes, speak to my wife, and meet you in the sickroom whenever you are ready, Lady Kurland."

Even before the door shut behind Patrick, Lucy started speaking. "Do you really intend to confront Edward?"

"I don't think I have a choice, do I?" Robert replied. "The last thing we want is him setting the law on us for kidnapping his brother."

"But what if he turns violent?" Lucy asked.

"I'm not going to accuse him of murder, my dear. I'll just inform him that Peregrine is in my house and cannot be moved until he sufficiently recovers."

"Please be careful."

He reached across the table and took her hand. "I will. I promise."

Lucy leaned over the bed and studied Peregrine's flushed face. Dr. Fletcher had given him some laudanum to ease the pain, but she could already see that he was fighting a fever.

"I cleaned the wound out and used some of Grace Turner's herbs to make a poultice to put over it," Dr. Fletcher murmured as he removed his hand from his patient's brow. "I've noticed that whatever she puts in that mixture works much better than what I have used in the past."

"Then let's hope for the best." Lucy straightened up. "Has he said anything this morning?"

"Not much and nothing that made sense." Dr. Fletcher hid a yawn.

"I am more than happy to sit with him for a few hours, Doctor," Lucy offered. "I intend to have a quiet morning after the excitement of last night."

"Then I will go and sit with my wife. She isn't feeling well herself today and is insisting that I shouted at her and treated her as if she were a servant."

"You shouted at me, too, but I understood why," Lucy reminded him.

"You are much more . . ." He hesitated as if trying to think of an appropriate word. "*Robust* than my wife."

"Indeed." Lucy walked over to the door and opened it. "If you could ask Foley to come and speak to me when he has a moment, I would be very grateful."

After Dr. Fletcher's departure, Lucy reorganized the space around Peregrine's bed to her liking. When Foley appeared, she asked him to fetch her workbasket and bring another branch of candles. She was still finishing up some baby clothes for Penelope, and as the birth was likely to be earlier than anticipated she didn't want to have things half done.

She sewed quietly for a while, occasionally glancing over at the bed to see that Peregrine remained unconscious. Anna came in to offer up her services for the afternoon, and Lucy told her to speak to Dr. Fletcher. She knew that Robert had gone out to speak to Edward Benson, and she was rather worried that he hadn't yet returned.

A groan made her set her sewing aside and walk quickly over to Peregrine. His eyes were open and he was staring directly at her.

"What the *devil?*" he whispered.

She held a glass of water to his lips and he managed to take a sip.

"You were attacked by pickpockets and injured. Dr. Fletcher is taking care of you."

He winced and grabbed hold of her wrist. "I don't remember what happened."

"You were lucky that my husband and Dr. Fletcher arrived just after you were attacked. They managed to fight the men off, and they ran away."

He blinked at her. "Is Dr. Mantel all right?"

"Yes, he received some minor injuries. You were stabbed."

Peregrine wet his lips, and Lucy helped him take more water.

"What did they take?"

"Your purse and watch are missing," Lucy said.

"Not much then," he murmured. "Hardly worth stabbing me for."

"I agree." She set the glass back on the tray. "As you once mentioned, it is quite *extraordinary* how often your family are targeted in these attacks, isn't it?"

He stared at her for one second and then closed his eyes, his mouth settling into a stubborn line that reminded Lucy forcibly of his father.

She waited for another minute, but he turned his head away and was soon snoring again. With a sigh, Lucy returned to her sewing. She had a sense that he would be feeling far worse than he was right now and braced herself to deal with his fever.

"As I said, Mr. Benson. Your brother Peregrine is in the very capable hands of my physician. Dr. Fletcher said it would be unwise to move him at this point in case the bleeding started up again," Robert repeated himself patiently.

He'd been admitted directly into Edward Benson's study, and there was no sign of any of the other occupants of the house. For once his normally calm host looked remarkably out of sorts.

"But he would be better off here with his family, and with Dr. Mantel to care for him," Edward blustered.

"I'm sure that as soon as Dr. Fletcher thinks it is safe, he will bring your brother back here to the bosom of his family. I'm quite sure that Dr. Mantel would agree. Do you wish to consult with him before I leave?"

"Dr. Mantel was also injured in the attack and has taken to his bed. I would prefer not to disturb him at this point," Edward said.

"Then if he is indisposed, he cannot possibly care for Mr. Peregrine Benson, can he?" Robert said smoothly, and rose to his feet. "I would certainly not expect him to endanger his own health."

Edward stood as well. "I will come over and see Peregrine this afternoon."

"I doubt he will be able to speak to you, but please do call at the house and Foley will let you know whether a visit would be advisable." Robert bowed. "I'd better be getting back."

"Thank you." Edward bowed stiffly in return. "Our debt to your family is substantial."

"Hardly that," Robert countered. "I'm sure that if the situation was reversed you would have done exactly the same. I'll keep you informed as to Peregrine's progress, and if he takes a turn for the worse, I will send for you immediately."

Edward frowned. "I thought you said he was on the mend?"

"He is certainly no longer bleeding, but Dr. Fletcher anticipates he will suffer a fever, and that is never something to take lightly."

He nodded again and headed for the door all too aware that Edward Benson was staring at his back. In the hallway he met Augustus Benson, who had just arrived at the house. He still wore his muddy boots and rain-soaked cloak.

"Sir Robert! I hear that my brother Peregrine has been grievously injured."

"Did Mr. Edward Benson inform you of that?" Robert asked.

"Yes, of course he did." Augustus shook his head, making his many chins wobble. "What is the world coming to when a man can be attacked by ruffians right outside his door? There is a lack of godliness in this modern world, Sir Robert, that I find quite appalling."

Robert had no answer to that. "Your brother is currently residing in my house under the care of my physician, Dr. Fletcher, who was the person who tended to his wounds."

"Not Dr. Mantel?"

"Dr. Mantel was also attacked and found himself unable to offer his professional services at the time."

"Ah, I see." Augustus untied his cloak and draped it over a chair. "Perhaps I should accompany you home and say a prayer over my brother Peregrine."

"I don't think he is ready for visitors quite yet," Robert countered.

Augustus stiffened. "I am hardly a *visitor.* Peregrine and I might not see eye to eye on everything but he is still my flesh and blood."

"And I'm sure he will be delighted to see you when he regains consciousness, but until then he is not receiving anyone."

"If you insist," Augustus sighed. "I suppose the best thing for me to do is to stay here and comfort the other members of my family."

"I'm not sure if anyone other than Dr. Mantel and Mr. Edward Benson know what happened yet."

Augustus frowned. "What about Lady Benson? She has never liked Peregrine but I'm sure that she would not wish ill on him." He hesitated. "With all due respect, Sir Robert, is it possible that my brother might die?"

"It is always possible, sir, and eventually inevitable."

"Then you will inform me if he needs my prayers, or any other services I might render him such as writing out his last will and testament."

Robert frowned. "One would assume with all this furor over Sir William's will that all of you would have written a will already—although I suppose in your brother's case he might not have a feather to fly with worth mentioning in a will."

"You mistake the matter, Sir Robert." Augustus's chuckle was somewhat forced. "Peregrine was the only one of us who had his *own* wealth. His godmother was our father's sister. She married a wealthy industrialist and had no children. She left her entire fortune to Peregrine."

Even though he was startled, Robert kept his thoughts about that interesting information to himself. "Well, I must be going. It was a pleasure to speak to you, Reverend Benson."

Robert left Augustus standing in the hall and made his way back to his own house. He paused as he went to raise the knocker. Should he have warned Augustus to be careful? Surely Edward wouldn't be stupid enough to attempt to murder another of his brothers? Augustus was hardly worth killing and would likely accept money to pay his debts in return for his silence.

Foley let him in and Robert repeated his orders about not allowing any of the Bensons beyond the front door without Robert's or Dr. Fletcher's express permission. He went upstairs to the drawing room and found it empty. Lucy was probably still in with Peregrine, and Dr. Fletcher might be having a well-earned rest—if his wife allowed him to.

His gaze turned to the local newspaper and he sat down to read it. If Augustus was correct about Peregrine having his own fortune his behavior toward his father and the rest of his family made a twisted kind of sense. But did having that wealth make him a murderer or a victim? Who would inherit Peregrine's fortune if he died? One had to assume it would be his brothers.

Robert checked the clock on the mantelpiece and settled into his chair. Whatever the answer, he'd stay home and guard Peregrine Benson until the man was capable of defending himself.

Armed with the very interesting information that Peregrine was a wealthy man in his own right, Lucy returned to the sickroom after dining with Robert and sent Anna down to enjoy her own repast. Dr. Fletcher was frowning down at his patient as she came in the door.

"He's burning up with fever."

"Then I assume you'll want me to keep him cool, try and get him to drink water, and summon you if he takes a turn for the worse."

"Exactly." Dr. Fletcher nodded. "You would make an excellent physician, Lady Kurland."

"I'd rather not." Lucy shuddered. "I've nursed Robert and my younger brothers through many such fevers, and I've simply learned how to read the signs."

He smiled at her as he turned down the sheets to Peregrine's waist. "I have complete confidence in you, my lady. If you need me, do not hesitate to call. I have to go to the apothecary to get some more supplies, but I will be as quick as I can."

"I will be absolutely fine, Dr. Fletcher." Lucy smoothed down her skirts and tied an apron around her waist. She'd already destroyed one gown and was reluctant to ruin another. "Please make sure that you take time to eat before you even think of returning."

"I will, my lady." Dr. Fletcher paused at the door. "Did Sir Robert mention if any of the Bensons attempted to get in the house?"

"Apparently, they all did. Even Lady Benson, who was quite hysterical." Lucy sighed. "Foley managed to fend them off, but I doubt they will allow themselves to be deterred for much longer."

"By the morning, Mr. Benson's fever will either have broken, or he will start to show signs of the wound being infected and grow worse." Dr. Fletcher grimaced. "He is a man in his prime, and one can only hope and pray he will fight this off."

"We will do our best to ensure he survives," Lucy said firmly. "I will call you if his condition worsens."

She lit the extra branch of candles Foley had

brought up for her and made sure the light didn't fall on Peregrine. His breathing was ragged now, his skin flushed, and he moved restlessly on the sheets.

Lucy bathed him in cold water with a sponge and laid a cloth on his forehead, which he immediately snatched off. She'd asked Foley to purchase some ice earlier and had used it to keep the bucket of well water as chilly as possible. Peregrine didn't appreciate her efforts in the slightest. She regularly had to avoid his flailing arms and prevent his attempts to pluck at the bandages around his chest.

After half an hour of wrestling with him Lucy was exhausted and was contemplating asking for Dr. Fletcher's help. To her relief, Peregrine suddenly went still and started snoring. Lucy sat down in her chair by the fire and wiped her brow. If he grew more agitated she would struggle to control him and might have to ask Silas to aid her.

She sipped her tea, which had cooled down considerably, but decided not to bother ringing for another pot. If she started asking for things, Foley would inform Robert, and then poor Dr. Fletcher would insist on coming to Peregrine's bedside when he clearly needed to rest.

An hour passed in relative quiet. Lucy finished sewing a baby bonnet and started embroidering the brim with yellow silk. The clock on the mantelpiece ticked away as the small coal fire cracked and popped. Eventually she stuck her needle into the fabric and walked over to the bed.

Peregrine's eyes were open, but he didn't look himself. Lucy took his hand in hers and smiled down at him.

"Do not worry. You have a fever, but you will soon feel much better."

"Dying," he croaked.

"Not if Dr. Fletcher and I have anything to do with it," Lucy corrected him. "You must concentrate on your recovery."

She offered him some water, and he managed a few sips before she lowered his head back down onto the pillows.

"Have to tell you something," he whispered.

"What is it?" Lucy asked, leaning closer to hear the faint rasp of his voice.

"Letters."

Lucy frowned at him. "I don't understand."

"Letters and numbers." He blinked hard, his throat working. *"Listen."*

She took his hand again, and he grasped her wrist, the heat of his fingers scorching her skin. "What can I help you with?"

"Key to it all. Thought it was amusing, but can't let it die with me."

"Let what die?" Lucy asked. "Does this have something to do with your father's will?"

A commotion in the corridor outside permeated

through the closed door, and Peregrine's gaze intensified.

"Shakespeare was a better playwright than me."

"I would imagine so." Lucy held his gaze. "Could you perhaps be a little more *specific?* I fear we are about to be interrupted."

Just as the door opened, Peregrine's eyes closed as if he was exhausted by his efforts. "As you like . . ."

Lucy turned to glare at Edward Benson, who stood in the doorway, Robert and Dr. Fletcher behind him.

"Please have some *decency!* Your brother is very ill, Mr. Benson."

Dr. Fletcher came in and took over Lucy's position by Peregrine's head. "His fever still hasn't broken?"

"Not yet." Lucy walked away from the bed and went to stand next to Robert.

Her husband regarded Edward, his blue gaze frosty. "As you can see for yourself, Mr. Benson. No one is trying to deceive you. Your brother is gravely ill."

Edward looked from Robert to Lucy and a now oblivious Dr. Fletcher, who was busy concentrating on his patient.

"I do beg your pardon." He loudly exhaled. "My concern for my brother overlaid my good manners and common sense."

"There is very little you can do for him at

this moment," Robert said quietly. "If you wish to stay here and keep vigil with Dr. Fletcher and my wife's maid tonight, you are more than welcome."

"No, I'll call in the morning." Edward touched the brim of his hat. "I do apologize. I don't know what came over me."

Robert and Lucy followed him out into the corridor and escorted him down the stairs. Edward paused in the hallway.

"Has he asked for anyone? Has he spoken about what happened?"

"He has barely been conscious, Mr. Benson," Lucy replied. "And when he does speak, his words are somewhat garbled and nonsensical."

"Would you object if Dr. Mantel came to sit with him tomorrow in my stead?"

"Not at all." Robert bowed.

"I have to meet with the magistrate about Brandon and speak to Mr. Carstairs about returning to Yorkshire." Mr. Benson bowed. "Again, I do apologize for my impatience. After the recent death of my father I am very reluctant to lose a brother as well."

"Of course, Mr. Benson." Robert held the door open and bowed their visitor out. "Good evening."

Robert shut the door with something of a bang and turned to Lucy.

"What the devil was that about? Edward pushed his way past Foley, almost knocked him down, and demanded to be taken up to see Peregrine!"

"Maybe he thought we'd spirited him away somewhere," Lucy said.

"Or he's worried about what his brother might be saying about him and thought to finish him off." Robert blinked as his wife marched off in the direction of his study. "Where are you going *now?*"

He followed her into the book-lined room to find her studying the shelves, a candle in her hand.

"What exactly are you doing?"

"There must be a volume of Shakespeare here *somewhere.* Every library in the land has the Bard's plays," Lucy murmured.

"Why this sudden interest in Shakespeare?"

"Because of what Peregrine told me—or tried to tell me. I do hope I understood what he was saying because it did indeed sound *quite* nonsensical."

Robert caught hold of her elbow and firmly turned her to face him. "Start at the beginning, and then I'll help you search."

She sighed as if he was being a particularly dense pupil. "Peregrine said he had to tell me something in case he died. That it had all been a bit of a joke, but perhaps it wasn't funny anymore."

"And what does that have to do with Shakespeare?" Robert demanded.

She wrinkled her nose. "I'm trying to remember the exact words he used. He said it had *something* to do with numbers and letters, and that was key. Then he mentioned his plays weren't as good as Shakespeare's."

"Well, that at least makes sense," Robert muttered. *"And?"*

"I asked him if he was talking about his father's will, and he didn't disagree with me." She frowned. "And then all that noise started in the corridor, and he started to lose consciousness again."

"It sounds like a lot of fustian to me."

"But remember, Peregrine and Sir William loved riddles. Perhaps he was trying to give us some clues as to how to find the will."

Robert considered her hopeful face. "All right, then let's go over what he said again." He found a piece of paper and started writing.

"Letters, numbers, and Shakespeare." He looked up. "That's rather a daunting task. Where on earth are we supposed to start?"

"I don't know." Lucy bit her lip. "What relevance would that have to Peregrine and Sir William?"

"Lots of hawks in Shakespeare," Robert offered. "Not sure there were any peregrines, though."

"What an excellent thought!" His wife smiled approvingly at him. "Who else has a name that might have appeared in Shakespeare?"

"Practically all of them," Robert groused. "There's definitely a few Edwards and probably an Augustus in *Julius Caesar*, and then Miranda appears in—"

Lucy held up a finger. "Arden!"

"Also from Shakespeare." Robert nodded. "As is Brandon."

"But that makes sense of the last thing Peregrine said before he lost consciousness!" Lucy said.

"The thing you didn't mention, and that isn't on my list?" Robert asked.

"Only because it didn't mean anything until I thought of *Arden*. I asked Peregrine to be more specific, and he said, 'as you like . . .' At first, I thought he was merely *agreeing* with me." She gazed at Robert expectantly.

"*As You Like It*," Robert said slowly. "And the Forest of Arden. I had to study that one at school." They smiled at each other in complete accord. "Now let's see if we can find that play on these shelves."

"Don't you remember it?" Lucy asked.

"Good Lord, no." Robert shuddered at the very thought. "I hated every minute of the damned thing."

"If we can't locate it I'm fairly sure they have

it at one of the circulating libraries in Milsom Street," Lucy said. "We can go and search tomorrow morning."

They both took a candle and started at either end of the wall of books, but there was no sign of the play.

Lucy sat down with a thump, her face dejected. "Well, that is disappointing."

Robert perched on the corner of the desk. "I doubt we would've done much with the information tonight, anyway. Are you *sure* Peregrine didn't utter anything else that might indicate where we're supposed to be *looking* for the will?"

"One has to assume that the will is somewhere in Sir William's room or secreted in his belongings." Lucy looked up at him.

"Agreed. But *where?* By all accounts the rooms and baggage have been thoroughly searched on numerous occasions and nothing has turned up."

"But knowing Sir William's love of puzzles maybe the will is hidden *inside* something obvious that needs a key or a code to let you in?"

"That sounds very likely."

"Then the only thing we can do is search for ourselves. Knowing that we are looking for something that needs *opening* might help us see things in a different way to everyone else."

The hall clock struck eleven times, and Robert helped Lucy to her feet. "Let's check on Peregrine and go to bed."

He held the door open for his wife to go ahead of him and they ascended the stairs together.

"I do hope Peregrine survives this," Lucy commented as they walked through the silent house. She knocked on the door of the sickroom and peered inside. Patrick came out to join them in the corridor.

"He's still fighting the fever," Patrick said, and nodded to Robert. "With your permission, Sir Robert, I'm going to ask Silas to stay with me tonight to keep Mr. Benson safe."

"Of course. I don't need him." Robert nodded. "I'm perfectly capable of undressing myself. Do you think Peregrine is going to get better?"

"I'm hopeful." Patrick met Robert's gaze without hesitation. "If his condition worsens I'll send Silas to let you know, and you can fetch the Bensons."

"Thank you." Robert patted Patrick's shoulder. "I appreciate your skills more every day."

His friend went back into the room, closing the door behind him. Robert looked at Lucy.

"Let's go to bed and do our best to get some sleep. I suspect tomorrow might be a very interesting day."

Chapter 19

Lucy deposited the library book on Robert's desk and went to find her spectacles, which she realized she'd left with her sewing basket in the sickroom. She tapped on the door and was admitted by Anna, who was smiling.

"Mr. Benson's fever has broken. Dr. Fletcher is very pleased."

"That's wonderful." Lucy crossed over to the bed where Peregrine was now sleeping soundly, his expression so devoid of mischief and malice that he looked quite unlike himself. "Is the wound healing nicely?"

"Dr. Fletcher cleaned and dressed it this morning, and detected no sign of new swelling or the odor of decay."

"Then let's hope he makes a full recovery." Lucy smiled at her sister. "Have you eaten breakfast yet?"

"I will as soon as Betty comes to relieve me. I promised Penelope I would spend some time with her today as she is feeling somewhat neglected."

Lucy rolled her eyes. "Penelope is *terribly* selfish."

"I do have *some* sympathy for her, Lucy." Anna hesitated. "She is expecting her first child and her husband is rather busy dealing with another emergency while she quietly worries about giving birth."

"Quietly?" Lucy snorted. "Penelope doesn't know the meaning of that word. She just hates it when she isn't the center of attention."

Anna bit her lip. "I honestly believe that beneath her rather shrill exterior she is quite afraid, and I'm hardly the right person to alleviate those fears, am I?"

"You can only do your best," Lucy reminded her sister. "I promise that as soon as Mr. Peregrine Benson and his entire family leave Bath I will give you and Penelope *all* of my attention."

She turned to leave. "If you need me, I will be in Sir Robert's study, and then we might be visiting the Bensons."

Lucy pondered Anna's remarkably forgiving nature as she descended the stairs. She had to concede that her sister might have a point about Penelope being somewhat alone. Neither of them had a mother to guide them through the process of childbirth, but Lucy at least had helped out at many births and knew what happened. She had to suspect that even though Penelope was the wife of a doctor her sheltered upbringing had not offered her the opportunity to observe a birth.

On an impulse, Lucy changed direction, and went back up to the rooms Penelope shared with Dr. Fletcher and knocked on the door.

"Come in?"

Lucy went in to find Penelope sitting by the window, her hands folded over the large mound of her stomach. Penelope held her fingers to her lips and struggled to her feet. Her belly appeared to have dropped even lower.

"Dr. Fletcher is sleeping next door. I was just about to come down to the drawing room."

"Then I will walk with you." Lucy held open the door and stepped back to allow Penelope's bulk to pass through ahead of her. "How are you feeling today?"

"I'm exhausted," Penelope said without any of her usual snippiness.

"Do you need to go back to bed?" Lucy asked.

"I can't sleep." Penelope sighed. "The baby kicks me all night long."

"How horrible for you." Lucy gently rubbed Penelope's back as they walked. "Have you tried raising your feet up?"

"I have tried everything my husband has suggested, and nothing works." She smoothed a hand over her belly. "I cannot wait until this baby is born."

"From the look of you, it won't be long now."

Lucy settled Penelope by the fire and placed a footstool under her feet.

"Why are you being so nice to me?" Penelope asked.

"Because you are stuck here, without your sister, and away from your home when you are going to give birth," Lucy replied. "I want you to know that I will do everything in my power to make sure you are supported through this."

Penelope's lip trembled. "I think that is the nicest thing you have ever said to me, Lucy, and I probably don't deserve it."

Lucy sank down onto the footstool and took Penelope's hands. "We have had our differences in the past, but when it comes to this—bringing a new life into the world—we are all women together. I want the best for you and Dr. Fletcher."

"Thank you," Penelope whispered. "It *is* rather upsetting not to be home, and I am aware that my temper has perhaps been a little *uncertain*."

Lucy squeezed Penelope's fingers. "We will get you through this, I swear it."

Penelope nodded and found a smile. "Dr. Fletcher says the same thing. He insists that his professional reputation demands that I will not only survive the experience, but positively *enjoy* it."

"Easy for him to say," Lucy murmured. "When he isn't the one doing the actual birthing."

This time Penelope's laughter was more

genuine, and Lucy was still smiling when she continued down the stairs to Robert's study where he was awaiting her. As soon as this matter with the Bensons was concluded she promised herself she would dedicate her time to Penelope and Anna.

Robert was already engrossed in the book and barely looked up as she joined him.

"Did you find anything yet?" she inquired.

"Yes, and I didn't have to go far. This is the first mention of Arden Wood and it's right at the beginning of the play in Act One."

Lucy read out the lines.

"They say he is already in the Forest of Arden, and a many merry men with him; and there they live like the old Robin Hood of England. They say many young men flock to him every day, and fleet the time carelessly, as they did in the golden world."

She wrinkled her nose. "What does that tell us?"

"I have no idea," Robert said. "I've copied it out and I thought we might take it with us when we search Sir William's baggage tonight."

"Tonight?"

"Yes, I thought we'd sneak in up the servants' stairs. Foley still has a key to the back door."

"Peregrine said it had to do with letters and numbers," Lucy reminded him, "so perhaps it is a puzzle or a code or a play on words?"

"It could be any of those things." Robert took out another sheet of paper and handed her a newly cut pen. "Perhaps we should just work out as many possibilities as we can and hope we find the right combination."

"We should look at the letters Peregrine and his father exchanged," Lucy said. "There might be a clue in there."

"That's an excellent idea." He grimaced. "Do you think there's any chance Peregrine might wake up and tell us the whole truth?"

"Dr. Fletcher is reluctant to awaken him at this point. He says he needs healing sleep." Lucy opened the inkwell and dipped the nib of her pen in the ink. "And now that Peregrine is going to live I somehow doubt he will be willing to reveal his secrets anymore."

An hour later, Foley knocked on the door to let them know that Augustus, Lady Benson, and Dr. Mantel were seeking admittance to the sickroom. Robert stood up and stretched.

"I'll have to let them see him, but I'm not letting them go up there alone. Will you excuse me for a moment?"

Lucy put down her pen. "Seeing as I am getting nowhere, I'd like to at least *see* the Bensons. Perhaps I could offer them some tea after their visit and find out if they are willing to talk about anything in particular."

"As you wish." Robert nodded. "You're much

better at getting information out of people than I am. Perhaps you could also ascertain where everyone will be tonight."

"I'll certainly do my best." Lucy rose and smoothed down her skirts. "The Bensons do love to share all their secrets with us, so goodness knows what they might reveal now?"

Lucy had already settled herself in the drawing room with Anna and Penelope, and ordered refreshments when Robert ushered in Lady Benson, Augustus, and Dr. Mantel. She went to take Lady Benson's hand and led her toward the couch.

"Please sit down, my lady. I cannot imagine how you must be feeling at this moment."

Lady Benson uttered a mournful sigh. "You cannot imagine, Lady Kurland. You truly *cannot!* My beloved husband is dead, my youngest son had deserted me, and now *this!* Peregrine has never liked me, and one has to suspect that he is positively *enjoying* causing me such anxiety and grief."

Lucy frowned. "I hardly think he deliberately allowed himself to be stabbed purely to annoy you, ma'am."

"Oh, you'd be surprised." Lady Benson made a dramatic gesture. "He probably hoped my dear Dr. Mantel would be killed, and *he* would be the one who 'escaped' with minor injuries."

Lucy looked at Anna, whose stunned face reflected Lucy's own reaction.

"I don't think that's what happened at all, Lady Benson. You are naturally distraught and don't mean what you say." Dr. Mantel hurried into the conversation. "Mr. Peregrine Benson was as startled as I was when those men set on us."

"He was always a passable actor," Lady Benson sniffed. "And his hatred of me knows no bounds."

Lucy glanced over at the tea tray. "Would you like some tea, Lady Benson? Hopefully, Mr. Peregrine Benson will be recovered enough soon for you to take him back to your house where Dr. Mantel can care for him."

She smiled at the doctor, noting the scars on his hands and face. "How are you feeling after such a horrible event yourself, Doctor?"

He made a face. "Remarkably embarrassed by my own behavior, to tell you the truth, my lady. I panicked rather badly."

"Not all physicians are as used to dealing with bloody wounds as Dr. Fletcher, sir," Lucy reminded him.

"That is very gracious of you." Dr. Mantel took his cup of tea and sat down.

Even as Lucy smiled at him she decided she would insist that Dr. Fletcher not release Peregrine into Dr. Mantel's hands until he was capable of defending himself and he wouldn't relapse. She suspected the Benson doctor would fail his patient again.

The rest of the visit passed without any more revelations although Lucy discovered that all the Bensons were planning on being home that night. She reassured herself that the only room close to Sir William's was Miranda's, and that the widow was remarkably fond of laudanum to help her sleep.

Whatever happened, she was determined that she and Robert would succeed in finding the will and finally working out which one of the Bensons was a murderer.

"Are you ready, Lucy?"

"Yes, I'm just coming."

Lucy gathered her notes into a pile and folded them carefully so that they would fit inside the pocket of her darkest dress. She wore soft kid slippers and had decided not to bring a shawl or reticule that she might accidentally leave behind. She went down the stairs and found her husband waiting for her in the hall. The candles and lamps had been lit, and the house was quiet as everyone else had retired to bed.

Robert wore his black coat and waistcoat, which made the whiteness of his shirt and cravat stand out even more. He had a large key in his hand and was talking to Foley, who was describing which door they could use to enter the Benson residence and exactly where the backstairs were located.

Foley turned to Lucy as she came down the stairs. "Are you quite certain that you wouldn't prefer me to go with Sir Robert, my lady?"

"I'd rather go myself," Lucy reassured him. "We wouldn't wish to get you into trouble."

"As you wish, my lady." Foley sighed and opened the door that led into the back of the house. "There is a path from the mews that leads directly to the door you need, Sir Robert. Please be careful."

Lucy followed Robert out of the house and was surprised at how bright the moon was. If anyone were looking out of the Bensons' house they would spot them in an instant. But there were no lights burning in any windows, and no sign of any people.

Robert followed the path and located the door at the back of the house without much trouble. With most of the houses in Queen's Square being rented out rather than owned, there were not many dogs to advertise an intruder's presence.

The door clicked open, and Robert stepped inside, pausing to listen before he beckoned for Lucy to follow him in. The servants' stairs were close to the back door, which meant that they didn't have to go into the kitchen.

Luckily, Robert had an excellent sense of direction whereas Lucy found the darkness rather disorientating. When they reached Sir William's dressing room, Robert cautiously opened the door, wincing when it squeaked.

"Stay there," he whispered. "In case we have to flee. I'll make sure the other doors are locked."

He disappeared into the gloom, leaving Lucy holding her breath and clinging to the doorframe. Even as her nerves tightened, her eyes adjusted to the darkness, and she made out the shape of the furniture and proportions of the room, which weren't the same as in their rented house being on the floor above.

The strike of a flint and a flicker of light focused her gaze on the far side of the room where Robert was lighting a candle. He carried it over to her, his hand shielding the flame.

"Let's start in the bedroom. It's farther away from Lady Benson and most of Sir William's bags are in there."

Taking his proffered hand, she followed him across the room and into Sir William's bed-chamber. Robert shut the door behind her and set the candle on the side of the bed.

"We'll need some more light."

Lucy wondered why he'd decided to break in at midnight when it was hard to see anything, but kept her thoughts to herself as he lit another candle.

"Let's look through the cupboards and the

tallboy just to make sure nothing has been left behind," Robert said.

"And make sure there aren't any secret panels or places to hide anything?" Lucy suggested.

"Seeing as this house is rented, I doubt that any of the furniture here would have that purpose, or that Sir William would know about it."

"Oh." Lucy nodded. "Of course not."

"That's not to say that we still shouldn't be on the lookout for anything odd."

Despite gently tapping every surface and running her fingers over the backs of the drawers, Lucy found nothing of interest.

Eventually, Robert turned his attention to the three pieces of luggage that Sir William had brought with him from Yorkshire.

"Which one do you think is most likely to contain a secret drawer or a concealed container?" Robert crouched down and Lucy followed suit.

"The biggest one." Lucy patted the huge trunk, which was about three feet high and three feet wide. "Is it locked?"

Robert undid the clasps and the top of the trunk opened easily. "No, thank goodness."

He held the candle up over the contents and grimaced. "Now I wish we *had* brought Foley with us. I have no idea how we're going to pack this all up again."

By the time they had taken everything out of the trunk and piled it up behind them, Lucy was beginning to agree with Robert. They'd spent precious minutes examining the inside lid of the trunk but had found nothing within the lining except a folded ten guinea note. She'd meticulously checked every pocket of each garment and gone through Sir William's potions and lotions, but to no avail.

"Wait . . ." Robert was feeling around the edge of the bottom of the trunk. "The lining continues beneath this piece."

He roughly measured the inside of the trunk with his hands and compared it to the outside. "I suspect this trunk has a false bottom. Let's see if we can remove it."

With both of them working together, they managed to lever off the thin wooden base to reveal what lay beneath.

Robert smiled at her. "I think we've found it." He carefully lifted out the ornate black lacquered box. "Let's put everything else back, and then we can take a good look at this."

"There appear to be some kind of barrels to turn to release the hasp over the latch," Robert murmured. "I assume this might be the code Peregrine was referring to." He looked up at Lucy. "Now all we have to do is work out what that is."

"How many letters or numbers do we need to find?" Lucy whispered.

"Six, by the looks of it." Robert moved the candle even closer so that he could see what characters were etched in the brass. "They look like all numbers except the first one, which is a letter." He sighed. "I don't even know where to begin."

"Start with the letter *A*," Lucy said. "It's the first letter of Arden's name."

Robert used his thumb to turn the dial until it reached the *A,* and heard a faint click. "Well, that was lucky. Now on to the rest of it."

"If it's only numbers, then it can't be any words from the actual text," Lucy mused. "I wonder if it's the numerical equivalent of the rest of Arden's name?"

"Too short," Robert said, "unless you repeat the *A.*"

"Let's try that. *R* is the eighteenth letter of the alphabet."

"Which won't work as the numbers go from nought to nine."

"Then maybe it is a one, followed by an eight, followed by four for the *D,* five for the *E,* and fourteen . . . That's too long, isn't it?" Lucy sighed.

"Then what else can it be?" Robert asked. "Was there any particular pattern to the puzzles Sir William and Peregrine liked to play?"

"They did use a lot of Shakespearean quotes," Lucy said slowly.

"In what context?" His leg was starting to hurt from sitting on the hard floor. "And can you relate it to a series of numbers?"

"I wish it was that simple." Lucy sighed. "Perhaps we would be better off taking the box back to our house and dealing with it there."

"I'd rather not steal anything from the Bensons," Robert demurred.

"Then what are we doing here if you don't intend to find the will and use it to solve the mystery?" Lucy hissed. "If we take the box, we can give it to Peregrine and get *him* to open it!"

"What if he's the murderer?" Robert countered. "Do we really want to merrily hand over everything?"

"For goodness' *sake,* Robert—"

He pressed his hand over her mouth, as a familiar voice spoke from the dressing room next door.

"I have to search again! I cannot allow all these terrible things to happen to my family!" Lady Benson wailed. "If we could only recover the *will.*"

Robert met Lucy's gaze and slowly removed his hand from her lips. There was no door to the servants' stairs in the master bedchamber. He took Lucy's hand and drew her to her feet. She scooped up the box in her arms and held it against her chest.

"Please, Miranda, do not distress yourself. You

and Edward have already agreed to go to court to split the money fairly between you."

That was Dr. Mantel's calm voice.

"But how can I *trust* him? Look what happened to *Peregrine!*" Miranda cried. "I can't trust *anyone.*"

"You can trust me, my darling."

Robert's gaze clashed with Lucy's startled one.

"Well, of course I can, but I still don't think you are telling me *everything.*"

"If I am keeping things from you, there would be a very good reason for it. I love you and cannot bear to see you upset."

"You are so *good* to me, so *kind* . . ."

Miranda went silent, and Robert imagined she was probably being kissed.

"Now, come back to bed and I will endeavor to keep you occupied until morning when everything will look much brighter," Dr. Mantel murmured.

Robert shuddered. She'd definitely been kissed.

Robert backed toward the door that led out onto the landing and fumbled behind him for the latch. If Miranda did decide to ignore her lover's pleas and come through the door, he would make sure he and Lucy had an escape route.

The next thing he heard was the click of Miranda's bedroom door and Dr. Mantel's low, satisfied laughter. After slowly counting to five hundred and keeping one hand in Lucy's, Robert set off back to the dressing room. He didn't draw breath until they were both safely within their own four walls.

While Robert spoke to Foley, who had waited up for them, Lucy placed the lacquered box on the desk and studied it. She couldn't believe that they had been at the Bensons' for an hour, and how close they had come to being discovered. She opened the volume of Shakespeare at the page where the Forest of Arden first appeared, and considered all the numbers on the page.

"Act One, Scene One," Lucy murmured, and then moved her finger down the side of the column of prose to the exact line of text where the forest was first mentioned. "Line . . . one hundred." She frowned. "Peregrine did say something about turning letters into numbers, and that was the key. And this is a device he used in many of his puzzles to his father. Could it be that simple?"

"Could what be that simple?" Robert asked as he came in and closed the door behind him. He carried a bottle of brandy under his arm, and two glasses in his right hand. "I thought we deserved a drink after that scare."

"You have one, but I'm wondering about the code. Sir William often used numerical references for particular lines of Shakespeare that he wanted Peregrine to look up to solve the cipher."

He took a seat beside her. "You don't want to discuss Dr. Mantel's presence in Miranda Benson's bedchamber?"

"We'll need to discuss that, too, but what about the code?" She tapped the open page of the book. "If Peregrine was suggesting we substitute numbers for letters, maybe the *A* is not a clue for Arden, but for Act One?"

Robert leaned closer and studied the list of numbers she'd made. "Act One, Scene One, line one hundred? Where did you get the one hundred from?"

Lucy showed him the text of the play and pointed at the relevant line containing the word *Arden.* "See?" She moved her finger across to the tiny printed *100* on the right-hand side of the column directly next to the printed words. "It's mentioned right here."

"Ah!" Robert nodded. "One zero zero. That makes five numbers plus the letter *A.* Shall I try it?"

"A, one, one, one zero, zero." Robert spun the brass tumblers, and there was a definite click. "Good Lord, Lucy. I think you might have done it."

He eased the box open and stared down at the pile of documents within, one of which bore many seals and was tied with a red ribbon.

"The last will and testament of Sir William Benson, Baronet," Lucy read out, and then looked at her husband. "Now what on *earth* are we going to do with it?"

Chapter 20

T o what do I owe this honor?" Peregrine inquired as Robert and Lucy came into his bedchamber. He was sitting up in bed and had obviously felt well enough to consume the bowl of gruel that sat on his nightstand. "Are you kicking me out?"

"Not quite yet."

Robert laid the black lacquered box on the bed. He and Lucy had argued for quite a while about what to do with all the information they had uncovered. Seeing as they now believed there might be a different reason for the murder of Sir William, he'd argued that Peregrine was their only chance of solving the rest of it.

"How on earth did you find that?" Peregrine exclaimed.

Lucy smiled at him. "With your help, and a little luck."

"When I was delirious with fever? You are an incredibly devious woman, Lady Kurland."

"You thought you were dying," Lucy pointed

out. "You *begged* me to find the box and break the code."

"I don't remember what I did." Peregrine sighed. "But it sounds like the sort of ridiculous thing I *would* do, so I can hardly blame you for my sins." He eyed Robert. "Why have you brought it to me, and not Mr. Carstairs?"

"There is the small matter that we were trespassing when we found it." Robert crossed one booted foot over the over. "And we thought you might help us understand exactly what is going on before we proceed any further."

Peregrine opened the box and took out the will. "I've already seen it."

Robert nodded. "We suspected as much, which begs the question of why you didn't destroy it, but put it back where your father had hidden it?"

"I thought it was amusing. The idea that they were all frantically looking for it and that not one of them thought to ask me—the favorite son." Peregrine shrugged, and then winced as if suddenly aware of his wounded side. "My father told me about his latest version over breakfast the day he died. That's why I followed him to the baths and argued with him. I stole it out of his pocket when he went off with Dr. Mantel to get in the baths."

"You didn't approve of his decisions?" Robert asked.

"Hardly. He was intending to leave everything to me."

Lucy blinked at him. "And you didn't approve of *that?*"

"How *could* I?" For once Peregrine wasn't smiling. "Firstly, I doubted it would stand up in court, and secondly, much as I dislike my brothers, I *did* think he was being rather unfair to them. The thought of them *all* coming whining to me when they went into debt was also quite fatiguing. I'm already wealthy in my own right, and while I like money, I don't need *all* of it."

"Do you know who witnessed the new will?" Robert asked.

Peregrine grabbed the will and leafed through the many pages to the end where there was a lengthy codicil. "You can read it for yourself. Mr. Tompkins and Dr. Mantel witnessed the damned thing."

"Dr. Mantel did?" Robert glanced at Lucy. "Was Lady Benson left nothing?"

Peregrine grimaced. "A pittance that would make her totally dependent on remaining in my good graces."

"Which explains a lot." Robert nodded. "I wonder if you would be so good as to look at the other documents Sir William kept in there."

"Of course." Peregrine set the will aside and took out another bundle of letters. "These are related to the Hall brothers and their father,

Dennis. I haven't seen them before." He sifted through them, his eyes widening. "It appears that there was no reliable evidence that Mr. Hall was dead, which means that Miranda is probably a bigamist." His smile widened. "Good *God,* how deliciously *scandalous!*"

"One has to assume that this was why Sir William decided to cut his wife out of his will," Lucy said. "She wasn't really entitled to *anything.*"

Peregrine stacked up the papers. "This is all well and good, but it still doesn't tell me who murdered my father, does it?"

"Actually, we think it does." Robert looked at Lucy, who nodded for him to go on. "We believe Dr. Mantel killed him, and Mr. Tompkins."

"Dr. *Mantel?*" Peregrine said. *"Why?"*

"Because he is involved in a love affair with Lady Benson. If he discovered that she had been written out of Sir William's will, don't you think he would've done something about it?"

"And he would know, seeing as he was one of the witnesses," Peregrine said slowly. "Why didn't I think he might be guilty of murder?"

"Probably because like us you believed he was a physician who took a solemn vow to *first do no harm,*" Robert said. "Our own physician is so trustworthy it blinded us to the obvious truth."

Peregrine nodded. "Dr. Mantel was also at the baths on that fateful day."

"The only thing we aren't clear on yet is how much Lady Benson knew about all this," Lucy added. "And that's why we need your help. . . ."

"Be careful!" Peregrine scolded the two footmen who were carrying him. "I don't want yet another injury."

Lucy and Robert followed a complaining Peregrine into the Benson house and up the stairs to the drawing room. Edward, Augustus, Lady Benson, Arden, and Dr. Mantel were all gathered there awaiting his return. While Peregrine settled himself in a chair with as much drama as Lady Benson usually brought to the proceedings, Robert went down the stairs again to make certain that Mr. Carstairs had also arrived.

He escorted the solicitor up the stairs, ignoring his muttered comments about the disorderly conduct of the Bensons and his desire to never do business with them again. When he reached the drawing room, Robert ushered Mr. Carstairs in and remained by the doors, blocking the exit.

Peregrine caught his eye and Robert nodded.

"It is good to be back with my family," Peregrine said, raising his voice sufficiently to drown out everyone else. For the first time, Robert could imagine him on a stage. "I thought that I was going to die, and that made me rethink my past choices." He sighed heavily and beckoned to Lucy, who brought the box over to him.

"I have a confession to make."

Edward scowled at him. "What have you done now, Peregrine?"

"I . . . stole Father's will."

A cacophony of noise filled the room, making Robert wince. When they all settled down again, Edward was the first to recover.

"Why?"

Peregrine shrugged. "I didn't want you all to see what was in it."

"Had Father finally disinherited you?" Edward asked hopefully.

"No. He disinherited you lot."

Edward visibly rocked back on his heels, and Lady Benson pressed a hand to her mouth.

"You mean . . . he left everything to *you?*" Edward said faintly.

"Yes." Peregrine held out the will to Mr. Carstairs. "You might wish to take hold of this before anyone in my family destroys it." He continued. "It's a good job I *did* steal the damn thing before someone decided it was better if it remained hidden. Mr. Tompkins was one of the witnesses, and he's dead, and dear Dr. Mantel was the other, and he was set upon by scoundrels along with me." He paused. "It's almost as if *someone* didn't want anyone to know there had been a new will."

Edward glared at his brother. "I do hope you're not suggesting it was *me,* Peregrine."

"I suppose it could've been you, or Augustus, or even my dear sweet stepmother, who would *hate* having to come and beg me for money."

Robert winced at the malice of Peregrine's tone, but for once he didn't blame him. Knowing the volatility of the Benson family and their propensity for open strife he was hoping everything would soon boil over in a satisfactory manner.

"Now, I say." Dr. Mantel stood up. "Leave Lady Benson out of this. She has done nothing wrong."

Peregrine raised his eyebrows. "Well, that depends on whether you believe *bigamy* is a sin or not, doesn't it? What do you think, Miranda?"

Lady Miranda's mouth dropped open and she drew in an audible breath. Dr. Mantel grabbed hold of her elbow.

"You do not have to answer him, my lady."

"Oh, I think she does," Peregrine retorted. "Did she fool you with her tears and protestations, too, Dr. Mantel? Did she promise you that if you helped her get rid of her ailing husband you could be her new one?" His laugh was unkind. "What a *shame* that she can't marry anyone because she is still a wife."

"My father is dead," Arden insisted. "He died when we were children."

"I'm afraid that isn't true." Peregrine held out the documents to Arden. "I assume this is what

Brandon was searching for at your mother's behest when he came across Mr. Tompkins and killed him."

"Balderdash!" Arden shouted. "Brandon didn't kill *anyone* and my mother *never* asked us to search for the documents!"

"Then who did?" Robert finally intervened, and caught Arden's furious attention. "Was it Dr. *Mantel* by any chance?"

"Yes, he *did* suggest it because he cares about my mother's health and knew she was distressed by the matter." Arden glowered at Robert. "What's wrong with *that?*"

"Perhaps Dr. Mantel can answer you." Robert looked across at the tight-lipped doctor. "Although one does have to wonder whether the *title* of doctor is actually yours by merit, or merely something you acquired so that you could get close to Sir William and Lady Benson. According to my physician your skills are *abysmally* lacking."

"I'm not sure what you are implying, Sir Robert." Dr. Mantel raised his eyebrows.

"He's *implying* that you murdered my father so that you could marry Miranda, and have now found out that she's actually of no use to you at all," Peregrine drawled.

"He *is* of use!" Lady Benson jumped to her feet and rushed over to Peregrine, her finger pointing at his face. "And I would *not* be a bigamist!"

Dr. Mantel briefly closed his eyes as everyone stared at Lady Benson.

"Are you . . . suggesting that Dr. Mantel is in fact your first husband?" Peregrine asked slowly.

Lady Benson raised her chin. "Yes, he is! Dennis *loves* me, and *everything* he has done is because of that!"

Robert stiffened as Dr. Mantel made a run toward the door, and stepped forward to stop him. The doctor lowered his shoulder and rammed his head into Robert's chest, sending him sprawling backward onto the floor. Behind Robert, Lady Benson screamed, and Edward and Arden shouted.

Lucy appeared at his side. "Are you all right, Robert?"

"Yes, I think so." He stood up with her help and shut the door, blocking the Bensons' pursuit. "He won't get far. I have some men positioned downstairs to take Dr. Mantel into custody."

He walked over to Peregrine, who was smiling at him. "Perhaps now that we have established that Dr. Mantel is a murderer, we might sort out some of the other pertinent details. I assume Dr. Mantel killed Mr. Tompkins because he was the only other person apart from Peregrine who knew what was in the new will."

"*And* he got me stabbed by footpads," Peregrine added.

"Precisely." Robert nodded. "It was clever

of him to receive minor injuries of his own."

Robert deliberately half turned to Lady Benson, who was sobbing her heart out while Arden attempted to comfort her and raised his voice. "If Dr. Mantel *did* murder both men then perhaps you might drop the charges against Brandon, Mr. Benson?"

Lady Benson's head shot up. "What charges?"

Arden took her hand. "Brandon's being held in Bath Gaol on suspicion of murdering Mr. Tompkins."

"Why didn't anyone *tell* me?" she wailed.

Lucy spoke up for the first time. "Perhaps Dr. Mantel intended to blame Peregrine for both murders after he died from his wounds, and thus set Brandon—who presumably is his son, free?"

"If Dennis did that to his own *son* . . ." Lady Benson bared her teeth. "I will kill him *myself!* He wasn't *supposed* to murder Mr. Tompkins! I knew *nothing* about that. I just asked him to help me make certain Sir William would not suffer anymore. He *hated* being old."

"You think my father would've thanked you for putting him out of his misery?" Peregrine's voice was full of scorn. "You disgustingly self-centered *harpy!*"

Robert had to step in front of Lady Benson as she launched an attack on Peregrine. It took Arden to calm her down and restrain her.

Eventually Lady Benson was escorted up to

her bedroom and locked in. Robert received word that Dr. Mantel, or whatever his name was, had been apprehended and was on his way to Bath Gaol. Edward went down to his study in somewhat of a daze with Augustus in tow to write a letter releasing Brandon from all charges and presumably to compose a new one accusing Dr. Mantel.

Mr. Carstairs picked up the will and put it in his case. "This family is an abomination. As soon as I get back to my office in Yorkshire I am going to pass the whole circus on to another partner."

"An excellent idea, sir," Robert commended him. "Perhaps Mr. Peregrine Benson will soon sort the sorry business out with you and make sure all the Bensons are happy again."

"Indeed I will." Peregrine grinned at the sour-faced solicitor. "I can't wait!"

"So let me get this straight," Dr. Fletcher said as he stood in front of the fireplace in the drawing room. "Dr. Mantel wasn't qualified to be a doctor, and was an *actor?*"

"*That's* what worries you?" Robert asked. "The fact that he also murdered two people is rather more important."

"I know that." Dr. Fletcher waved an impatient hand. "And he is, or was, Lady Benson's husband?"

"Correct." Robert nodded. "He came back to

her at some point after she married Sir William—I'm not sure if she *knew* he was alive when she got married again, but that might come out at the trial. She did encourage Dr. Mantel to pretend to be her physician and do away with her husband when they came to Bath. They probably reckoned that fewer questions would be asked than if he'd died at home where everyone knew him."

"They didn't reckon on you and Lady Kurland and your nose for murder, did they?" Dr. Fletcher said. "From a medical standpoint I assume Dr. Mantel might have stabbed Sir William as he helped him into the baths, shoved his head under the water, and then walked away assuming nature would take its course while he was far away bargaining for herbs."

"Which is exactly what *would* have happened if you and Sir Robert hadn't been at the baths that morning," Lucy added. "No one would have noticed a thing if Sir William's own doctor certified that his client had drowned after suffering heart failure."

"Lady Benson also confessed that she and Dr. Mantel tried to get the will by bribing the servant you spoke to, Lucy," Robert said. "That's probably why Miranda went through all the clothes so thoroughly when you brought them back to her. I'm still not quite sure how involved she was in the planning or whether Dr. Mantel kept her in blissful ignorance."

"What a mess," Lucy sighed. "And if *Peregrine* had died . . ." She shivered. "Then we would not have been able to solve any of it."

The door to the drawing room flew open to reveal Penelope looking rather perplexed. She pointed down at her gown.

"I am all *wet!* What on *earth* is going on?"

Dr. Fletcher started stuttering while Lucy rose to her feet, went over to Penelope, and took her hand.

"Your baby is coming. Let's go up to your bed-chamber while Dr. Fletcher remembers what he's supposed to be doing and joins us."

Later that evening, Robert looked up as Lucy came into his study.

"How is everything?"

She beamed at him. "Penelope and Dr. Fletcher have a fine, healthy son."

He raised his glass of brandy to her. "How wonderful for them."

"And, of course, Penelope had the easiest and quickest birth I have ever seen, and is boasting that she doesn't understand what women complain about. She will be insufferable now." Lucy sighed as Robert pulled her down to sit on his lap.

"Did Anna assist you?"

"Yes, and thank goodness she was there because Dr. Fletcher suddenly became an indecisive, bumbling fool." Lucy paused. "Although I *do* think it did Anna good to see such an easy birth. She confided to me that she is considering writing to Captain Akers and asking him to visit her in Kurland St. Mary."

"Well, that *is* good news. Have the Fletchers decided on a name for the child yet?"

"They were still arguing it out when I left." Lucy struggled not to smile. "Dr. Fletcher wanted to call the child Robert Declan, and for some reason Penelope was *quite* against it."

Robert chuckled and wrapped an arm around Lucy's waist, his fingers spreading over her rounded stomach. "I do hope that when *this* one arrives, you won't object to adding a Robert in there somewhere if it is a boy?"

She put her hand over his. "You *knew?*"

"My darling girl, I am a trifle unobservant, but not about such an intimate matter as what goes on in my own bed."

"Why didn't you say anything?" Lucy asked.

"Because I assumed that you would tell me in your own good time." He looked up at her. "Which I hoped would be before I had to stay in Bath for another six months."

"I was too afraid," Lucy confessed. "I'm not sure I even want to talk about it *now.*"

"Then we will not speak about it until we get home." He kissed her very carefully and held her gaze. "Let's talk about something else."

"The Bensons?" Lucy suggested.

Robert scowled at her. "Good Lord, no! I've had quite enough of that family to last me a lifetime!"

Center Point Large Print
600 Brooks Road / PO Box 1
Thorndike, ME 04986-0001 USA

(207) 568-3717

US & Canada:
1 800 929-9108
www.centerpointlargeprint.com